Reviews For

Where The Heart Is

Masterful in style and form, the narratives in Andrew Chatora's *Where the Heart Is* are intensely provocative.
-**Memory Chirere**, University of Zimbabwe

***

Where the Heart Is, is a compelling story told against the backdrop of Brexit era Britain, where it is becoming increasingly difficult to live as an immigrant.
- *(This is Africa)*

***

A masterful exploration of what living in post-Brexit Britain is like through the perspectives of immigrants. Offers unvarnished insights.
-**Stan Onai Mushava** – Author, Poet

***

Through an expertly woven tour de force, criss-crossing the streets of Harare, London, and Bangkok, Chatora's characters seamlessly forge their own stories and identities in a poignant, immersive way which will enthral you.
-**Gift Mheta**, Durban University, South Africa

***

Beautifully written and evocative, *Where the Heart Is* shines an illuminating light into diverse migrant experiences as they struggle to forge ties and make sense of their lived experiences.
-**Malvern Mukudu**, Author, Rhodes University, South Africa

i

***

Where the Heart Is offers an unforgettable tableau of the struggles so endured by many immigrants.

-**Tichaona Chinzowu**, Westminster University, UK

WHERE THE HEART IS

ANDREW CHATORA

KHARIS
PUBLISHING

Eulogy to My Grandmothers

To Mbuya Emma Chatora (my paternal nan) and Mbuya Renna Matare-Makaya, (my maternal hero). Both my grandmothers, you're dear to my heart. My true diamonds. Eccentric and exceptional women in different measure. I love you dearly both.

Rest in perpetual peace.

"Because the story is a metaphor for life, we expect it to feel like life, to have the rhythm of life...So the rhythm of life swings between these poles."

Robert McKee (1998)

CONTENTS

Chapter 1

Return to the Source – Kurukuvhute

I have been living a lie for the twenty years or so that I have been in England and living under an assumed name and identity. I've been living in the shadows, the labyrinthine maze that is the British underworld. But now they are closing in on me...

It was a strange funeral. I had mixed emotions and felt conflicted within myself. In fact, I was bristling with anger, incandescent with unbridled rage. I was deeply perturbed and could not make sense of how Sekuru Fari, my mother's brother, a man of means, a man of letters, after spending all those years in England, should have such an ignominious end in the back of beyond, buried in an obscure Gatsi village cemetery, with a scarce, measly, trickling of mourners there for his send off. Something made me feel uneasy. This wasn't on, for a man of Uncle Fari's stature to have such a demeaning send off without his children or grandchildren in attendance. *"Even paupers had decent burials, not this..."* I mumbled quietly under my breath.

"And so, to dust, men will return, for you are mortal," droned the vicar's voice in insipid monosyllables as he sprinkled gravel on the brown wooden coffin which the villagers had hastily put together the previous day. It had actually been whispered, Sekuru would most likely be buried in a mere blanket, covered by a traditional reed mat, *rukukwe or bonde*, if the village carpenters took long to construct his makeshift wooden coffin! Time was of great essence. Fortunately, the collective effort had prevailed, and out of the effort came his hurriedly built, not so imposing wooden coffin.

"Well, that wasn't a befitting burial for someone touted as a university lecturer in England, someone who used to teach even white people. Such a damp squib of a burial, but how did it come to this? I mean, does it make sense to you, Tapera, because to me, none of this is logical in any way, shape, or form," I remarked to one of my distant nephews who had helped with coordinating the funeral proceedings.

"So much for staying in the diaspora, *haa havana musoro madiaspora aya, havana kurongeka;* they are not sensible at all How can you spend half your life in England, yet you don't think of a basic thing like having a funeral policy and repatriation plan in place. Do you know that his body stayed in the morgue for over six months?"

"Bloody hell, six months!"

"Yes, for six full months, no one could raise the fee for repatriation to Zimbabwe."

"Come on, did he not have a wife?"

"Nope, as far as I know, they divorced many years ago, and he was living with this white woman who kicked him out when he started to be in and out of hospital."

"Wow! What of his children?"

"Not remotely interested, I'm told. You see, another ill-effect of divorces, the children never saw eye to eye with him, Tapera. The children blame him for the acrimonious divorce from their mother. Word has it, there was a massive fallout between Uncle Fari and the children, which dates back to the rancorous divorce he had with Mbuya Maidei, Mai Muchi, the wife."

"I get that," remarked Tapera. "People do fall out, that's a fairly normal part of human relations, but this is a funeral we are talking about here. The death of your parent, for heaven's sake, the man or woman who brought you into this world, this is the time to say the last goodbye. Surely, in accordance with our culture or the spirit of *Ubuntu*, as fellow humans we set aside our differences in times of bereavement. Whatever the children's beef with their dad, today was not the day for it. They should have been here to pay their last respects. I'm sorry, dear, but with this no show, all the stuff about not having funeral arrangements in place, the kids are bang out of order, here! I'm not having this. You know there are some things which set us apart from animals, and one of those attributes is common sense and decency which, as I can see, we have a dearth of here."

2

"True, *muzaya* Tapera, but remember we are not entirely privy to Uncle Fari's family's shenanigans. We are talking of a family which uprooted and ostracised themselves from the entire Mupawaenda clan when they relocated to England over four decades ago. We hardly saw them at other family functions, except Sekuru himself, bless him. Perhaps, their no show at other important family gatherings, no communication, not keeping in touch with anyone were a sign of deeper problems laid bare by their failure to attend, let alone pay their last respects, to the passing on of this lovely man who made them to grace this earth." I spoke with so much passion and fervour; I was almost choking with rage at the brazenness and uncouth nature of Sekuru's family who had seen fit to turn their backs on him in his death. Heartless sods!

"We all know Sekuru Fari had a heart of gold. Who didn't pass through his hands, in the entire Mupawaenda family? With Sekuru, you just had to ask for assistance and, boom, it was done before you had finished asking. Now, how do people repay his munificence? Aah, thank you but no thanks, with a crappy pauper's burial, hardly attended by any close family members. This is totally disgusting and out of order, my friend!"

"You know very well how Uncle Fari was emotionally blackmailed to look out after his extended family here, paying school fees, and university fees for his sisters' children, even though the parents were still alive but couldn't be bothered to exercise their filial duties. This 'taking the mickey' became increasingly absurd when people came to expect him to pay their *lobola* for them. These are able-bodied men and women we are talking of here, Tapera."

"And then there is the case of Senda, Uncle Fari's brother. Sekuru used to send money to Senda to look after their aged mother, Mbuya Matipa, but Senda then decided to take a second wife, who gave birth to twins to 'fully secure her place in the Gumbi homestead,' as she put it. That was it. Mbuya Matipa's upkeep money was diverted to his two wives' living expenses. It took quite a while before Sekuru cottoned on to this subterfuge, and what's more, I'm told there were additional cases of chicanery from Sekuru's kith and kin taking advantage, milking the man's good-natured way. What a life we live!"

"Possibly, all this may have quickened the poor bloke's demise. Who knows? I know he'd been unwell, but it was way too quick the way it happened."

"Far too quick, I agree, and look at it, even Senda, the brother who benefitted so immensely from Sekuru, is also not here today to bid farewell to his own brother! No! Not right. Beats me how some people sleep at night with this kind of odious behaviour."

"It's all weird, the way things have turned out with the Mupawaenda family. Something is not right with this crooked family."

There had been so much innuendo and double speak, gossip, half-truths floating around Sekuru's funeral. I couldn't help picking up some of the snippets of unkind innuendo-infused conversations.

"Some say he was living with a woman from Thailand, who kicked him out once he started getting ill again," remarked Aunt Tambu, another distant niece in conversation with Kumbirai a local Gatsi villager.

"Really, did he not have a house of his own? Aaah, these women from foreign lands. Better to stick with your very own devil that you know."

"True. Can you imagine? Word has it, for all those years he lived in England, he was renting a council flat?"

"Renting a council flat my foot!" She rolled in derisive laughter and said, 'Why couldn't he have the good sense to secure a mortgage for his own house?'"

It hurt me exceedingly, picking Aunt Tambu's snide remarks. The courtesy of Sekuru Fari's benevolence paid for her education, from primary school right up to university. Aunt Tambu really had a field day, like other village mourners, with their jeering laughter, taking pot shots at Sekuru's low key pauper funeral.

Then, there had been the mystery woman's presence, to add to the brutal drama surrounding Sekuru's burial. A tall, posh looking woman, elegantly dressed, thereby underscoring her being an outsider and enhancing the sense of enigma surrounding her. Amidst the sad, sombre, dreary funeral proceedings, she had provided an animated talking point backdrop as we tried to work out who she was and what had been her connection to Sekuru. This was something she didn't try to demystify to us. Perhaps she was revelling in the mystery. There was no doubt she was a woman with extreme composure, very much cultured. She exhibited the assurance of a connoisseur. She had a certain poise of grace and elegance which I found sexually alluring. Even as I felt the stirring in my trousers, I was embarrassed to be thinking of sex at a funeral, more so, the funeral for one I so venerated as Sekuru Fari. What could she possibly want to do mingling with us mere mortals, here in Gatsi? What could have been her connection with Sekuru? A flurry of these and other questions flooded my troubled inner psyche. She had a sophistication and unmistakable, well-groomed lyrical twang in her voice when she spoke. *Ndidzo mbingaka idzi, paita mbingakadzi apa;* she is well posh a woman, Tapera had knowingly remarked to me as if he was privy to the strange woman's bank balance.

"Nematambudziko," she'd said, extending her long, slender, diamond encrusted, supple fingers into my palm. "He was a true diamond to me, your uncle, with a beautiful personality to the core. It breaks my heart to see him gone. Here lies a man who never was fully acknowledged and cherished in life; perhaps death will reward him with his cherished place amongst mortals. Accept my heartfelt condolences." With those cryptic remarks, she left without providing any clue to her identity. The opulent silver Toyota Landcruiser she entered, further adding to the mystery surrounding her identity and her yet unknown link with Sekuru Fari.

Chapter 2

Milton Keynes

Maidei and I met Ben and Taurai at Palmers Butchery in Bletchley, near Milton Keynes town. Many Zimbabweans in the UK tended to throng this place in droves to buy succulent beef, *bhuruvhosi, boewors* sausages, *maguru nematumbu,* cow tripe, cow intestines and other different sorts of meat, meat offals and traditional dishes like *madora, mancimbi* termites. "It all reminds us of home and quenches our nostalgia," is what my fellow citizens were wont to say. Draped in Zimbabwean colours, the couple were standing next to us in the long, meandering queue that sweltering Saturday afternoon. In her overly friendly but typical way, Maidei started small talk, *"inga harisi kumbofamba* line," literally translated: the queue is moving at a snail's pace, to which the short, charcoal black, plump woman we later knew as Taurai, gave a jovial rejoinder. She said, "Typical of Zimbabweans, once we obsess on something we never give up do we?" She began to cackle with laughter, "Why can't we get ordinary meat like everyone else does from Tescos or Sainsburys supermarket? Would save everyone the hassle in this Covid era."

 "Aaah, so says a woman who is always moaning about how Tesco meat tastes like plastic," interrupted the tall, lanky man whom I later learnt was Ben, Taurai's husband.

"Palmers butchers' meat is tasty I have to agree. I give them that, *inyama yekumusha chaiyo.* It transports me back to Harare kwaMereki," I remarked as I joined in the fray, not to be outdone.

Memories of KwaMereki instantly flooded back to me. KwaMereki was a popular braai barbecue spot in Harare's Warren Park suburb which drinkers like me used to frequent in my heydays as a young university lecturer at UZ. Ask any guzzler in Harare, and they will initiate you into the wonderful world of Mereki, Mai Musodzi and her braised steak, *sadza* with pork bones at that legendary watering hole. I had that nostalgic reverie summarily popped when Maidei poked my ribs, saying, "They need our numbers baba waMuchi. You know I have a bad memory and can't even tell my own phone number."

We soon exchanged numbers with the couple after introducing ourselves by our first names. Unbeknown to us at the time, it later turned out, by a sheer stroke of coincidence, that both Ben and Taurai were our neighbours in our local Milton Keynes hood. We visited each other in a friendship which blossomed over the years. They had twin daughters, Makanaka and Mazvita, who were completing their sixth form at the local girls' Aylesbury High Grammar School. Aylesbury was an adjoining town to our very own Milton Keynes. The twins became friends, or more like big sisters, to our teenage daughter Yeukai, because, as *my better half* Maidei liked to put it, "The twins are positive role models and will certainly do Yeukai some good to have big sisters to look up to."

Over several years, we had a great friendship with Ben and Taurai, an amity which flourished and lasted, though I was openly contemptuous of the white way of life Ben and Taurai pursued, at least in private to my wife Maidei, that is. Maidei bore the brunt of my cutting edge, stinging criticism of the couple's veneer of "whiteness" they liked to flaunt.

"The problem with Ben and Taurai is, they have no sense of belonging and identity whatsoever. They are ignorant of their identity and culture, *havazive kani*! They remind me of the old age saying, *kungopeperetswa nemhepo*, more like a rolling stone. Forgive them, for they know not what they are doing," I would often cynically remark.

"Who are you Fari, to be spouting such hogwash?" You know not everyone is like you, with your strong Jindwi rural background," Maidei chided me.

"I would rather retain my strong rural background as you diss me than be a coconut," I laughed derisively at this. "You know what a coconut is Maidei, I doubt you do. I'll just clue you in, nonetheless. Ask any Ghanaian friends you come across, they're well-schooled in coconuts and their goings on. Well, I digress my love, a coconut, put simply, is Ben and Taurai."

"That's hardly a cogent explanation, is it?" Maidei remonstrated.

"Easy, easy, Maidei, let me finish first, then you can butt in for all you like.

So, I was saying, a coconut is any black person who is not culturally woke, so much steeped in whiteness and trying to imitate a white culture or way of life, like your friends next door, but their tragedy is, they're rejected by the very whiteness they pine for: The system they're trying so much to emulate, being whiter than white." At this I burst into sarcastic fits of laughter.

Perhaps, it came as no surprise, years later, I was even more derisory when Ben's daughters were both married by white boys.

"Aaaah ndoo chii ichocho; kuita mukuwasha wemurungu; what is this having a white son in law?" I quipped. "Our forefathers and ancestors must be turning in their graves, to have their bloodline corrupted with this interracial marriage thing!"

"Does it not strike you at all that not only are you being a rabid racist, but you're showing off your ignorance full scale at being unable to integrate in a country which has given you a home all these years?"

"Given me a home my foot!" I said, rolling my eyeballs in remonstrance; "I don't know about you, Maidei. I wouldn't call this home. There's only one home for me. PO Box Gatsi, Zimbabwe."

"Oh, let's see whether you'll ever get to live there again! Back of beyond."

"My goodness Maidei, how can you have so much self-hate? And you call yourself an educated woman, yet you have no sense of self-appreciation and confidence in your own identity? All traces of your Zimbabweanness have been wiped away, Maidei. What for, if not for vanity's sake?"

I had let that one pass. With Maidei, I'd learnt to pick my battles wisely. In that way, I retained my sanity. Besides, it also kept the peace in the house.

Chapter 3

The Early Years

I could never get used to how men like Ben tried to sanitise their spectacular fall from grace, reconciling the sort of odd jobs they now pursued in England and the quality of life lived in comparison to the good old days of Harare, Zimbabwe. Many times I wondered, *Does it mean people like Ben now prostituted their intelligence under the guise of eulogising immigrant life in Britain, even if the realities obtaining on the ground pointed out otherwise?*

I mean, how does one even begin to make comparisons between two diametrically opposed lived experiences?

Ben used to be a civil engineer in Joubert Crushers and John Sisk, a large construction company in Southern Africa, with a very posh title to go with his monthly fat paycheque, *Area Regional Manager*. He gallivanted all over Southern African capitals, Harare, Mbabane Swaziland, Gaborone Botswana and Windhoek Namibia among others, but now he cuts a pale shadow of his former ebullient self. Instead he spends the greater part of his life shuttling between *r and r* jobs in England; *r and r* is a derogatory term in common parlance among fellow Zimbabweans in the diaspora. It was a pejorative term, denoting *rese-rese* as in "any type of job will do for me," ranging from bum cleaners of geriatrics in care homes (BBC as they were mockingly called British bottom cleaners), factory workers, heavy industry workers, stacking boxes in Tescos and Sainsburys supermarkets. Instead of r and r, some fellow Zimbabweans persistently ridiculed it. CIN was another insulting term, *chamuka inyama*, implying that as an immigrant one couldn't afford to be choosy in terms of jobs. You just take what comes your way, as at the end of the day, that's what pays the bills. It puts food on the table; that's called being practical. This was a conversation I had overhead many times amongst my fellow immigrant brethren and sisters.

I knew Joe's case, another Zimbabwean fella, who was an accountant back home with Deloitte and Touché, at one time. He also worked for Ernst and Young in Harare, but now was a bin man here. Not that there is anything wrong in being a bin man. A job is a job if it's taken as a means to an end. I get that! I am not daft. What I am against is people like my wife and her gullible band of followers who liked to whitewash the black immigrant experience in England. Maidei's cheerleaders, as in Ben's wife Taurai, liked to go on and on about Joe's case, putting an exaggerated spin on it. "Eeh people were taking the mickey on Joe and his bin man job, but you know what *mabin ake aya amutengera imba kumasabhabha, kumadale-dale* is literally translated; his being a bin man has earned him a posh house in Harare's Mt Pleasant Heights, an upmarket, leafy suburb.

"But why didn't he just stay in Harare, at Deloitte and Touché? He was doing very well you know, living in Harare's Belvedere and you can't tell me living in Belvedere is a sign of penury?" I countered.

"There he goes again," remarked Maidei, rolling her eyes at me, much to my delight, now that I knew which buttons to push. I thoroughly enjoyed winding her up on purpose.

"But, Maidei has a point, Fari," Ben cut in, not to be outdone.

"What kind of point, when a man who had a cushy life in his home country ditches it all for vanity's sake, so he can brag to all and sundry on Facebook©, Instagram© and Twitter© that, 'Hey you know what, this is me, Joe, I am living in England, the Queen's habitat, and of course I won't tell you of my live to work life, no work life balance at all,'" I remarked with an exaggerated flourish of my hand and a mischievous smirk on my face, imitating how Joe would have flaunted himself on social media as most airheads are wont to do.

"So, why are you here then, seeing that all you do as your favourite pastime is to persistently diss the very place which has given you a home and sanctuary? Was it not you who nearly claimed false political asylum when the home office took so long to sort out your papers?"

"Why am I here?" I repeated Maidei's question, sarcastically throwing it back at her. "I am here because of you Maidei. If you forget, I am married to you and you are the mother of my two children, Muchadei and lovely Yeukai. If my memory serves me well, Maidei, was it not you who threatened me with divorce if I didn't play ball and ditch my UZ lectureship job for a grandiose life in England?"

"Aaah, I have got this job as a staff nurse at a care home in England; we will all be covered on my work permit. We can't let this once in a lifetime chance pass Fari, was it not you?"

Perhaps I sounded a tad accusatory in the tone of my voice, and it must have hurt Maidei's feelings.

"Aaah, shame on you Fari, *inyaya dzinotaurwa pane vanhu here idzi*. How can you be so uncouth to flaunt our dirty linen before Ben and Taurai?"

"Ben and Taurai are no strangers to us. If anything, they are brothers to us, to which I have no shame for them knowing the nitty gritties of my life. *Kugara nhaka huona dzavamwe,* we all learn from each other's lived experiences. My brother Ben here and Mainini Taurai can actually be a repository of wisdom," I remarked back slapping Ben with a friendly chuckle.

I had an unexpected ally in Mainini Taurai who leapt to my defence for once. "True, there should be no secrets amongst friends, as Babamukuru Fari just said. I totally agree we can always bounce ideas off each other you know," she remarked with a mischievous glint in her eyes.

"But the thing is, can Fari ever take other people's ideas, or it's his way or no one else's way, like his usual modus operandi?" butted in Maidei, one accustomed to craving a stage and an audience. This fired her up. I could see how animated and upbeat she was.

"Maybe it's a man thing, not wanting to acknowledge any input from us women, no matter how good that word may be?"

"I'm afraid I beg to differ there," said Ben, seeming to have awoken from his slumber. "Men we do listen to our womenfolk, you know."

"Oh really? Good to know." There was that exaggerated incredulity in Taurai's voice.

"Of course, I do listen to you Taurai, you know I do," Ben remarked with a knowing glint in his eyes.

The first few years of our friendship as a couple with Ben and his wife Taurai, were marked by this constant verbal sparring over our perceptions of life here in comparison to back home Zimbabwe. As it happened, I was always the odd ball in this trio, which sadly included my wife of many years, Maidei, not siding with my views, which, in a way, hurt.

I often wondered at Maidei's blatant deprecation of me, such brazen duplicity, as I termed it. Always ganging up against me, publicly disagreeing with me each time we had a robust discussion with Ben and Taurai. What kind of woman does that to her husband, of all people? Inwardly, part of me felt hurt at this blatant display of what I termed disloyalty to one's husband. Wives are supposed to close ranks with their husbands in public, aren't they? Even if they disagree privately, in front of the public, you put up a united show. Maidei never seemed to be able to do this. Why?

Once, I pulled her on it. "So much for your loyalty to your dear husband, Maidei," I sarcastically sneered at her. "How is it you never support me publicly each time I have a spat with Ben and Taurai?"

"Am I not allowed to have an opinion Fari? It's called having an independent mind, freedom of thoughts. I dare say, agency, as the more erudite would call it. Is that not what you used to teach your undergraduate students at Law School in Zimbabwe?"

"Freedom of thoughts, huh? Whatever happened to, 'I will support you in sickness and health' mantra, or was it all for the pulpit? You playing to the gallery on our wedding day?"

"I can't believe you're saying this," she said, looking at me quizzically. "Are you for real Fari? Seriously?" The disdain and contempt were palpable from the way she contorted her facial features as she spoke.

"Of course, I am. I don't understand why you're being snooty, Maidei. Truth is, you're disloyal and disrespectful to me. And you know what, honey, it hurts. Yes, it does, especially as you publicly give me a flogging and dressing down, right in front of Ben, another Zimbabwean man. I've seen the way he looks at me with that, *oh god, look at him that emasculated man!* It's an awful look, I tell you."

"Are you sure that's not your paranoia setting in again? At the rate you're going Fari, next, you'll be telling me you're hearing voices."

"Aaaah, so you think it's a laughing matter, do you? Typical Maidei tomfoolery, where everything is a joke. But this ain't a joke, I'm telling you. Sweetheart, you've really got to be loving and respectful towards me."

"Fari, you'll never cease to amaze me. What you fail to get is, you don't demand or coerce love and respect, you earn it, my dear! Where are you getting it wrong? Perhaps, you need to enrol for some love and relationships classes, so you are correctly schooled in how to properly relate to women, let alone to your wife. We are wired differently, I can tell you this," and with that she stomped off upstairs, leaving me aghast.

Chapter 4

Makanaka and Mazvita

It was a huge moment for both Ben and Taurai when the twins, Makanaka and Mazvita, smashed their A Levels and were accepted into Leeds University medical school. *"Aaah makorokoto Mainini nababamunnini,* warm congratulations your way, folks."

"We're all happy for you on this momentous family occasion, and certainly for our Yeukai who will have big sisters to emulate."

I joined in the fray, saying, "Do you follow, Yeukai, my daughter? Makanaka and Mazvita have set high standards for you which you must now strive to achieve," as both twins modestly took all this in. We had arranged a graduation bash for them, a befitting send off to the duo before they departed to commence their undergraduate degrees.

"So, are you both going to study medicine?" Yeukai joined in.

"No, it's only Mazvita reading medicine. She's the clever one pursuing the Hippocratic Oath studies, the family's medical doctor if you like," chuckled Makanaka. "I'm taking an actuarial science degree."

"Aaah, I see. What is actuarial science? That's way above my head," chipped in an over-awed Yeukai. This was something I liked, for I felt such a relationship with Ben's two girls would do her some good.

"Acturial science is insurance studies in layman's terms. The risks and strategies that big corporate businesses have to take and avoid, etcetera," Makanaka said.

I could see the adulation and admiration on my daughter's young face as it lit up like sparkling diamonds. She was both enamoured and bamboozled by the twins' academic prowess. Inwardly, I felt happy. Yeukai had some positive role models to whom she could aspire. Mazvita and Makanaka were more like her big sisters. It was all too easy for kids to go off the rails in this county.

17

I had seen it far too often in England: county lines, drug gangs grooming kids, sadly, mostly young black children from broken homes. Gun and knife crimes were the order of the day and typified most inner-city ghettoes like London, Liverpool, and not least our very own Milton Keynes. It broke my heart each time I saw on telly the perpetrators of these seedy juvenile crimes were mostly young, black kids. My skin recoiled in horror even thinking of this; no wonder I was overprotective of both my kids. "They need the harsh Zimbabwean upbringing and sensibility," many-a-time I remarked to a be-mused Maidei.

"And what exactly is that? Being heavy handed on your kids so they grow up scared of their daddies and mummies? No thank you. I won't have that," remarked Maidei, in her bid to always undermine whatever I said.

"Eeh, allow me to raise my children the proper way, Maidei, whatever reservations you may have. No one has their best interests at heart more than I!"

"Well, excuse me, is my input then, not needed? You seem to forget I am also a parent to both these children."

"Whatever," I shrugged as I made my usual exit once the heat escalated in my usual spats with Maidei. These tiffs had come to typify our marriage more and more.

As I sprawled on our king size matrimonial bed, I reflected deeply on how things were panning out in England. My mind wandered to many other variables and permutations, life with Maidei now, as opposed to our lived experience in Harare. Were things better here than our laid-back life, at home? I wasn't convinced. Besides, deep down I resented coming here. I felt I had been arm-twisted by Maidei against my will. By and by, I had fully immersed myself in the drudgery and monotony of my failed marriage with her.

I reminisced and reflected on how I missed my weekends in Harare, the slow pace of life and things in general, unlike here where I felt I was always in a hectic, frenetic marathon of work, work, work, bills, bills, bills, all the time being drip fed into my psyche, constantly making me feel guilty. I had to work constantly, even when I wanted a day off. Increasingly, I became taut, edgy, and worked up. I felt like screaming at Maidei, Ben and Taurai at times, *"I want my life back, not this bullshit, pretence, façade existence!"* But then, I had long realised, I was on my own. They all didn't care, no one cared. My son, Muchi, hardly spoke to me. My daughter, Yeu, was the one who seemed to have a semblance of a relationship with me; good old Yeu, my beautiful flower.

I also mused on the lived experience of my fellow citizens now residing here. I knew of many fellow Zimbabweans who took false pride in showing off to folks back home that they were living large in the diaspora, England, Australia, Canada or the United States, yet their habitats were threadbare. Some, like, my neighbour in Milton Keynes, drove posh cars bought on extortionate car finance rates but he lived in a one-room matchbox, squashed like rats with other East European immigrants from Poland, Lithuania and Romania. All they did was work non-stop, literally 365 days a year, sending huge sums of money home monthly as they bragged. "I'm building an imposing mansion back home," Chris would trumpet his horn at us, every now and then when we cared to listen. At times, he would brandish his mobile phone to show off pictures of men apparently at work on one of his many mansions, back home. "See, that's my sixth mansion in Harare," said Chris, tugging aggressively on my arm, as if trying to convince me to believe in his narrative, which I doubted in any case.

"See, Fari, that's my dad in the blue workman suit, commandeering the builders. And you know what, my dad said to me the other day? He's become the envy of all and sundry in Harare, courtesy of my unfolding property portfolio." There was an air of unfettered arrogance and zeal in the way Chris spoke, which made it ring hollow all the more.

"Why don't you get a mortgage here, instead?" Maidei would brazenly ask.

"Why should I get a mortgage, when, if I grow old, the Queen will dispossess me of my house, sell it against my will to pay for my care, and throw me in an old people's care home?" countered mountebank Chris. "A mortgage is for wimps and fools like you and Fari," he said amid guffaws of raucous laughter in that gruff voice of his, revealing the gaps in his front tobacco-stained brownish teeth, as he puffed at his pungent smelling rolled joint. Inwardly, I have to say part of me agreed one hundred and one percent with Chris's sentiments, for I had been equally vociferous against buying the Milton Keynes house when Maidei floated the idea to me, "But we need it baba wa Muchi, we can't keep paying rent to Mister Abubakar. Frankly, that rent money is like flushing money down the toilet cistern every month we do it, like the Halifax woman mortgage advisor said to us."

19

"Well, but we do have a house in Harare, don't we?" I tried to rationalise with Maidei.

"I'm not disputing that, dearest, but look, it's been quite a number of years with us renting. Besides I really want my own kitchen where I can bake cakes and exercise my culinary skills like yester-year," went on Maidei. "You've lost all your chubbiness and glow; you could do with my Nigella Lawson recipes."

In the end, I gave in to this mortgage foolish talk and that's how we moved into 8 Snowberry Close, Bancroft, Milton Keynes, but my feelings of uneasiness and dissent remained within me, lying dormant. I felt personally aggrieved. *"How could you take twenty-five years to pay for your purported house, and having that mortgage millstone, tied round one's neck?"* I mused to myself because I couldn't rationalise or justify this Herculean financial commitment. Then, there was that moment of truth two years after paying for the mortgage through our noses. We discovered that the woman who'd been our mortgage advisor had mis-sold us an interest only mortgage, as opposed to a capital repayment mortgage.

"So that's it, we've paid off two years of our mortgage, twenty-three more to go," quipped Maidei as we sat before an office in Nationwide Bank in front of the plump, bespectacled mortgage advisor, who was trying to arrange a better deal for us. "You've done two years, you say ma'am? I think you're mistaken. You have an interest only mortgage not repayment, so, you're only chipping away at your interest and not the capital. Was this not explained to you when you took out the mortgage?" she asked, peering at both of us over her horn-rimmed, antique looking glasses.

"No, no! There must be a mistake," exclaimed a visibly distraught Maidei who always liked to be on top of situations. "We were told we took out a twenty-five-year mortgage two years ago. Are you sure you have our correct details, Maidei and Fari Mupawaenda?"

The mortgage advisor calmy glanced at her screen and nodded in the affirmative as she spoke, "Yes, I do have your correct details, can I call you Maidei?"

"Maidei," she went on, unperturbed by her trance like gaze, "it looks like both you and your husband were mis-sold a mortgage product by your original lender. What you have here is an interest only mortgage like I keep saying. These are old school mortgages used to hoodwink desperate first-time buyers and home seekers. They then fall under the illusion and excitement of owning a home, but really, with this type of mortgage, you are only sinking your money into a bottomless hole. Why do I say so? You will find, at the end of twenty-five years, all you've done really is pay off the interest on the mortgage and not the capital which in this case is £240 000.00 for your three bedroom house."

"What is this baloney?" I almost shouted at the woman. "Forgive me, I know it's not your fault, you are not the one who misrepresented this mortgage product, but where do we go from here? We're keen to right this travesty, believe me."

"What are our options out of this morass?" a belatedly composed Maidei finally butted in.

"You're in perfect hands, please call me Elaine," said the mortgage advisor flashing her disarming smile at us. "First things first, I can be able to get you a better deal, but..."

"But what?" I interrupted.

"There are trade-offs to be made, as we are converting an interest only to a capital repayment mortgage. It means significant charges will be incurred, and most importantly, your monthly mortgage payment will increase from the current £856.56 to £1132.31 monthly. How do you feel about that?"

"Well, you have to do what you have to do, Elaine, to extricate us from this jam," shrugged a dejected looking Maidei, "but I am suing Northern Rock after this, those bastards!"

"Maidei, will you stop this," I interjected.

"There is some recourse on what you both can do," offered Elaine by some way of advice. "You can take your case to the Financial Ombudsman. They are more like a financial regulator or referee if you like, and they should be able to sort you out in your current dispute with your lender. In the meantime, I will proceed with your application. If you're both happy for me to go ahead, then I'll just schedule another meeting with you to sign some of the remaining paperwork. I've done a credit check whilst I was talking to you, and you're all good to go, as you're both squeaky clean. It's just the paperwork, and we should be sorted."

"Thank you. Please, Elaine, do go ahead as early as you can. We can't carry on a minute longer, paying interest only when we could be making inroads into our borrowed capital, and thank you for your time once more," I said as we rose. We shook hands and with that, we both left Elaine's office.

"Now, don't you start blaming me for this palaver," began Maidei once we were in the car.

"The guilty ones are always afraid, Maidei. Can't you see how pathetic it is, you're quickly going on the offensive, so I don't make you accountable for your oversight on this? You told me you were sorting our initial mortgage application and all you needed from me was my signature which I duly complied with, and now this, Maidei?" I remonstrated with her.

"The onus was on you to also have checked the paperwork before signing, mister university lecturer! We're both in this together; you can't blame me alone for this cockup."

"Aaah, I see, whenever things go pear shaped, then you have to taint me as well," I sarcastically sneered at her, and for that I got the silent treatment in the car right up to home. I was lucky to escape the doghouse that evening.

Chapter 5

Maidei

I am Fari's scorned and maligned wife.

I was married for a good two decades before I saw the light and the proverbial scales fell from my eyes. I started doing it behind Fari's back later into our marriage. It was all because of the overbearing and stupid burden of responsibility on Fari's shoulders that partly killed off the spark and eventually our marriage. Killed it all. Now, imagine a husband who was like Father Christmas to his family. Always slaving away for his brothers, sisters, all and sundry kith and kin, at the expense of his children and myself, his wife.

So I refused to play second fiddle. I refused to be a door mat. I refused. I took myself out of my misery. I indulged into a clandestine relationship with Mudiwa. That is the beautiful name of my toy boy lover. I needed a release and I got it. Mudiwa has been that well-needed antidote all these years. I'm not sure whether Fari is privy to my dalliance with my Boo. I don't think Fari sees me as smart enough to pull off something like this. So, it's been quite a feat, pulling this off right under Fari's unsuspecting nose. Frailty, thy name is a man's puffed-up arrogance! Fari knows not what will hit him. All men are arrogant. That's their weakness. Fari is no exception to this dictum. His arrogance pretty much gave me a free reign to pursue my other life with Boo.

At one-point Fari had five that were not from my womb to feed and send to school. That was nigh tough. It broke my spirit and will to live. It broke me to pieces.

"It's a very common story for many in the diaspora, you're not alone, *mwanangu*," remarked *mai Mufundisi*, the vicar's wife at our local Milton Keynes Pentecostal church, as she tried to soothe and cajole me. "Give him a chance; *ndoo zvinoita* marriage." But I was having none of it. Much as I took the barrage of insults, the invectives from his extended family, and was demonised as "selfish, unloving, unAfrican, with a Western viewpoint of the world," I found the whole thing with Fari's wider family morale sapping and draining. I admire the white way of doing things. It can only be in Africa where grown-up men and women expect handouts from their siblings. Only in black Africa.

It's unfortunate that Fari couldn't see what a mug he was when he was being taken advantage of by his family back home. They blatantly milked his benevolence big time. Time and again, during the course of our marriage, some of the perennial messages from his side of the family were thus.

"Sekuru ndikandire kawaya kemapondo, ndookuona monthend."

"Can you send me £100 and will repay you end of the month," they said, and because he'd done it once too many times, they felt entitled to that £100 every month, which was never paid back of course. Grown ass men unable to plan and expecting a bail out every month. These unreasonable monthly demands for financial bailouts from his burgeoning family back home were the cornerstone of my squabbles with Fari. Many times, over these ludicrous demands. I snapped angrily at him, "I refuse to bankroll lazy, greedy sods, back home. These gits have no sense of appreciation at all. They think London streets are paved with gold, which is not the case. Do you see how we work our socks off to earn this elusive pound?"

"Aaah, Maidei, that's not a very kind thing to say. Where is your sense of family?" quipped Fari.

"'But who will look after your own kids and wife, if all you do is bask in this telescopic philanthropy?'"

Usually, my saying this would just kill off any further conversation with Fari. "'Aaah, I see, it's your madness again woman, you're back to your games, needlessly dissing my family again. It's that time of the month when you lose your marbles, but fortunately, now that I know your wiley ways, I won't give you the satisfaction, Maidei. I refuse you conversation,'" and he stormed out of the living room, just like that.

And then our squabblings would take an ugly trend. They would escalate to those physical fights. The constant fights over Fari's extended family in Zim. Their sickening perennial demands. Somehow Fari couldn't see through their duplicitous nature that he was being spectacularly played, used as a mug. "For heaven's sake, Fari, grow up, have some balls, like the man you are, and see it for what it is. Your family are subjecting you to daylight embezzlement," I would repeatedly shriek at him in exasperation, as he gave it back in equal measure. To and fro! Oh, damn!

"Why do you have to set yourself on fire to keep others warm? Ha? Learn to say no! NO is a full sentence and needs no elaboration! Otherwise, you'll end your working life a destitute! The diaspora is designed to keep us work-dependent, like a trap, get that!" Sadly, it turned out my protestations fell on deaf ears. Fari would go ahead abetting, extending his charity to them. It was as if I didn't exist, and my voice didn't matter. Alternatively, he would lash out at me with his vile, patriarchal, cultural values, Zimbabwe bullshit crap. "'You don't get it do you Maidei? No matter where you go, you carry your birthplace; it's part of you always. One can't eviscerate themselves from it. There is always that spiritual bond prevailing, which is how I feel about Zimbabwe, which is why we should never forget our people back home. We shouldn't turn our backs on them.'" Of course, I exercised selective hearing to this mumbo jumbo stuff. That had becoming part of my coping mechanism.

There was a general, disgusting avalanche of vile misogyny directed against me by my inlaws and wider extended family, particularly my being *too white* as they called it, in my ways of life by refusing to be a doormat. "Your misogyny doesn't faze me; I will not be intimidated out of the room by hate. Get it, suck it," I would defiantly remark many times, and that made them despise me more, *an independent free-spirited woman, who could speak out was anathema to the wider extended family.* Once, I had abrasively given it back to Auntie Nyari, her vitriolic war of words after she started in on me again, casting aspersions on my whiteness. "'Your problem Maidei is, your inflated ego and loss of identity, identity crisis if I may put it that way. Really Maidei, whom do you think you are?'" Auntie Nyari had the nerve to place a long-distance call, all the way from Zimbabwe, just to pick a fight with me early in the morning, but I swore under my breath she would get what was coming her way that day. Did she not have something productive to expend her energies on?

"I see Auntie, so you tell me, this is how you would rather spend your hard-earned money, placing a long-distance call, just to insult me?"

She had replied, "'Well, about time you know your place *muroora*, seeing you don't seem to get it, you are a daughter-in-law in the Mupawaenda family, but you seem not to want to interact with anyone in the family at all.'"

"I see Auntie Nyari, and so it's on you to school me on my duties as a daughter-in-law?"

"'Of course, why not?'" she rudely interjected, oblivious of the inherent sarcasm in my retort.

Then I decided to go for the jugular: "Tell you what, Auntie Nyari, being a woman isn't all about curves or a pretty face. You should also have a functional brain, an enduring spirit, and a praying tongue," and with that salvo delivered, I banged the phone down on her, much to my delight for having the last laugh over her.

Good gracious me, it gave me so much peace of mind and unmitigated pleasure, knowing I wouldn't have to interact with those bastards again, Fari's harem of sisters. The bastards!

The strategies and techniques they used on Fari were wide and varied ranging from emotional blackmail: "'If you don't send any money for school fees then the kids will be chased away from school,'" was another usual line from his sisters, and aunties. Auntie Tambu's mother, Tete mai Chagwiza, was the most cunning of them all, adroit and manipulative, so her daughter Tambu could have her school fees paid.

It's no coincidence, therefore, that commencement of school terms was the worst period for my husband when the relentless phone calls, WhatsApp© text messages came full steam galore. I tell you, if not properly grounded, you go off the rails, which is what eventually happened with Fari, as he went overboard in his misplaced duty of care and purported selfless charity. And the sense of entitlement and ungratefulness on the part of the benefactors made me sick and depressed, as the requests bordered on rude demands for material assistance.

Oft times I had pointed out to Fari, "Why not empower your siblings so they won't perpetually drain your fiscus, you know, the kind of 'teach a man to catch a fish' scenario, for want of a cliché."

"Trick is, love, not to pull the ladder on the way up as a family. Why not try to bring your siblings across the shores for them to help themselves, without needless expectations, but with a few exceptions. This has worked for others, like the Gapare family in our hood. In time, this will lessen the pressure on you. Once your siblings are over here, you can help each other out as a concerted effort." You guessed it. Fari had no time to listen to a woman's word, let alone his wife's.

At times, his family would hound him with group WhatsApp© messages in which he would become an object of ridicule and be openly caricatured for being "governed" by a woman -- me that is -- and the running commentary was, "'No wonder he doesn't think of us as his family or help us out anymore.'"

But then, as with Fari, perhaps it was a macho thing with him. Anything which came from me was never good enough to accept, unless it came from someone else. The same odd stubbornness resurfaced when I tried to encourage him to buy our own property in England as a form of investment, as opposed to the, "I will go back to live in Zim mantra."

"Buying a house in the diaspora and paying into a pension is a must to avoid penury!"

"Why would I want to buy a house in a foreign land?" retorted Fari in his usual arrogant, sanctimonious, *mister know it all* odd way.

"Why would you then?" I retorted sarcastically to him.

I doubt he ever got to understand my sarcasm, or perhaps, he chose to ignore it, but such squabbling pretty much typified our marriage. And the sad irony is, the people instigating our squabbles were thousands of kilometres away, ensconced in a cushy life in Zim, being bankrolled my husband. Damn!

Everyone wanted a piece of Fari. He was for grabs from sisters, brothers, distant nieces, nephews; all and sundry in the Mupawaenda clan wanted their stake in his ever-shrinking, family financial pot. Yet on looking closely at the bonds of kinship, it was hazy and murky with some of these people. There was no clear-cut family relationship to talk of. Such was the captivating spiderweb fabric of extended family taking its toll on us. Is it any wonder I felt aggrieved?

"This is not what marriage is about, Fari! I didn't sign up for this!" I had remonstrated with him on numerous occasions till my voice had become hoarse and dry.

It was always the same old shit with his usual standard response, "'Marriage is a collective thing, suck it or leave it!'" So blasé, just like that, as if it was some kind of virtual reality game like he played on his usual PlayStation 4™ when he wanted to avoid conversation with me.

I was fed up with this unending palaver. As far as I was concerned, Fari's relatives lived in a different realm, far removed from mine, a world I preferred not to step into. I couldn't care less about them seeing I was their constant source of vilification and punching bag.

Once I got Taurai's hubby Ben to knock some sense into Fari's head; Ben had once walked the same road my husband was hellbent on pursuing. Was it not the proverbial saying, *kugara nhaka huona dzavamwe*, in order to do well in life, we learn from others, emulating their good practice? It was, however, an interesting spectacle, savouring Ben's and Fari's conversation that evening.

"Look, Fari, hear it from me, this is personal experience stuff. In September 2017, after eight years in South Africa, I resigned and went back to Zim in Oct 2017. Nothing works in Zim. The November 2017 coup gave me hope. I almost transferred my kids also. I couldn't survive in Zim, and after six months I took my old job back. I have lost over R800 000 in Zim, at least I tried. Fortunately, we were able to relocate to England for a fresh start after Taurai secured a job here. But you can't say we didn't try. We learnt our lesson though, we learnt it well, the hard way that is. My fingers were certainly burnt with the Zim experience."

Ben added, "Good luck to you, if you insist on wanting to relocate there, but it might be necessary to keep your medical insurance active in your current host country, in case you ever need to get back for treatment."

"I'm determined to give it my best shot," interposed Fari.

"You know what our problem is here Fari, as fellow diaspora citizens?" Ben asked, as Fari shook his head. "Well, today I'll spell it for you, it's what I call the black tax."

"Black tax?" Fari repeated. "What's that?"

"We as black people have black tax and that never ends. We are still paying here too. That's our spirit of ubuntu, which is our undoing. We feel we must carry the world's troubles on our shoulders. It gets us in a permanent fix.

"I know I went through it, Taurai butted in, "at one time I had three children that were not from my womb to feed and send to school. Imagine?"

With a cheeky wink at Taurai's sentiments, I commented, "Damn! That must've been tough on you. It can break your spirit and will to live, I tell ya! You're a strong woman."

"Don't you think it's a shame that grown up men and women expect handouts. Nowhere do you see a person expecting free money, only in Africa. A white man will not accept free money and will pay you back whatever favour you give them. You buy him a drink, he will work hard to return the favour," remarked Ben, addressing the question to the floor. At that, I readily acquiesced with his sentiments, nodding my head in approval, much to Fari's disapproving scowl and glares, which I interpreted as, I'm seeing you, I know your feelings on this subject.

"Yes, Ben, you actually see some family and friends even taking advantage of their diaspora kith and kin's benevolence. 'Can you send me a small amount? what is £100 to you,' they say dismissively, as if they're privy to my monthly incomings and outgoings." Both Taurai and I laughed mockingly at this insouciance.

"Thankfully, we cottoned on a very long time ago. Years will go by and you'll retire a renter! And too ashamed to go back home because the very people you used to bail out every month will laugh at you for coming home with nothing!"

"That I'm here -- temporarily, I will go back home, *kumusha,* mentality is a trap. Some have citizenship in nations that offer everything, yet they're like someone who still romanticizes about an abusive ex, Stockholm syndrome, constantly banging on about wanting to go back home. My advice: "'Invest where you are. Home is where you lay your head.'"

Taurai, who had been exceedingly quiet all along, now jumped into the fray, seeming to agree with me. "That is what they do best! So, better you start looking after yourself! Grown-ups must learn to look after themselves, except our parents of course, I make an exception there, in looking out after them. That's our filial duty, if I may say. Even the Good Book says it, 'Honour thy father and mother, so your days maybe long on earth.'"

"You know our difference with white people? They don't have the moral obligation to look after their elderly parents and siblings. Most of them simply move out and move on, some don't visit their parents for years, despite them living in the same town. What they earn is THEIRS! While on the other hand, we have this unending dependency syndrome vortex, which perpetually holds us back from progressing with our lives. We can't do anything by way of social mobility advancement. How can you when you are looking after the entire clan's children? In the end your very own children suffer by losing out," Ben said.

"This is all very true Ben. Failing to say no also prolongs this chain of dependence and extended families. People think you must do this and that for this one before you develop yourself first, or before you marry or get married. They failed to do what they want you to do. Draw a line and do what you please; that's my advice."

"I helped many people too, but I am here. It's just the way our African culture is structured. People have many kids that they don't plan for and expect a relative, who seems to have money, to send them all to school and university. It's stressful," Taurai contended.

"My rule is: You look after your own child. You enjoyed the night you sired that child and today you want to share the burden of your enjoyment? Enjoyment is equal to responsibility. There's more to fatherhood than being merely a sperm repository. I will donate if I have extra, but it's not my duty, not my business," I remarked amid chuckles from the trio, though I wasn't so sure of Fari's exact stance with all this.

"We were raised that way. My brother took care of us and others in turn. I was the last to take care of the last borns. We moved and sometimes those people will not; they'll stay expecting you to take care of them and their families. Mind boggling how they still expect you to carry on looking after them, all these years."

"Maidei, you can say that again. People should shoulder their responsibilities without constantly asking for handouts from others, being related is not a crime."

"*Unenge waakunzi iwe une luck saka tibatsire*. It's okay to prioritize yourself. If people knew what we go through in foreign lands, they would cut down on their expectations and empathise with us. You put your head down and work every available overtime shift. It hurts to know that your qualifications and experience don't count for much in the diaspora. I have seen the much-touted, high-profile engineers, human resource managers, accountants from back home, being reduced to mere bbc workers: British bottom cleaners of geriatrics. But now that the tables are turned here in the diaspora, where most Zimbabwean women are nurses with a secure incomes, even earning high incomes, trouble brews. They start playing up in the house, dictating things to their husbands. No wonder you see the high divorce rates amongst fellow Zimbabweans here in England, and even amongst most immigrant communities, *inongova njake njake, donga watonga,* do as you please in marriages."

"I'm glad we're actually talking about this, folks. Someone had to say it, relatives feel entitled. They blackmail you with family curses if you don't meet their needs. Most people will ask you for money, but close to none will ask you about your goals and dreams, or even if you're happy. This includes parents. It's like you are born in debt."

"Diaspora remittances have caused a spoonfeeding mentality such that citizens will never take part in protests because they 'have it all' at the expense of diasporans."

"Well said, Ben," I exclaimed. "I was in Zim recently, and I witnessed people straight from Mukuru with Western Union money remittances to Chicken Slice and Pizza Inn. After that, they go home in a USD kombi, while others were waiting for Covid infested ZUPCO buses for 50c Bond. You wonder *vanoshanda kupi,* then reality sets in *imari dzana mukoma vari Joni, Randani.*"

"Zim folks have mastered the craft of exaggerating their woes. One would be forgiven, they are about to die. *Kuchema chema* is a talent, they act like they are about to die in Zim. Christmas shopping is a need, but when you talk about investing in something productive, no one wants to listen. They're not interested at all."

"Society teaches guilt from a young age, *'ukasapa mwanangu, mangwana ndiwewo'* and at your expense; no one teaches us about boundaries. It's something we start learning as adults, saying no without guilt. People just want to take from you just because you are related, but they never give you something back or some credit to your efforts."

'The problem with some mainstream thinking amongst some of our folks is that a child is considered a retirement plan, '*Aaah anozondichengetawo ndakura,*' he/she will look after me in old age. What if they die first? Why can't we ever think of such eventualities? Even life insurance policies do have risks embedded within them. *Munhu akazofawo wani.*"

Much to my delight, Tauri remarked, "Now that's a whole clan and surely your spouse would have every right to grumble if you're going to take everyone related to you under your wings. The money simply won't be enough to go around." Inwardly I was thoroughly enjoying this talk. Every now and then, I glanced at my husband's scowling face, which gave me kicks; I knew this wasn't the kind of talk Fari would appreciate.

"Bravo Taurai," I remarked, clapping my hands in sadistic jubilation. For was it not the sort of conversation I tended to have with Fari in our marriage, every now and then? And boy, it was reassuring; my sentiments were being echoed by another disinterested party. I surreptitiously glanced at Fari and could clearly see he was getting pissed off at the way the conversation was going.

"Some of my fellow diasporans have been duped by the very relatives they supported. Many have lost their hard-earned money when they send money home that is meant for building their houses. Relatives simply pocket most of the money, buy a few stones, and take pictures of someone else's piece of land and misrepresent it as yours. Some are duped by unscrupulous Harare land barons connected to the ruling mafia. They sell residential land on wetlands, and come the rainy season, we have an unfolding tragedy, as people's so-called houses are swept away in floods. This happened in Chitungwiza and Budiriro that other year."

"I remember one colleague at work, Jamie from Gambia, always banging on about having had a six-months plan when he initially came here. Double digit years later, I'm still here, mate."

"You only need to see how some of these recipients feel so entitled. *Kutozvarira vana ana Sekuru vari Randani.*"

"One thing with the diaspora, you can't afford to be ill. Almost every call from home is about money, even when you say you are ill. No one pays attention to that but they're quick to say, 'So when are you sending money?' If a relative dies, they don't make arrangements. I tell you it's tough. You become the funeral director, arrange the hearse, and foot all the funeral costs, yet over here, one still has to honour their monthly mortgage commitments and utility bills."

"You're spot on, Taurai, the economists factored it all in. There's no better worker than one who has to support people abroad. It's a win-win for the host country."

"Never be depressed about our folks' home but be enlightened with the reality of life and our Zimbabwean situation! These stories we share are inspiring; for me they provide answers and clarity to some of the questions I had as an immigrant navigating my way in this morass and labyrinthine called England."

"Black tax causes depression, especially for young people who start working earlier in their lives and are suddenly have responsibilities and a crisis of expectations thrust upon their lean shoulders. Worst is when you are expected to support an adult who failed to hustle for themselves. Some people will take a decision of staying where they are without ever visiting home because the expectations are impossible. I swear, I've seen this trend with my own eyes, and you wonder why some people never talk about home, let alone visit home, even in the case of a funeral and the loss of a loved one."

"Maybe they are undocumented immigrants who can't afford to blow their cover," interjected the unusually quiet Fari, who seemed to have found his tongue at last.

Not to be undone, Ben remarked, "My experience is, I keep abreast of events back home and visit regularly. Every time I come back after seeing how tough life is in Zim, I come back to England to endure, it's not easy to have glass ceiling."

"You are already on your way! The entrapment of the diaspora is subtle but real!"

"Having lived both in England and South Africa, my advice is, build your life where you are. Support family as necessary but enjoy life where you are. That's what I and others have done. Life is too short."

"This is very true. Failing to say no also prolongs this chain of dependence and extended families. People think you must do this and that for this one, before you develop yourself first. Instead, they failed to do what they want you to do for them. Draw a line and do when you please, otherwise you will eventually be left behind whilst others prosper. I've seen this first-hand in this ephemeral life I've lived."

"I helped many people too, but I'm here. It's just the way our African culture is structured. People have many kids that they don't plan, for but expect a relative who seems to have money to send them all to school and university. 'Tis stressful."

"With the way things are, home is now wherever you are. Sink those roots now and naturalize, if at all possible. Painful to accept, but that feeling is not uniquely Zimbabwean. Holding on to the hope of a normal Zimbabwe any time soon seems like a stubborn denial. Visits, yes, but to think we will ever live in those houses, those stands we buy in Zim, is very much pipedream stuff."

"Main problem with diasporans is having two minds. You cannot live two lives, one in Zim and one in the diaspora. Once you do that, you are doomed and going nowhere slowly. Home is where you lay your head, where the heart is. And there is more to investments than houses!"

"I do understand but disagree with the home is where you sleep sentiment, maybe because I have lived in countries where you're constantly reminded that you are the other, and that alone makes me yearn for a better Zim to go back to, someday."

"That is the main concern for some of us who have already attempted to return and settle back home. I think, once you are used to functional public services and state institutions, it becomes difficult to readjust backwards to a system where such services come at a very high cost. A system where public servants feel entitled to get a bribe for doing their jobs, for which they will still get paid, come end of the month."

"Enough of this diaspora talk and your needless philosophising, folks. Why can't we talk about something else more productive?" Fari finally cut in, visibly irritated at the way the conversation had drifted and had appeared to largely marginalise him throughout.

"But, what else can we talk about Fari? If we talk premier league football, you're a sore loser, you get so wound up, your team is wallowing mid-table with other mediocre clubs. About time you switch allegiance, mate."

"I'm a diehard Arsenal fan Ben, however you lampoon my team. Forget it, I'm not an unashamed glory hunter like some of you! In any case, we are not doing badly as you make out."

"Haha-ha... we are not doing badly. Listen to yourself speak Fari. Being beaten by West Brom the other day, newly promoted West Brom, a team fighting relegation for that matter, and you say you're doing well? Are you living in a pararell universe of some sort?"

"Coming from a United fan, this is not surprising Ben. You guys and your lot are experts in these snide remarks. But let's talk football mate, proper, beautiful football then, Arsenal is right up there in the top echelons with the greats of European football! The pride of European football teams if I may say. I'm talking of the likes of Barcelona here, Barca, Real Madrid, Juventus, Manchester City, not your so-called charlatans United!"

"Remember the days of the Boss, Arsene Wenger. four-time Premier League title winners, 14 FA cup winners, cup champions, not to mention *The Invincibles* 2003-04 season dream team, in which we were unbeaten for the entire season, it's all out there in the public domain. Dare I go further?" He spoke with an animated pitch to his voice raising both his fingers as if to emphasise the wins to Ben, who by now was writhing in raucous laughter."

"You're so comical, Fari," Ben replied. "You know this, you come here, swooning around about your mere four Premier League title wins, hahaha... this is a sick joke for you to utter such hogwash. You know very well it can only be us, Manchester United, the greatest of the greats, who've won the Premier League more times than any other team in England's football history, and yet we don't shout from rooftops. Hahaha, hear, hear...And don't get me started about your so-called prowess in European football. How many times has Arsenal won the Champions League? No need to answer that one mate; I'll just leave it here as a rhetorical question. Earlier on you said you liked facts, well in this instance, let the facts speak for themselves."

Taurai and I had quietly slithered into the conservatory, where we savored the late afternoon July summer breeze amid cocktails while the men talked about their beloved football. At least I could see English premier league football was one passion that still visibly excited my husband, especially his unparalleled zeal for his beloved Arsenal Football club, AFC as he called them in his heady moments. I remember, when things were still kicking between us, on my fortieth, he'd surprised me with two FA cup final tickets, Arsenal was playing Manchester United at Wembley that afternoon. It had been a memorable afternoon, I have to give Fari that credit, as Arsenal, who were the underdogs in the match, went on to spring a surprise, beating the favourites Manchester United 5-4 on penalty shootouts after playing a whopping 120 minutes extra time. That afternoon had been big for Fari, epic in stature! Then, Fari had been one happy fella. We drove home from Wembley with his car stereo blaring the *Mukanya's Maiti Kurima Hamubviri* tune. As my man chugged along the M25 motorway in his guzzler BMW X5, and then careered on to the M1 motorway to Milton Keynes doing 90 miles per hour, I had to chide him, "That's enough baba waMuchi, I'm equally happy for you, you've won your record FA cup, but pipe down a bit on your speed. You don't want to be zapped by the M25 speed cameras, do you?"

"Who cares about bloody speedy cameras when we've fucking won the FA Cup again! We are Arsenal FC. In Arsene We Trust, this is what we do at AFC, Arsenal Football Club," he continued singing along to the music, and I let him be. It was his day after all. It's a free country; every man deserves to be happy. That evening we had made love with a certain renewed ferocity and tempo hitherto unknown, which could only remind me of our earlier years of marriage, when we used to do it non-stop, be it on the washing machine, on the dining room settee, kitchen table, or in the bathtub amidst fits of giggles. I can still vividly smell Fari's aftershave and strong, alluring aroma of his *Jean Paul Gautier*™deodorant as he strummed my nubile body in the darkness of our master bedroom. It was as if he was playing an acoustic guitar, skilfully and patiently thrusting in and out, as I gyrated my hips in ecstatic unison, in full acquiescence of his stiff manhood, till we both exploded together in a vortex of crescendo. "Oh, handsome, that was just what I needed. I had so much pent up energy and work stress, and you just about gave me the much needed panacea my man, thank you," I'd remarked, as I wiped off his semen from my bits. Looking back, it is only now poignantly hitting me that, at some point, things were not this bad with Fari. We did have something going on between us at some point, a strong connective vibe. So, where did we possibly go wrong? It wasn't only his love for football we used to share, though I mostly did it for him, humouring him, for is that not one of the tenets of

love: "Your interests will be my interests also?"

Fari also used to reciprocate my appreciation and enthusiasm for cricket and tennis. In the early years of our marriage, every July, he would get Wimbledon tickets for both of us, even though I knew he had no clue about tennis, let alone understanding its rules and maxims. I kept having to explain the basics to him: Tennis games comprise sets; tennis scores are *Love, 15, 30, 40;* and it's game point, which wins matches, among other little titbits. I remember we were there when Supreme Serena Williams, as I liked to call her, clashed with her sister Venus Williams in that herculean, titanic Women Wimbledon duel of 2009. That was the Venus and Serena's epic Wimbledon meeting on the grass courts. What a belter of a match it was, featuring "big hitting" and "big serving" on the part of the two sisters. It was certainly a memorable day in Wimbledon tennis history, a sublime match between Serena and Venus, what John McEnroe, former renowned tennis player and commentator dubbed, "a borderline classic."

Such was the grandeur of the epic duel between the sisters; it elicited myriad joyous responses from tennis fans the world over, myself, not the least. Although Venus went on to win the match by 7-5, 6-4, pipping my favourite Supreme Serena, still I wasn't disappointed as the Williams sisters later teamed up to win the doubles title that year, and later a second Olympic Gold medal together. These are some of my red-letter-day highlights with my handsome boy Fari, not to mention the litany of Ashes cricket matches we used to attend.

I digress from Supreme Serena and her sister's tennis victory. The latter's win seemed to have positively bounced on my sex life with Prince Handsome Fari. But there is no way I can fail to acknowledge one other memorable shared experience with Fari: The Oval 2005 Ashes, Kevin Pieterson inspired "victory." It had been another one of Fari's brilliant surprises, something he was really good at throwing then. He said, "*Sugar Lips,* cover your eyes, I've got something to share with you. Please, no cheating, Maidei."

"Okay, no cheating," I agreed.

"Ready, are we, 3-2-1, you may open your eyes," and boom, there they were, right in my hands, The Oval Five Test series match tickets for that coveted Saturday match against the mighty Aussies.

"Oh, you're wonderful, handsome, thank you so much, love." In gratitude, I had flung my arms around Fari, smothering him with an avalanche of warm kisses, ecstatic at the chance to savour the cricket royalty match, the Ashes biennial tournament. Who would want to miss such an epic tournament? Throughout the preceding week, it had generated a buzz at work, becoming a key talking point. Never underestimating the Brits and their love of cricket, I was certainly not an exception, having joined the bandwagon, also.

"You are so good to me, handsome," I said. That evening I had cried tears of joy, perched up on Fari's lap, in our exquisite foreplay, which preceded our volcanic lovemaking. I felt him come as he thrust his manhood into me hard and fast, like he was high on some substance, possibly weed. The sex was rough and fiery; Fari liked it that way. As I showered afterwards, I could feel his semen trickling down my thighs, and I smiled contentedly to myself. My bottom felt sore from too much lovemaking, but that didn't matter. I had thoroughly enjoyed it. I could swear I was so overwhelmed with Fari's kindness and sweet gestures. We were so much in love then. The Oval 2005 Test series hadn't disappointed either, as it became folklore history, a stuff of legends kind of thing. That memorable September day with my handsome, we witnessed a 25-year-old batsman, Kevin Pieterson, announce himself to the cricketing world by trailblazing his way to "victory" against Australia.

Yes, we thumped the Aussies 373+335 to 367+410, thanks to Kevin Pieterson's brilliance. And you know what? I was there to witness it all. This dazzling win, to cap what was rightly regarded as one of the best Ashes matches of all time, resplendent in cricket history as both teams fought tooth and nail for that little urn.

"I can only thank our hero of the day, Kevin Pieterson, for the outstanding inning. Bravo, my fellow Brits!"

Although a draw was declared, still this gave England, this gave us, our first series win over the Aussies since 1987. Get that! Top notch, resounding success, which enabled us to bring that little urn back to England. England won! We won the Five Test series 2-1.

And of course, thanks to my handsome for the surprise tickets to The Oval. Always more of a football person, I'm not sure Fari had grasped the enormity of our win over the Aussies. "Did you enjoy it? Looks like you had a perpetually pained expression on your face, and you would have needed someone to take you out of your misery," I had playfully teased him as he drove us back home.

"Sort of. You know I have no clue about cricket, but it was all for you, of course."

"I know that," I told him. Playfully, I said to him, igniting the foreplay way in advance as I sought to whet his appetite, "That's why I'm teasing you, dummy. Thanks, you will be rewarded handsomely, love, in the quiet comfort and privacy of our bedroom, later tonight. King size bed, beware..."

"Oh yea," and we both had a quiet chuckle. What a blast we'd had then, those formative years of our marriage. And now I found myself reflecting, my mind wandering back in a labyrinth of nostalgia, on this, another momentous day, as Fari drove us home again after the glittering Serena-Venus Williams Wimbledon duel.

I had been chuffed enough to get an autograph from both Serena and Venus after the epic match. In a replay of the Arsenal victory over Manchester United FA cup finals night, that night, I had given it to Fari, in leaps and bounds throughout the night till he begged me, and panted, 'Thanks ,*sugar lips*, I'm really grateful, but I'm sore down there. Can we adjourn for tonight, please? The boy is flacid now and will need recharging tomorrow," he had begged me as I playfully teased him with my luscious boobs buried in his face. So many memories, such intimate moments.

That was then! Something had certainly happened to drive us asunder and agonising over this missing link only further helped pull me out of my reverie to the present moment.

'Thank you both, Ben and Taurai, we really have to go; baba waMuchi, are you done with your football banter, with Ben? We really have to take our leave..."

"Well, not until Ben acknowledges Arsenal are the real deal in English football," Fari had shouted back, and we left with Ben still protesting to the contrary.

A few weeks following that robust, no holds barred, fiery roundtable discussion with Ben, Taurai and Fari, one would have thought Fari would have seen the light afterward. But no, that was not the Fari I knew. The Fari I knew had gone somewhere. I'd once remarked to him, "But where have you gone, Fari?" A bemused Fari had responded in bewilderment, looking at me askance. With a sly smile curling his lips and quipping, he said, 'But I haven't gone anywhere, Maidei, I'm still here with you."

That was the problem with Fari, he now saw a joke in everything I said, perhaps inwardly dismissing me as a caricature. Inwardly, I couldn't help reflecting that this was not the man I had married, my partner in crime during those FA cup matches attendance, Wimbledon matches at centre court and grass court, early July mostly.

How had Fari become this other person, a monster of gargantuan proportions? I pondered within myself many times. *A person I did not recognise anymore. This was not the man I had married.* Somehow, I felt duped within myself.

Where had this headstrong, sometimes foolhardy loony came from? I was none the wiser. Bizarrely, in his own foolish, obdurate way, Fari still pressed ahead with his relocation to Zim plan. In fact, the next few days following this group chat, Fari was tetchy and grumpy, as if he blamed me for stirring the conversation, saying it was a pre-planned stitch up at my behest to make him toe the line. "Of course, nothing could be further from the truth Fari," I remonstrated. "In no way did I engineer that conversation to go that way, in the manner it meandered. Why don't you grow up for once and stop this needless paranoia and siege mentality? People have different ways of seeing life, and it's not always the case that your views will be absolute. Suck it in!"

That was it, as it only made Fari dig in further. "I want to see how things pan out. I am off to try my second chance in Zim," he had opined. "I don't see any viable prospects here anymore, Maidei."

"Why don't you give it time, Fari?"

"Give what time?"

"Your knee-jerk reaction to return home is not a well-thought out idea, believe me, and listen to me as your wife for once, I implore you."

"What is there for me here in England? Nothing other than the cold, miserable weather. I don't see any future at all, Maidei. I don't know about you, but I do miss my old lectureship job at UZ. I've made up my mind, I am returning to Zim and see how things pan out. Better to err trying than continue to wallow in misery, methinks."

"What about our marriage? And where exactly does it fit amidst these grandiose plans of yours? Are you returning to a godforsaken place on a whim and fanciful notions?"

"Well, if you care so much about our marriage, perhaps about time you close ranks with me as your husband. Then we should be having a consensus on our return journey home."

"Poor Fari, all these years in England and you're still behaving like a fuddy-duddy!"

"You'll never cease to amaze me Maidei, especially with your newfound identity. Somehow, in your own twisted mindset, you've now taken a shine to Ben and Taurai since you all started this anti-Zim tirade. Is it any wonder that you now speak like a votary of this couple, our neighbours, and now you sing their gospel, their general loathing and distaste of anything Zimbabwean?"

"That's not a fair indictment, Fari, and you know it!"

'Then you shouldn't throw stones if you care so much about your glass house," he triumphantly smirked at me.

"Aaah, I see, brilliant idea isn't it Fari? It's all well-thought out, just close shop and leave everything at the drop of a hat to return to Zimbabwe. Has it even once crossed your mind that we have the mortgage obligations hanging over our heads like the sword of Damocles? And what of Muchi and Yeukai's feelings? Do we uproot them, just like that, from their new lived culture here, where they've made friendships, to massage the ego of a dictator? Why do you behave like Mugabe in this marriage? It's like only your voice matters, how can you be so obdurate?"

"Oh, do come off it, Maidei, and spare me the corny platitudes... given your frigid heart, where is this family, lovey-dovey stuff coming from? A new heart? Are we on a conversion path here? Is this your pseudo-Damascus moment? I'm sorry, I can't take that, I'm allergic to bullshit."

"Don't belittle me please! This is not what I signed up for. I have been to hell and back in this marriage. I'm fed up with your antics, Fari. They stink to high heavens! I've had it up to here!" I gestured, raising my palm to my neck.

"Bloody hell! Stop it, Maidei! This is not about you! It's about my life and my choices to go to Zimbabwe or stay here, and I'll pretty much do as I please! Don't play the blame game with me; it won't work. Besides, what difference does it make, Maidei, consulting you or not? It's not like you would ever take my side, would you? How many times have you ever listened to my point of view yourself?"

I flipped these to her as rhetorical questions, Fari told himself. He mused further, *That was enough for poor Maidei, who almost brusquely left the room without a word. I must have floored her breathless with my biting sarcasm. Looking back, I didn't feel affirmed in my decision from the trio, even though I knew I was doing the right thing, following through on my convictions, returning to Zimbabwe. I wasn't really surprised they were knocking my ideas down. Why would Ben, Taurai and Maidei support me?*

That night we went to bed without talking to each other and with unresolved issues between us. Can you imagine the bloody cheek when Fari tried to touch my boobs! The idiot! I roughly shoved his grubby hand away. I seethed, "Leave me alone will you, you sick pervert! Go fuck your gobby tongue." With that I turned around and gave him my back for the entire night.

I was fuming underneath, raging angry at Fari, although I can't be certain whether this was the turning point in our increasingly fractious relationship. But one thing is for sure, when the tears start pouring down, you pretty much know the shit has hit the fan. The battle lines had been drawn long ago. Somehow, I was under no illusions. We had crossed the Rubicon in my troubled marriage with Fari. The centre could no longer hold, and perhaps it was now merely a question of time...Perhaps.

Chapter 6

The Lure of Home

Persistent frustration with the lack of social life in England, coupled with my failure to integrate after two decades, and add a troubled marriage in the fray, I summoned my inner courage and decided to set residence in Zimbabwe. The second coming, as I called it. I know, I had been talking about it a long time, in my sparring with Maidei and our neighbours, fellow Zimbos, Ben and Taurai. *So much for talking, now is the time for action from me. I have to walk the talk, let the men be counted from the boys*, I found myself saying to my inner psyche.

Just over twenty years ago, when I first landed on the English shores, I thought I'd be here for three years maximum; work and go home, and set up an electrical contracting company. Twenty-two years later, I was still in the Queen's country. I didn't think I would be there for long.

In my little head, I had brilliant ideas which made perfect sense when I decided to relocate back to Zimbabwe from England. Part of me had never jelled and accepted England as my natural habitat, despite the long stay. Perhaps this wasn't surprising. I had grown up in Zimbabwe, where I had forged my identity, maturing as a little boy in Gatsi rural areas, Honde Valley. I didn't see eye to eye with my wife Maidei on my relocation plans. Our views couldn't be more diametrically opposed on this. "Get used to the idea, England is now home for us," had become her usual refrain as she was wont to rebuke and trod on my "second coming mirage" as she called it. "It's a hopeless dream Fari, it's not gonna work. It will end in tears, I can see through this, your vacuous plan."

The more she said this, the more I squared up to her, and became increasingly obdurate and defiant in my dealings with her, so when I mooted the idea of my eventual reverse migration back home to Zimbabwe, I kept some of my plans to myself. *Why would I share with her, when all she did was constantly pillage and knock them down?* I rationalised within myself.

Call me rustic, but as a young lad who had grown up in rural Gatsi District, herding goats and cattle; running barefoot and skimpily dressed; experiencing the raucous laughter in the Samaringa rain; walking to Samaringa School barefoot as the morning dew laced my feet, and playing hide-and-seek in the Msasa bushes. I knew so well the allure of village life: The smell of cow dung; the chirping of the birds; the buzz of the grass insects… all these nostalgic memories greatly appealed to me. Never mind the bright lights of the city where I moved in later years, the greater part of me still harboured notions of setting up my retirement home in rural Gatsi Village. With this at the back of my mind, I secretly liaised with my nephew Gumisai, my sister's son, to oversee my project for having a borehole sunk at our Gatsi family homestead, where I had cut my teeth into puberty and popped my cherry.

The plan was *muzaya* Gumisai would help with the borehole construction project first.

"So, Muzaya this is the plan," I had said to Gumisai over the phone. "I want you to drill a borehole at the family homestead, then we'll do solar installations thereafter. We move in phases. Fence a piece of land for the borehole project to insulate it from the village communal use."

"Consider it done, Uncle Fari." That gentlemen's agreement marked the onset of my committing huge monthly sums of money to Gumisai as he set up the borehole project, from its infancy right up to its fruition. The plan was he would send me periodic pictures of men at work doing the borehole drilling and keep me in the loop on the different phases of the project. I ensured that I hid this from my wife, as she was adamant that she was now done with Zimbabwe and would not hear of anything to do with Zimbabwe ever again, come hell or high water.

"What for? What is there to go back for?" Maidei would sarcastically retort, throwing this barb back at me each time I broached the subject, therefore, this meant my Zim projects were conducted in absolute secrecy.

The borehole project went on very well as Gumisai successfully delivered on this and now it was time to move on to phase two of the projects, installation of solar power on the four-bedroom homestead with the corrugated iron roof at rural Gatsi.

"I have gathered a series of quotes on the job, Uncle, and it's not looking good," Gumisai had alerted me.

I enquired, "What do you mean it's not looking good?"

"Well, let me give you a lowdown of the figures." True to his word, the figures from four different contractors were astronomical. In the end, we settled on $6500USD. This was a lot of money and I had to think of ingenious ways to hide this from the prying eyes of my wife Maidei; she had a sharp, hawkish eye on the family pot's income and outgoings. I also knew this was a big commitment financially and trusted, like the borehole project, that *muzaya* Gumisai would deliver. For some unexplained reasons, I had a pensive sense of unease and dread, which I brushed aside anyway. I rationalised doing these projects was the genesis of my eventual move back to Zimbabwe to be rid of the stresses of England, where we had to keep two or three jobs running concurrently, just to stay afloat. I had seen how most exiles had swollen feet, as if they had elephantiasis, on account of the constant run-around of keeping multiple jobs, the long-standing, gruelling hours in factory jobs being one of them.

My friend Lester worked in the factory where, he told me, "We are not allowed to sit down Fari. You have to be constantly standing in a line like a food chain, passing heavy objects to the person standing next to you. And woe unto you, if you dare sit down because of back pain. The managers will descend on you with full wrath like a sledgehammer, or you will be called for a disciplinary hearing. A full-scale disciplinary hearing, just like that."

"But surely, they have to be human?' I countered. Lester reaffirmed, "Human, they don't do human, you're in the wrong industry if you talk human, I'm afraid." To compound matters, he told me, "The factory is clogged with huge swathes of dust particles which are making most of us ill; that's why I have these unending spells of colds and chest infections. Given these days of coronavirus, I live in mortal fear of contracting a cold, lest it degenerates into that awful illness. And yes, you guessed it, one can't afford to be ill in these isles, as you well know. Who is going to pay your bills in England when you're ill? No one. I can tell you this for certain."

Now reflecting on these conversations with Lester, I couldn't, for the love of Mike, understand why my wife wouldn't simply get it and agree with me to close shop, that England wasn't the place to be. How could one see a future in this shithole? I just couldn't get it, but then I have to give it to Maidei, she has always been shallow and exhibitionist in her persona. Once a show girl, always a show girl; give her a stage, she would dance for an imaginary audience. She certainly enjoyed the kicks showing off to her other siblings in Zim. "Hee, we live in England." "So what, you live in England, as if it's anything to write home about." "Just a misplaced show of vanity, nothing else." And so, mindful of my reservations about staying in England for the long haul, I scrimped on doing long shifts in my other weekend care job, where I looked after geriatrics, cleaning their bums, a demeaning job by all standards for one who used to be a university lecturer back home.

Within three months' pay cheques I was able to send Gumisai the money to kick-start the solar installation project. Things went on well for about the first three months until Gumisai texted me the bombshell news on WhatsApp©: "Uncle Fari, the solar pump was stolen last night. Not only that, but the robbers managed to cut the fence housing the borehole, so it's a double blow, and to replace the pump we are looking at half the amount you sent me for the job, so that's nearly 3 and half thousand US dollars, not taking into account that the men still need to be paid for their labour." I was gutted and visibly dejected by this setback. I had no choice other than to shelve the project, as there was no way I would be able to raise that kind of money again at short notice. So, I let it be and called time on the solar project, though it hurt me on the financial loss I incurred. I lived to fight another day like the reputed cat of nine lives infamy.

Chapter 7

Business Empire – Dream Big

When I arrived in Harare for my second coming, I was brimming with grandiose plans to set up a thriving transport business industry which, according to the plan in my head, would not only bankroll my retirement, but would eventually sever the umbilical cord with England.

The plan was two-fold: To have a people passenger carrier fleet and cross-border, heavy haulage truck business empire, *magonyeti*, as we call them in my mother tongue. I had secretly stashed my savings and hid this from Maidei. I knew she would have dissuaded me anyway, and conveniently found other alternative uses for the money. Having grown up in a polygamous setting, my father had schooled me well and proper in the art of deception when dealing with one's wife. "You see son," Dad was wont to say, "a real man does not declare all his finances to his wife. You stash some money aside for the proverbial rainy day. That's what a clever man does, lest you're left out in the cold, should you declare all your earnings. Look at me Fari, how else do you think I have managed to consistently juggle having two wives concurrently, yet I still manage? Well, it's quite simple. I'm smart with my finances and none of my wives knows the true extent of my finances. It's all shrouded in murky waters and secrecy…" then Dad would burst out laughing after imparting his piece of wisdom.

I may have been a little boy, but I had taken to Dad's tutelage and lessons very well, the way a duckling takes to water. And true to his words, after Dad's funeral years later, the events only proved to the wider family how the man had been a Machiavellian prince of darkness and past master of deceit, especially as all the insects came crawling out of the woodwork, not the least of which was the litany of children and his myriad satellite families who came out claiming they were his. It was through his death that it dawned on us: The man had certainly been a dark horse. Mother was thoroughly heartbroken at this to her last days. "Talk of not really knowing a person," she would often remark to anyone who dared give her an audience.

I digress, but following my Harare arrival, all together my savings were able to kick-start my transport business. Besides, where I needed to supplement my coffers, I was also able to dip into my pension pot from my erstwhile UZ job as a don.

As I attempted to acclimatise to life in Harare, I did my market survey and saw a possible future in the *kombi transport* industry; these were informal emergency taxis which would ferry passengers to and from the myriad locations into the city centre. Thus, I invested in this venture. I started with six 18-seater kombis plying City Tafara/ Mabvuku, and also Chitungwiza city routes. Part of the arrangement was that I would use my trusted nephews, *wana* muzaya, as the drivers and conductors to oversee the business portfolio on my behalf, with myself coming in as the overarching overlord, policing the enterprise.

Out of all the trusted nephews, my sister's son, Munyaradzi, stood out from the mainstream, and I tended to trust him with the day-to-day running of the transport business, alongside another *muzaya*, Chabuya. For the first few months, things were looking up; I did manage to branch out and diversify into cross border heavy vehicles, haulage trucks plying, Harare, Lusaka, Joburg, Harare, and also Gaborone Harare. Things were really beginning to look up for me, and I reflected to myself, *How smart I've been leaving England, its horrible weather, and dry psyche.* Gosh, how I would have loved to gloat to Maidei and her dual naysaying prophets of doom, Ben and Taurai. I surely didn't miss them beating the drums of their despondency tune and the *"it can't be done"* mantra.

There's one area, though, where I increasingly failed to make a breakthrough: salvaging my long-distance relationship with my irascible wife, Maidei. I have lost count of the litany of phone calls I made to her in earnest, imploring her to ditch England and join me in Zim, as things were on an upward trajectory, but she would hear none of it. She would constantly remonstrate on the phone, "You can't convince me otherwise, Fari. Why don't you just come to terms with it? How many times do I have to tell you, I long ago severed my umbilical ties with Zim?"

Perhaps I am too much of a glutton for optimism, but I kept harbouring false notions. *Aah give her time; in time she will come round and join me and we will become a complete family again.* The kids didn't bother me much, though I didn't have much of a relationship to write home about, especially with my son Muchi, who had taken quite badly my decision to "dump Mom and retire to Zim," as he called it. He hardly spoke with me, but aired his sentiments when he did, saying, "I'm done with you Dad, you're excommunicated; don't bother making contact with me." But I think he was conflating issues here, as we had also fallen out on a delicate matter which I couldn't countenance.

How could Muchi dare to have chosen that dreaded, horrible path which had brought so much shame and obloquy to me? Even now, I can't bear to talk about it. I'm not yet ready, perhaps, and that's a subject for another day, my son's treachery and opprobrium.

Things were different with my daughter, Yeukai. We'd always had a healthy, robust relationship, but somehow something happened in her first year at university which made her drop out and subsequently soured our relation-ship. I was disappointed enough with her first pregnancy so soon after her first semester, and then when it happened the second time, that just about ruined it for me. That was the well-known last straw for me. I continued to feel a personal loss at the emotional distance which has characterised and sadly marred my relationship with my little flower Yeukai. So, on the home front, I inwardly mourn the spiritual loss of both my children. Perhaps, one day in the future, things maybe righted. Who knows? We live in hope and die in despair, as an amorous friend used to say to me. But it's worth holding out hope, methinks.

I can't say I am whiter than white myself. During my several years' sojourn in Harare, I stayed with Liz, an ex-childhood sweetheart whose own marriage had floundered. We had this mutual, unwritten, sexual agreement, initially according to where we would only meet for the deed as and when we both needed it. The youngsters these days term it, "friends with benefits." There was no love in this arrangement; it was purely a physical thing. I periodically needed sex, and Liz was there to unfailingly fulfil that need. Once, she started talking about marriage but I dissuaded her of those fanciful notions, saying, "Now, will you stop it, this silliness Liz? You know very well I have my wife in England. Why should I entertain getting married? You and I know that we're playing the field here, so let's enjoy it, make the most of it, is all I ask of you. Reciprocate my gesture, as I don't make any exacting demands or expectations on you."

"But I want you to myself, handsome. I want the security of us being together, with no spectre of outside impediments," Liz would pontificate.

With a dismissive wave of my hand, I said, "Why don't you give it time?" I wanted to buy time with her. In my heart of hearts, I wouldn't hear of ending my fledgling marriage with Maidei. In spite of my marital transgressions, I still had this irrational belief, that somehow things between Maidei and me would gradually be resolved. Talk of misplaced faith. Never underestimate the power of self-delusion. That was then, with me playing hard to get, but eventually, frailty, thy name is carnal pleasures. I ended up moving in with Liz to her plush Mt. Pleasant Heights Harare home. A senior accounting executive, Liz worked for one of the largest and most prestigious accounting firms in Harare, Coopers and Price House Chartered Accountants. She certainly had a privileged background and I found her on point intellectually. What an immersive draw, especially her knack for intelligent conversations. Add on that a brimming sex life, then I was one happy fella. Liz surely knew how to keep my scrotum empty.

The sex between us was always mind-blowing. Liz was a tigress, tireless in bed, full of boundless energy and creativity. She always kept me on my toes. Many times, I was left huffing and puffing for more, but too far gone to perform any further. The sexual chemistry between us helped cement our bond over the years I spent in Harare. She was a tall, buxom woman with wide hips and a disarming smile, very much a fashion connoisseur who dressed extremely well in her designer labels… Luis Vuitton™, Dolce and Gabbana™, Lorenzo™, sporting equally expensive fragrances in her all-inclusive repertoire of exclusive, lavish fur coats. Many atimes, I had multiple orgasms in the inner warmth of those broad hips as I navigated her inner crevices.

One of my trusted muzaya, whom I regarded as my top right-hand man in my transport business, Chabuya was a war veteran who shocked me one afternoon when he announced his intention to quit from being my lead point man in the transport business.

Incredulous, I inquired, "But how can you just say you want to leave like this *muzaya?* What's become of you? You can see how things are increasingly difficult in this shambolic economy, yet you want to throw your job away, just like that! Are you out of your mind Chabuya?"

"But haven't you heard Sekuru?' he interposed animatedly, wringing his hands in the air.

"Heard what?" I was getting visibly frustrated with him.

"The high-profile demonstrations. The war veterans have been demonstrating for recognition and financial compensation, and now the Mugabe government has relented."

"But why do you demand recognition, let alone financial reward, for your war effort? I didn't realise you were mercenaries when you took up arms against colonialism," I chided him, my disapproval all too obvious.

"Whatever you say, Khule, but we deserve it, we're in line to get a windfall, we're talking of heavy, imminent, gratuity pay-outs, free healthcare, and free education for our kids, up to university. No disrespect to you, Sekuru, for these past few years, but now I don't see the need to be working for anyone again. I'm still grateful to you though Khule."

"So much for being greedy," I sniggered at Chabuya derisively. "Is it not only over two decades or so ago, that you lot were paid $50,000 reparations? So why should you be paid for the second time, as if the liberation war of this country was not a collective effort? Did we not talk of the freedom fighters as the fish in water, with us, the masses, being the very water which shielded them? So, you tell me Chabuya, are we, the *povo*, also going to get these so-called financial rewards, handouts, what have you? Have the powers that be not learnt anything from that mistaken decision of yester-year?" I let this barrage of questions hang in the air, clearly discomfited by Chabuya's greed and misplaced sense of entitlement which was clearly grating on my nerves.

I felt worked up and nigh exasperated. I couldn't understand the wisdom, let alone see the logic, of Chabuya quitting his job on a mere government promise yet to be honoured by this dishonest mafia government. Was he not smart enough to realise how this government had failed the nation? Inwardly reflecting to myself, I began musing on what I had observed of the downward spiral of the Zim economy within the last few months but had refused to openly acknowledge it for fear of bursting my reality check bubble.

I had been braving it all along, but the economy seemed to have taken a turn for the worse, and none was so intense than my business interests. Running my informal business had gradually become nigh difficult in Zim, because of the high inflationary environment. Once your vehicle had a breakdown, you knew it was on its knees and on its way out. At least that had been my experience with my aging fleet; spares to vehicles had to be imported and given the useless bond paper currency, it was nigh exorbitant sourcing for the scarce foreign currency on the parallel market to facilitate buying spares. And now that there was talk of this huge unbudgeted expenditure on the national fiscus, $30,000 us dollars pay-outs to each war veteran, which was the second time they were getting financial handouts! I had a weird sense of déjà vu and apprehension that things were about to take a turn for the worse. My heart skipped as I thought of Maidei's usual anti-Zim, anti-rulers' diatribes, and my friend Ben's cynicism with the Mugabe administration. Inwardly, a little voice told me, *there's no way should I agree all these people had been true in their scepticism of my relocation to Zim and trying to eke out a living. It's far too early to panic,* that inner voice reassured me. *Hold tight, hang in there and see how things pan out.*

Chapter 8

Zumba

"Right, girls move sideways! Yes, Emily, let's see those hips sway sideways, to the left, to the right, to the left.... Now, chest forward and keep going, up down, up down, keep the rhythm going," Mudiwa, our Zumba class instructor bellowed to us in the well-ventilated auditorium hall, encouraging us with our body moves as we gyrated on the floor serenading to Abba's *Fernando*© playing in the background. Mudiwa was always full of life, an animated figure, as he belted out the instructions. He would jog up and down the long Zumba room's wooden floors, clapping his palms, egging us on in our Zumba gymnastics and body rhythmic movements.

It was coming up to thirteen months now, five of which had been fruitful rich months in which I had come to know Mudiwa as my young, fit, fitness class Zumba trainer. There had been something in the way he looked at me. Mudiwa! Something like a signal, perhaps. A sexually alluring inviting smile, a flicker of interest which flattered me, my ego, that at 52 I could still pull young attractive males like Mudiwa? Indeed, he was a good-looking young man. I put him at maybe early thirties just a few years older than my firstborn son Muchadei.

A couple of times we'd bumped into each other along the corridors to the changing rooms. Good Lord! I swear, on more than one occasion, I'd caught Mudiwa ogling at my boobs, undressing me with those lecherous eyes. "You wanna check my tits out, you're welcome, Boo," I surprised myself one afternoon uttering such an open invitation to this flirtatious young man.

"Of course, why not, sunshine, would be such a pleasure," he'd thrown the gauntlet back at me in equal gaiety and defiance, which I found sexually irresistible.

"Can I invite you for a drink at Kingston shopping centre, Maidei?"

O boy! He need not have asked, given my floundering relationship with Fari at home. I was all too flattered to be accorded attention. I hadn't done it in a long time with Fari, as he increasingly upped the ante about his wanting to relocate to Zimbabwe, which mostly put me off. The few times we'd done it had degenerated to a more or less insipid, sombre, mechanical, rhythmless chore devoid of emotions. It had all become reduced to more like a hardcore duty. "Have you finished? Okay, get off me then, and make sure you clean up your mess Fari," I'd remarked one evening, chiding him, perhaps inwardly for coming so soon, as I rolled over the bed sexually frustrated. I lay prostate, my mind elsewhere. *Some men! They come too soon and that's it. Gone, just like that! After a few faffing and fumbling about, they think they've done the job. Yet, I've barely felt anything.*

That summed up my increasingly drying sex life with Fari. Sadly, I think we both felt it, even though it was unspoken between the two of us that this thing called passion, love as the more hopeful call it, was fast dissipating between us. And then, he'd called my bluff, much as I had hoped he wouldn't follow through on his threats. Fari had packed up shop and left for Zimbabwe in what he brazenly and foolishly called, "the second coming." Can you imagine that? Turning his back on the family? It was now coming up to nearly eight months since he'd jumped ship. And why should I put a stop to my life when his own life was moving forward in Zim? Why would I want to cry myself to sleep as if life had ground to a halt because of a silly old man? Why? Why? Why?

"Are we cool, Maidei?" Mudiwa's polite cough momentarily jolted me back to reality.

"Aaah, sorry, Kingston shopping mall, yes, I would be very much delighted to grace your presence, personal trainer," I remarked coyly, as I didn't want to appear too keen, though I was elated inside. I was burning up.

"No need to call me personal trainer, Mudiwa will do as everyone else calls me in our Zumba classes," he'd remarked, the mischievous glint clear in his eyes. I felt like there was a subtle dare in those eyes, and I wasn't going to let the dare pass unreciprocated, I vowed within myself.

"Okay, I hear you, Mudiwa," I had flashed back his disarming smile. "I'll tail you behind your car, as Kingston mall is five minutes from here."

That had been it. That was the genesis of my amorous liaisons with Mudiwa, whom I henceforth called "my Boo," following our frisky maiden romp in the Zumba changing room one afternoon. By all accounts, within the Zumba community, our class comprising a bevy of different shades of women, Mudiwa was considered a catch. He was a tall, light-skinned man. He would have passed for white, and with a lithe body that came from working out long hours in the city gym. He had a certain aura; call it charisma. When Boo walked into a room, he commanded instant attention, which is why he was such a sensation at our Zumba classes. His physical presence in a room made many women turn their heads to look at him, and boy, was I not chuffed with such a catch!

He was certainly a catch to me and a validation of my insatiable libido. For one obsessed with my strict dieting regimen, it was a bonus having my Boo who could double up as my fitness trainer. Why would I complain at those long, marathon sessions at Winterhill gym? I could have had any excuse in the world just to have Boo's supple fingers massage me. In any case, workouts gave me a rash that could only be rivalled by sex.

I felt wet and receptive as Mudiwa's expert fingers playfully stroked my now super erect, super-charged clitoris. "Oh yes, my Boo, give it back to me..." I couldn't restrain my ecstatic moments as Mudiwa released his hot-warm manhood into my inner crevices with my nails digging into his supple, tanned body, my feet cupped around his shoulders. I could feel his hands comfortably cupping my bum in unison and he bellowed my name several times as he came. My body pulsated with mind-blowing pleasure as I reached orgasm. My saviour!

Minutes later, we lay revelling in the post-coital afterglow, contented and spent.

"Did you come honeypot?" he playfully teased me, stroking my still erect nipples with the tips of his fingers. The cool cat!

"Yes! Yes! Thank you, Boo, one hundred and one percent, you do know how to get the better of me love," I purred with contentment as I playfully stroked his manhood in reciprocity.

"Thanks for the vote of confidence," he responded, a sly smile curling his luscious lips. We had a vibrant sexual chemistry which consolidated the bond between us. My heart constricted each time we had our snogs and I snuggled up to his sexy beard. There was something secure and protective which oozed from him, offered by his masculine protective embraces, and equally enhanced by his lingering aftershave.

Mudiwa energised me and constantly kept me on my toes, especially given our explosive marathon romps. It was bloody brilliant, I give him that! The sex and austere exercise regimen meant my body was kept trim, toned and in top form. I was chuffed to lose my folded belly fat and middle-aged woman's wobbly bits! Woo hoo! Life is beautiful! Many atimes I would squeal in unmitigated delight to myself, feet up on my bed remarking at how lucky I was to have Mudiwa by my side to help me cope with my husband's shenanigans.

What I had with Mudiwa was exciting for the spontaneity, impromptu nature in which we could just do it, especially on the Zumba dance floor or in the changing rooms. The rough tussle, orgasming on the floor, gave us the kicks, the sheer excitement and daring overtures of knowing we could have been caught right there in the throes of passion and thick of it by other users of this public facility, Milton Keynes Zumba Auditorium centre. Once I emerged from the changing rooms with my hair crumpled after our rumpus and I nearly jumped out of my skin when Emily, one of my Zumba classmates, remarked, "A very good afternoon to you Maidei, I hope you enjoy it while it lasts; you certainly won't be the last either..."

"Aaah, aaah Emily, you too Emily?" I struggled to compose myself as I wasn't sure whether Emily had heard my noisy lovemaking with Boo, and what on earth did she meant, I hope I enjoy it? Not to mention her sarcastic statement thereafter, which I tactfully ignored. Perhaps, the guilty ones are always afraid as the saying goes.

"We really have to be careful Boo, last night I bumped into Emily after our frisky bathroom nooky."

"Careful of what? We are two consenting adults honeypot, no need to freak out on the little Emilies' of this world;" Mudiwa had derisively laughed it off.

"I do get your lackadaisical attitude Boo, but I have a lot more to lose than you, if this our relationship ever gets found out, remember, I'm still legally married to Fari, if I can remind you, my love."

"Whatever you wish, honeypot, we have the luxury of my apartment, seeing as I'm a free bird myself," he'd remarked, laughing. And that's how our trysts eventually moved to his Milton Keynes bachelor pad, to which I could always slip, sometimes for a quickie after my nursing shift at Milton Keynes NHS Trust hospital, or during the early mornings when I would go jogging. I started religiously monitoring my figure, now that I had my young toy boy lover, about whom I was jealous enough and protective so he couldn't look at other women. It was integral for me to keep my trim figure intact.

But I could swear some of the women in my Zumba class started giving me dirty looks each time we bumped into each other in the changing rooms. Sometimes it could be an odd, snide, cryptic remark dropped amidst the strident changing room gossip. "You're looking very bright these days Maidei, your skin is certainly glowing, the pipe certainly agrees well with you," remarked Becky the busybody as she strove to stifle a laugh.

"Oh, thank you, Becky, maybe it's the season of blooming," I tried to diplomatically cut her off but that was before Emily butted in, "Glad you've confirmed my observations Becky, I thought I was the only one noticing these changes in our vixen Maidei." And with those remarks both women exited the changing rooms amid giggling fits.

I couldn't care less about their suspicions while Fari and my two children were oblivious to my nocturnal shenanigans. That's all that mattered to me, not what every Tom-Dick-Harry-Julie thought. In any case, I was having the time of my life, good, fiery, vibrant sex from my youthful lover Mudiwa. Notwithstanding my age, Mudiwa seemed to have reawakened something in me, my smouldering embers of burning passion that felt like an awakened volcano in my loins. Each time I was with Mudiwa, I felt deep stirrings in my inner loins. The young man certainly knew how to pleasure a woman ad infinitum. Not only that, but he was well endowed for a thirty-two-year-old young man. Many times, the night provided a cloak of discretion over our shady activities.

Perhaps Emily and Becky may have been right about the physical change on me. Here I was, leading a duplicitous life cleverly concealed to the outside world. Before he'd left, I had had a difficult home life with my husband in my other parallel universe. With Mudiwa, I had my de-stress moments of bliss and unmitigated ecstasy, especially with our marathon love sessions. I doubted if Fari and my two children, Muchadei and Yeukai, suspected anything. This suited me. I was happy to keep stringing the idiot along, cuckolding the unsuspecting Fari. Why wouldn't I, especially as I regarded it as his comeuppance for the shitty marriage he gave me? Why did it have to be his family in Zimbabwe coming first all the time, being put ahead of my interests as his wife? It was about time I looked out after my own interests. And now that he was away, I felt pretty much emboldened and nigh justified in my infidelity.

But in the early hours one morning, I awkwardly bumped into both Ben and Taurai as I exited Mudiwa's apartment. With my hair crumpled and my skin still smelling of Mudiwa, boom, there were both our friendly neigbours taking their morning jog together. "Morning, Maidei, how are you," they'd both politely inquired after me. I politely acknowledged their overtures, saying; "Morning love birds, I'm well, thank you." Although they had briefly stopped for small talk and didn't directly confront me about what I was doing exiting a block of upmarket Milton Keynes flats, there was an awkward atmosphere permeating. Once or twice, I caught Ben and Taurai giving each other knowing looks, after which they would glance at me quizzically, but I was not going to make life any easier for them by giving out or volunteering any information. If they were to ever find out about this secret aspect of my life, I was adamant that it would have to be accidental, their knowing this. No way would I willingly embarrass myself.

The takeaway lesson for me from that near slip incident was, each time I exited Mudiwa's flat, I would do a bit of prior reconnaissance, checking, craning my neck, head over the cycle footpath, cross-checking there were no morning joggers milling about. In addition, I now took the double insurance of using a long circuitous route home, just so I could cover my tracks.

Then there were those moments when Fari would take both children to Zimbabwe on holiday, although to give him credit, I did refuse to be party to these trips. The other reason I did this was to excite jealousy in Fari. As a woman, I still wanted to feel loved by my man Fari. I wanted him to exhibit it, flaunt that love, as he used to do wooing me in Harare during our courtship years, going to those cricket matches at Harare sports club. But I didn't get that attention anymore, which further riled me. Why couldn't he show me that love of yesteryear, anymore? Perhaps that's why I felt justified in my amorous liaisons with my Boo. Thus, as the chill of Thames Valley bit into my fingers as I exited Mudiwa's flat one wintry evening, it reminded me of the chill of my marriage to Fari. I looked at my gold wedding band and thought of Fari, all the way in Zimbabwe, on holiday with the kids, never calling to ask how I fared. *Where had we gone wrong?* I silently mused to myself as my mind drifted back to our wedding day, years back. Merely being here assailed me with so many memories as snippets of our past flashed before me.

Goodness knows, I had looked exquisite on our wedding day with Fari at that exclusive Mount Hampden resort in Harare, with my sisters craning their necks like everyone else among the excited guests, looking at me enviously as I fluttered my heavy makeup-encrusted eyelids at them all. And how I had revelled in the spectacle. My sister Wadzanai had done me proud, sending me a magnificent wedding gown all the way from down under, Melbourne, or Oz as we then called Australia. *Good sis, thank you,* I mumbled under my breath as my eyes moistened at the nostalgia and reflections on the road we'd travelled, Fari and I.

I recoil in horror at the ugly spats when our pettiness degenerated into ugly skirmishes. Those physical fights were usually preceded with Fari playing *Bhundu Boy's* hit tune, *Ndoipunza Imba Iyi: I will destroy this house!* Each time that song filtered throughout the house, a dark cloud descended as if to forebode the imminent violence, and god, I knew it was coming that night, an avalanche of it, left, right and centre, Fari's blows and fists raining fast and loose on my flesh, as he snarled through his anger-gritted teeth, "I will not have you disrespect me, woman. Do you hear me Maidei?"

If I was up to it, I would fight back, lashing back at the beast in equal measure. At times, I would escape into the haven of Mudiwa's bachelor's pad, unbeknown to Fari, who all these years thought I sought sanctuary at Ben and Taurai's place. On my return, I would subliminally give Fari a coded message through playing Tina Turner's, *I don't Wanna Fight no More*© on auto repeat, and especially exaggerated singing with the chorus: I don't care who's wrong or right Fari, I just don't wanna fight no more...Such were the darker phases of our marriage on which I would rather not dwell.

Bloody hell! Marriage is a dirty game, I mumbled under my breath as I quietly reflected on the vicissitudes of my marriage over the years. I get it. I'm an old timer and not naïve. Every marriage has its ups and downs and we'd been coasting along just fine these past few years. But that was before Fari became a fucking arsehole.

For crying out loud, I had had enough of this! I was tired of picking up the pieces and rebuilding the blocks of our faltering marriage. I wanted out of this charade of a marriage but didn't have the guts to live through my fantasies. Being with Mudiwa offered me escapist consolation of some sort.

There was no way I would accept going back to Zimbabwe again, after the failed politics and the life of penury as a nurse, a civil servant at Harare hospital again, and Fari with his *two cents pay packet* as a UZ Law lecturer. Just thinking about my former employment made my skin crawl in petrified horror. England was bliss. England was progress. Taking me back to Zimbabwe would have been regression. And I'm not having that! I've put up with a lot of bullshit in this marriage, about time I put my foot down on this madness. Why did we always have to bear the brunt of other people's burdens? I could never really get that Father Christmas persona Fari liked to project about. Silly old man, as if he had the money to splash about!

How could Fari even dare contemplate going back? I despised him more for his obduracy and poor decision-making. The fool!

Funny how things had turned out with Mudiwa. Each time we made hot passionate love, I would gush at Mudiwa's libido, and he would quip, "See, that's why you need to leave that bastard husband of yours. I swear, I'll give you this holy treatment every night, without fail."

"It's not that easy Boo, there are many things at stake here."

"What sort of stakes would you possibly allow to stand in the way of your happiness? I thought you're always moaning about how shitty he is?"

I was quiet for an exceedingly long moment as I played with my wedding band. Granted, lovemaking with Mudiwa was out of this fucking world. Still, I wasn't sure I was ready to leave Fari yet, despite all the grief he gave me. Part of me feared the social opprobrium if it ever came out: *A middle-aged Zimbabwean woman has left her husband because of her toy boy lover, Zumba-fitness instructor. Possibly, mid-life crisis or menopause kicking in.* Some of the more judgemental would certainly remark in that way, casting aspersions on my persona. But much more dreadful to me was what Ben and Taurai would say. I just couldn't face the shame and attendant scorn. What about our two children together, Muchadei and Yeukai? Would they ever forgive me, knowing I had walked out on them for someone close to their age?

Besides, much as I was flattered by Mudiwa's protestations of love and attention on me, I wasn't sure if he was in it for the long haul. Perhaps it was because, deep down, our huge age difference nibbled at me. Would this dashing young man really stand by me out there in the real world where he could easily snap any attractive woman of his choice? So many questions, so few answers; perhaps it was better to remain in this kind of limbo whereby I had one foot in my farcical marriage, whilst at the same time enjoying my wild romps with my Boo. *Everybody wins, we can all have our cake and eat it at the same time*, I quietly rationalised within myself.

"It will happen when it happens, Boo," I had finally remarked to Mudiwa, who by then was tenderly giving me a back massage as I cooed with delight."

Chapter 9

The Storm

I had been feeling a bit under the weather for some time. I kept going as the nature of my being a self-employed entrepreneur meant I needed a lot of behind-the-scenes follow-ups and policing and sometimes *blitzkrieg* spot checks on my *mushika-shika* kombi drivers. For if you give them leeway, they will pull you down under, conniving both driver and conductor to fleece you of the day's takings.

"If you give them free rein, carte-blanche freedom, they will sabotage your business interests Fari," Liz had wisely warned me on numerous occasions.

"Perhaps the pressure of my fledgling transport business is getting to me, Liz. I passed out in my car this morning," I remarked to her late one evening after our evening meal.

"What do you mean passed out? Were you driving?"

"Fortunately, not. Would I be here, if I'd been driving? I would be mincemeat by now. I was parked at Avondale shopping centre, waiting to tail Chabuya's *kombi* when it happened."

"I think you need to get checked out, Fari. You haven't looked right in ages, and each time I've raised this, you brush me aside. Look at you, you're downright flushed! What's happening with you, love? What if it's something serious?"

"Of course, it's nothing serious. Don't be silly, Liz!" I brushed her aside dismissively with a peremptory wave of my arms. I was even annoyed at her for shooshing me about, like she was my mother. So I carried on with my brave man stunt. Perhaps it's an inwardly man thing which drives us not to want to confront our frailties and mortality. One thing about me, I hated going to the doctor if there was any ailment afflicting me. I would always brave it out with a grin-and-bear-it face. "Aah, it will go away, be it a cold or cough, it's nothing to worry about," I would say to allay my inner misgivings. This was not helped by the fact that I hated taking tablets; there was something horribly jarring about medicine tablets which made my skin crawl in revulsion.

However, in a somewhat dramatic turn of events, it took two quick successive panic attacks I had in Liz's presence for her to frogmarch me to our family physician, Dr. Bvirakare, whose medical practice was housed at Harare's Baines Avenues Medical Chambers.

A lanky, slim fella, Bvirakare was easygoing, and I soon warmed up to him as he asked me lots of questions that breezy Friday morning. "How long have these passing out phases been going on Fari?"

"Oh, it's nothing really Doctor, just a couple of times," I tried to shoosh him away. "I wouldn't be here, were it not for Liz's perceived hypochondriac tendencies," I said glaring at Liz menacingly.

"I've run a series of tests. Please be back here tomorrow morning for results and thank you Liz for dragging Fari here. About time we shy away from this macho thing of not wanting to seek medical attention. Earlier detection for ailments is really a virtue, something I always encourage in my patients."

"I couldn't agree with you more, Doctor," interposed Liz, as we bid farewell to Bvirakare and took our leave.

As Liz drove me back home, I playfully chided her in the car, "Oh you goody, goody two shoes Liz. So, you reckon you'll get some brownie points and shiny stars from the good doctor by dragging me to him against my will? I can assure you, I'm well Liz. This is just a minor blip thing, temporary phase kind of thing, nothing to lose one's sleep over."

"Thou protest too much, Fari. Why don't we wait until we learn the outcome of the series of tests done on you tomorrow?" quipped Liz, at which I let it rest. We drove home in comfortable silence.

In hindsight, nothing could have prepared me for the seismic, cataclysmic events which were to unfold, as Liz and I sat before a grim-faced Dr. Bvirakare at his practice the next day, that bitterly cold, wet Saturday morning. I can assure you, what followed was something completely out of the blue that I hadn't envisaged at all. Perhaps the unexpected rains in the middle of August in Harare may have been an ominous omen, a harbinger of grisly news to come.

"I'm afraid I do have some grim news to share with you both," spoke Dr. Bvirakare as he peered over his antiquated glasses, shifting awkwardly in his chair, as if he was sitting on pins. For the first time, he had my attention, as my heart skipped, and I felt an uneasy sensation going through my now tense body. *Could it be, that's why I'd had a recurrent grotesque dream last night of Maidei constantly calling out after me to come back home and it would all be all right?* But not one for superstitious thoughts, I brushed these thoughts aside, as my befuddled mind tried to process Bvirakare's cryptic remarks.

"Please enlighten us. What is it, Doctor?" Liz's calm voice broke the uneasy silence which had descended in the room following the doctor's introductory remarks.

"I'm afraid it's not looking good. The initial results from yesterday's tests show Fari has stage 2 prostate cancer in its infancy..."

"What are you saying Doc? No, that cannot be true. There must be a mistake of some sort," I bellowed at Dr. Bvirakare, springing out of my chair with an unexplained zeal.

"Will you stop it, and calm down Fari, will you please?" Liz spoke authoritatively as she tugged at my jacket, and I resumed my seat, ashamed of myself, but still very much confused.

"My apologies, Dr. Bvirakare, I'm really sorry about shouting at you, but you must be mistaken, sir. With all due respect, are these my real results? I can assure you sir, I am in good health, is, is...is it not always the case, happening in Zimbabwean hospitals, that patient results get mixed up and later on, people are told, 'aaah we are sorry, we gave you the wrong results?' So, I can assure you both here, right now, it's a mistake of monumental proportions. I don't have prostate cancer at all. That is a huge case of mistaken identity, swapped results, I can assure you... Now, just admit the error, Doctor, then Liz and I can both go home."

"Are you done, Fari? Now, let the doctor speak," Liz said calmly.

"The thing is, this is always a very difficult moment for me in my career; informing patients of a cancer diagnosis has never been an easy thing to do. Fari's reaction is typical with most patients, but I am here to help you, so allow me to explain and share with both of you a viable treatment plan. The first important question I need an answer to, as unfeeling as it may sound is, "Are you on medical aid, Fari?"

I could barely answer him, as I shook my head to signal to him I didn't have medical aid coverage. Why would I ever have wanted medical aid, being always in vibrant health, as strong as an ox, as I used to call myself? No one would ever have convinced me to get medical aid. Besides, had there not been so many stories doing the rounds in the media about how medical aid societies were fleecing ordinary Zimbabweans of their hard-earned money, whilst not living up to their side of the bargain, while delivering a shoddy service. There were well-known cases of government big shots unashamedly helping themselves to medical aid societies' funds. In particular, the government-run Premier Medical Society had wantonly fleeced its hard-pressed employees through years of corruption and mismanagement of member contributions. In the end, I had reached a conclusion: "Medical aid is for gullible idiots and losers."

"Fari, are you with me?" Dr. Bvirakare's voice jolted me out of my momentary trance. I could only stare at him absent-mindedly. It was all too much to take.

"Please advise us on what we need to do, Doctor, in the absence of medical aid?" Liz quietly implored him.

"I will level with you both," Dr. Bvirakare spoke sombrely, looking intently at me. "Prostate cancer treatment costs are prohibitive, if not nigh astronomical, here in Zimbabwe. And as you intimated that you have no medical aid in place, then you will have to privately fund your treatment plan and attendant surgery, post-surgery treatment, also. I am truly sorry to be piling on you seemingly negative story after negative story, but I have a duty of care to be honest and transparent in my diagnoses and professional dealings with my patients."

He explained, "With an initial treatment plan of eight sessions of chemotherapy, surgery, and radiological therapy, it will be a shock to your system, and that's only the beginning. But on the plus side, most patients do get over this initial hurdle, barring excessive tiredness, general body malaise, and hair loss which comes with this treatment."

With my shoulders drooping at every word from the doctor, my heart sank, my knees wobbled, and I felt an uncomfortable perspiration, knowing I had no meaningful savings to talk of, neither did I anticipate getting help from my family in England. Relations had gone from being lukewarm to rock bottom between myself, Muchi my son, who hardly spoke to me anyway, my daughter Yeu, and my seemingly wife-in-name-only now, Maidei. I had not spoken of her in ages, if that can be called speaking at all. Our last phone call had been a slang-filled match in which Maidei had screamed obscenities at me for being a waste of space father, and I had angrily slammed the phone down on her. So, how could I even entertain thoughts of getting help from that quarter? It was unthinkable. It was just not doable. I was resigned to finding alternative ways to fund my cancer treatment, bypassing my family in England. I quietly rationalised that thought within myself.

"What sort of figures are we looking at, Doctor?" I inquired, arising from my self-pity and stupor.

"To start off, regarding your surgery, which is quite imminent I have to say, we are looking at a baseline of $30,000 US dollars."

"Holly crap! $30,000 US dollars!" I repeated incredulously, darting an unbelievable glance at the equally bemused Liz.

"Have I misheard you Doctor? Did you just say $30k?" I shot back at him.

"I'm afraid you heard me correctly, Fari."

Inwardly, I knew this was an enormous task, a big ask for that matter. There was no way I could raise that sum, even if I were to dispose of my ramshackle transport vehicles business, the three that were still running it wouldn't get me anywhere near that steep sum. The greater part of my fleet and cross-border heavy vehicles *gonyeti* had been severely hampered and depleted by the hyper-inflationary environment which had massively eroded my once lucrative savings in cash and unit trusts. The business had sadly become a casualty of wilful recession brought about by the huge war veterans US payments my nephew Chabuya had been upbeat about a few weeks earlier, the staggering US dollar second financial reparations payments made to war veterans of the country, but had not been budgeted for in the national fiscus. There was no telling the ensuing economic fallout in terms of galloping inflation and a contracting economy. My transport business had been one such casualty, taking a severe knocking from this, and here I was, with a terminal prostate cancer diagnosis, and yet somehow Bvirakare expected me to cough up $30,000 USD just like that, at the drop of a hat. Was he for real?

I couldn't even talk of my cross-border truck haulage business; it had long ceased to operate, once our Zim currency became worthless pieces of paper, a currency in which all and sundry became millionaires. It became increasingly imprudent to engage in a business which was now mired in liabilities and being sustained by a huge bank overdraft. Half the time, I found I was playing catch-up Russian roulette, chasing paying off the overdraft and its charges, and trying to maintain a dilapidated fleet in a country where getting simple car parts paraphernalia was nigh impossible. Once any of the cars had a breakdown, it meant I had to get spare parts from neighbouring South Africa, which added another conundrum, importing car parts from South Africa required forex. There was no forex in the banks, the only forex I could lay my hands on was available on the lucrative parallel market. The downside to this not only hinged on the illegality of the practice, but also on being at the mercy of being fleeced by the parallel market boys' merchants of death, as we derisively called them. Add to that cacophony of madness the internal sabotage from my work force, it was no longer viable to continue to run the truck business. Thus, with a heavy heart, I had been forced to wind up this once promising business enterprise and, because I was hugely in debt, the sale of any meaningful assets I had failed to even clear my business overdraft. And now I was staring at the prospect of huge medical bills for a potentially life threading ailment, prostate cancer.

It had been tough going in Zimbabwe. The second coming hadn't really worked out well. I was strapped for cash. I had been too ashamed to admit it to myself that my supposed second coming dream plan had been a foolhardy exercise in the long run, although there had been a false promise start in the beginning. However, in hindsight, it had gradually become an act of desperate lunacy. It was like in the books where you know the outcome, but you just carry on, playing it out and seeing how it ends. I didn't want to accept my project was pretty much doomed.

I'm not usually one to feel sorry for myself, but for once I reflected that fate had dealt me a heavy hand. Here I was, having ditched my life in England to return home, *kurukuvhute*, as I called it and things had turned pear shaped for me. Perhaps things would have gone well, had it not been that downward spiral instigated by the war veterans' pay-outs with the attendant gargantuan economic upheaval. But all this bullshit was neither here nor there. I had practical realities to contend with which entailed raising a well-nigh astronomical figure to help with my cancer treatment.

The doctor's cough jolted me out of my reverie. He could see I was shaken by the diagnosis, and he tried valiantly to reassure me, saying, "There's a significant chance we can save your life. The only thing is, a fine trade-off has to be established between now and when we commence surgery, but I wouldn't leave it too long. I am aware there's a lot to take in here, Fari, so, I will give you time to go and have a think with your other half," he said acknowledging Liz who'd been sitting quietly throughout the surreal life-changing exercise with Dr Bvirakare.

Suddenly finding her voice, Liz thanked the doctor and we left, promising to be in touch soon. The next few weeks following the diagnosis, I witnessed a nicer and so lovely side to Liz that I secretly wished she were my real wife. I had never been transparent with her with my business interests, partly as self-preservation mode, but also being aware she was merely a consort, and therefore on a no-need-to-know basis. However, I found myself opening up to good old Liz. "In all honesty, love, I can't afford this obscenely astronomical cancer treatment here. I have to seriously consider my options," I remarked to her one evening.

"What do you have in mind? Two brains are better than one?" Liz said. "Why not put everything on the table so we deploy our best option?"

"Well, the thing is, Liz, there's really nothing worth talking about from the remnants of my once thriving transport empire. You're all too familiar with the prevailing economic downturn and how it's negatively hampered business confidence and productivity."

"What about from your UK front, any investments likely to save the day?"

"Nope," I shook my head. "I've been away for some time and Maidei would rather see me dead first before raising a finger to help me. The long and short of it all is that $30k is just unattainable, given the way things are at the moment. Gosh, why is medical provision such an extortionate practice in Zim? Where have we gone wrong as a nation to treat our most vulnerable and infirm members of our society like this? Tell me Liz, how many ordinary fellow Zimbabweans could afford $30,000 USD for cancer treatment?"

"I completely agree with you Fari, the ordinary Zimbabwean wouldn't be able to fork out that much money, when they're struggling to even put a decent meal on the table. Have you not seen how, as a nation we've been reduced to doing go fund me online appeals for cash donations each time someone has a life changing diagnosis like cancer? The thing is, you can't blame yourself for this, Fari. It's no one's fault, but that's the way it is in Zim. We are a banana republic, for want of a better word. There must be a way out though. What's your take on herbal treatment options?"

"Herbal treatment of prostate cancer?" I scornfully repeated after Liz. "Sounds like a con to me. Where have you ever heard of herbs treating, let alone curing, cancer?

"Well, you need to be open-minded to enable you to widen your options and see what works for you, Fari. I know this Mupedzanhamo herbalist; Samaita. He has an impeccable track record of reversing cancer symptoms with some people having full remission. As we can't raise the $30k, I think it's worth giving Samaita a shout. We have nothing to lose but everything to gain. And, in any case, I'm only trying to help you out, dearest. You know I lost my job after our accounting firm relocated to South Africa. "Unfriendly business environment," as our senior management intimated. Were I still in employment, I would certainly have chipped in towards your medical fees, dearest. We're in this together."

It was very touching, especially Liz's last statement. I just mellowed and found myself crumbling before her. "Of course, love, I know you're only trying to assist. I'll give it some thought." With that I gave her an affectionate peck on the forehead as we retired to bed.

It took me over a week to finally come to terms and embrace my other half's alternative treatment therapy. I had my deep-rooted scepticism and cynicism about this much-touted herbal treatment. However, I reluctantly saw the wisdom in partaking some form of treatment rather than none at all. Besides, considering my tenuous money situation, the time for agency or being finicky was not now. If anything, my choices were greatly diminished, thus, I acquiesced to meeting Samaita, the "famous" medicine man by Liz's standards.

Chapter 10

Samaita Simboti

Liz and I visited Samaita, the self-styled Mbare herbalist whom Liz felt would cure my prostate cancer purely with his herbs. Medical science had suggested alternative treatment options, but for the dearth of money, I couldn't access hospital treatment options for cancer in Zimbabwe.

Samaita was a tall, skinny man, so exceedingly dark-skinned that he reminded me of Samanyanga, the late, famed music maestro, Oliver M'tukudzi, a fact I mentioned as we greeted each other, that Saturday morning at his Mbare, Chidzere home.

"Makadiiko Samanyanga?" I said, extending my hand to him in a jovial greeting. "How do you do as well *mwana wamai?"* he said taking my arm with a firm grip which exuded confidence and immersive strength. I immediately warmed up to the man even though I had agreed to see him with serious misgivings besetting me.

"In fact, I forgive you for calling me Samanyanga, though my totem is Samaita Simboti, but as you're not the only one to have made reference between me and that lofty icon Tuku, I forgive you," he said. "Many people say that I bear an uncanny resemblance to the late musician. And to be honest with you *mwana wamai*, who wouldn't want to be associated with that unique son of the soil? May his soul rest in peace." Samaita spoke with a broad grin revealing missing front teeth, which further reminded me of someone whom I couldn't place.

"How are you Mainini Lizzie?" Samaita spoke as he turned to Liz, making it so obvious they knew each other beforehand. "You're on time, Mainini, just like you said on the phone yesterday," Samaita spoke as he ushered us into his opulently furnished living room.

"Of course. I'm a stickler for punctuality Sekuru," said Liz amid her infectious smile.

We had small talk as we all attempted to break the ice, particularly between Samaita and me, as it was each of our first times to meet. Finally, Samaita broke the ice, "So, what can I do for you, *wazukuru*? Perhaps *Muzaya wangu* Lizzie you could shed a bit more light as we barely spoke in depth over the phone."

"Aaah *Sekuru*, let me start with proper introductions first, so we're all well acquainted. This is Fari, my other half. He was recently diagnosed with prostate cancer stage 2 and, *Sekuru Samaita*, I know very well how you are an herbalist of note, in Harare and beyond. If anyone can help Fari beat this monster of an illness, then that person is you Sekuru. Please, help us with your expertise Samaita, like you've done with others who've passed through your hands before. In short, that's why you see us here this morning," Liz finished off her little introductory plea with a bow of her head, a mark of reverence I surmised.

Inwardly, I felt touched and marvelled at the way Liz had made her opening pitch. In no time, within a few weeks, Liz had more or less assumed the role of a proper wife to me, and part of me felt ashamed at having fobbed off her pleas for commitment earlier at the start of our relationship. What a daft prick I'd been!

"*Aaah wazukuru*, I am sorry to learn of your ordeal, prostate cancer, we call it *mhuka*, in our language. Loosely translated, it's a ravaging, obnoxious animal which wreaks havoc on the human body. Once again, I am sorry *mwana wamai*, you're battling this, but if it's any consolation to you both, you are in capable hands. You've done well to come here and consult me. Together we will beat this monster, I can tell you *wana Muzaya*.

"Stage 2 prostate cancer is not as bad as they make it sound at Baines Avenues Medical Chambers. You will be surprised at the litany of patients they wrote off at Baines and St Anne's Hospital and they were resurrected right here in my own medical chambers. As we speak, there are people who have successfully beat prostate cancer and gone back to their ordinary, mundane lives with their families, I can tell you this!" Samaita spoke with an exaggerated flourish of his arms as if to hammer home his point.

"Really?" I exclaimed to all this, obviously taken in by Samaita's eloquence and medical prowess in treating cancer patients who'd been written off, with only herbs. For them to make a full recovery was a phenomenal feat by my standards. Surely, I had come to the right repository. I felt encouraged inwardly, even though I didn't want to openly flaunt my alacrity.

One thing for sure though, the man Samaita certainly had no time for pleasantries like modesty when dealing with clients, as he went full scale into a self-aggrandising eulogy of himself and his medical prowess. There was something about his voice, it was a gregarious, booming voice which reverberated throughout the entire house, underscoring Samaita's presence. The man certainly had an infectious presence. I could see he revelled in the spectacle he created. An exhibitionist, showman of some sort, if I may put it that way.

"My totem is Samaita, hence my name Simboti, Black Panther insignia, if you want the English equivalence. I run a successful and thriving herbal clinic of note, here in Harare, from the Mbare ghettoes, one of the oldest townships in the country. I must say, I find it humbling, I grew up in Mbare, playing plastic balls at Stodart Hall, and now one of the ghettoes' very own son is providing medical sustenance and recovery to all and sundry. Tell me, how good is that?"

Upon saying that, he bellowed into guffaws of uncontrollable laughter before he resumed his self-aggrandizing eulogy. "They know me quite well in Zimbabwe and beyond the borders. Do you know, I even run WhatsApp© consultations with needy patients abroad? See, this is my business card," he said, shoving into my face, a nicely manicured, laminated card as if to assert his medical credentials. On the card emblazoned in bold print were the following words:

> **Herbal Clinic. Free Scanning**
> **Herbal products for Piles,**
> **Fibroids, Prostate, Hypertension, Endometriosis**
> **Diabetes (boost your insulin production) Candida, STSs,**
> **Fertility, Reproductive health, Cardiac, Kidneys, Digestive,**
> **Acids, Ulcers, Arthritis etc**
> **Deliveries are done. Call/ or**
> **WhatsApp Samaita your medicine man at 0772358604**
> **Website details coming soon**
> *Upenyu hwenyu idambudziko romwoyo wangu/*Your health and wellbeing is my priority.

For one so pompous and gregarious, I quietly wondered why the mix in sentences between small and capital letters, but I let it pass within myself, and decided to share this later with Liz, in the privacy of the car on our way home. In the meantime, Liz and I allowed Samaita his show as he carried on extolling his virtues. It was all too clear the man certainly loved a stage.

But perhaps I had every reason to believe in this man's medical expertise and knowledge, given the litany of ailments listed on his business card, which he claimed were his areas of specialty or forte. Or could it be it's because my options had been severely hampered by the pre-required thirty-thousand-dollar hospital fees, that I found myself trying to convince myself to believe in this man's "medical prowess." I kept silently debating within my inner self as Samaita was rambling on, non-stop.

"Now, where was I?" Samaita remarked, taking off his glasses, looking at them intently as if they would provide him an answer, then carrying on with his mantra. "Oh yes, Muzaya, I have treated big names here, some in cabinet, but I have ethics to adhere to," he chuckled as he spoke. "I am not about to start naming my clients, now, am I? It kills your reputation if you disrespect your clients, and you know what? Reputation is everything in the kind of trade as mine." He sounded so all conspiratorial and philosophical as he uttered the last word.

"Be that as it may, however, I guess confidentiality ceases when one dies. All I'm saying is, amongst some of my departed clients who managed to beat prostate cancer are none other than Robert Mugabe himself, former head of state."

"Aaah, Sekuru, you talk too much," interposed Liz, "Why don't you stop blowing your own trumpet and attend to your newest patient?"

"Let me finish about Mugabe's battles with prostate cancer first. Mugabe died not because of prostate cancer but because of other underlying causes. I effectively cured his prostate cancer, never mind his countless trips to Singapore for his medical check-ups. If you remember very well that Julian Assange WikiLeaks cable, what year was it?" he asked, more as if he was directly addressing the question to me.

"2008 I think," I said shifting uncomfortably in my chair in case I got it wrong.

"2008 you're right, they'd been saying Mugabe is dying of prostate cancer, but did he die?"

"How many times did Mugabe always seemed to die at the beginning of each year and somehow managed to resurrect? Well, let me tell you the unknown story: I was Mugabe's private herbalist, physician, whatever fancy name you may want to call it. I successfully treated his prostate cancer; no wonder he went on to live for over 15 years after that infamous WikiLeaks cable and its insinuation Mugabe only had a few weeks to live. That is me, Samaita Simboti, living testament of my prowess.

"Mugabe ndini ndakamurapa uya, I successfully cured his cancer, many a time, I saved the day for that old man. I have to admit though the bastard had the proverbial nine lives of a cat," remarked Samaita amid his guttural laughter.

"Ask any of his surviving cabinet members for corroboration if you doubt me. I'm even prepared to bet my Nissan Qashqai car outside, if you're a betting man Fari?"

"Dare I talk of the late Proud Chinembiri, Kilimanjaro as well, the late boxing icon Zimbabwe has ever graced? He is also another former patient as well. Need I go on and on? Anyway, now turning onto you Muzaya Fari, stage 2 prostate cancer is child's play for me, *kutungana kwembudzi uku, hapana zviripo apa.* Look here, Muzaya Lizzie, you're the woman of the house so I will direct these herbs to your trust and ensure you look after Fari well. Listen to my instructions to the letter so you administer the concoctions and herbs well."

Since our short arrival and up until now, there had been something nibbling at me about who else Samaita resembled, particularly the gap where his front teeth should have been. Then, boom, just like that the penny dropped for me. Suddenly, I was able to make the connection of who else Samaita resembled. It was the constant off-the-cuff pomp and self-styled demeanour which made me realise what it was. There was something about this self-styled herbalist which reminded me of notorious, half-literate, caricature, war veteran simpleton, Chinotimba of the grass hat and his trademark smile fame, revealing a gap in his front teeth, but, somehow, I brushed this thought aside as I was trying to maintain my confidence in this medicine man Samaita and comparing him to Chinotimba wouldn't inspire confidence to a doubting mind

80

like mine. *Let me stick with the Samanyanga resemblance,* I silently spoke to myself, possibly discomfited by the war veteran analogy. Samaita's raspy voice jolted me to my present reality as he kept on talking. The man certainly had the gift of gab.

"We will start you with this herbal tea *Mufandichimuka;* it's a very bitter and ghastly concoction I have to say, Fari, but in that bitterness lies your salvation and cure, which is what we need, Muzaya. These other herbs you steam in boiled water then have a blanket over you, mouth and nose wide open, till you are sweating profusely. Remember; you have to produce excessive body sweat induced from both the herbs and boiling water, and you know you are on the first trajectory to recovery. See me after a month, then we review your progress. If these herbs don't do the job in curing your cancer, then I swear by my grandmother Mbuya Samaita's name, I may as well burn and throw away my medicinal herbs practice," he said, as he banged his feet on the ground as if to drive home his point, rousing his dog which had been sleeping on the floor but suddenly scurried away.

"Thank you, Sekuru, and what's your charges for all this?"

"I won't take any payment from you until you are satisfied the treatment plan is working. Only you can be able to tell the difference from your body, and once you're happy, then we can talk about my payments. For now, we need to conquer that menace in your body, Muzaya, and tell you what, we will, no doubt about that!"

Liz and I effusively thanked Samaita and we took our leave. On the journey back home, we couldn't help but reflect on the highlights of our first consultation, marvelling at Samaita the man himself, his quirkiness and self-praise on having had a former head of state amongst his patients. "What a remarkable man! Don't you think he was exaggerating on being Mugabe's personal doctor, Liz?"

"Possibly, but anything goes with Sekuru though I have to give him his due; he comes highly recommended from many men within the country who have successfully fought prostate cancer and fully recovered, so there may be truth in his unashamed personal aggrandisement and self-promotion."

"So you think his treatment plan will work on me?"

"Of course, Fari, you really have to be positive in outlook for this to work.

The battle starts right in your head. If you become broody and negative, then of course it's not gonna work, will it? There's power in positive thinking, my love, as cliched as it may sound! So, let's give this time and see how it goes."

We drove in comfortable silence for the remainder of our journey home. For the next couple of weeks, Liz was exceedingly good in preparing the concoctions for me, in addition to the bitter herbal brew *Mufandichimuka*. The latter was exceedingly hard to take, let alone swallow, because of its stinging on the tongue and putrid taste, but I persevered as I took solace in Samaita's words: "Therein in that bitterness lays your cure."

For some time, I valiantly tried to convince myself. Inwardly, I thought I felt better, though the excessive pain in my groin and persistent stomach cramps wouldn't go away. Once I remarked about this to Samaita in a follow-up review visit, but he dismissed it as a fairly normal process of the healing cycle. The smooth-talking uncle always seemed to have an answer for everything, and though I didn't want to admit it to Liz, Samaita's glibness and fast-talking suaveness reminded me of a conman, Zuwa, with whom we grew up in my Greenside hood. Zuwa was a con star who brought misery to many residents because of his crooked shenanigans. Given Zuwa's tongue, he had an uncanny way with people in which he could pretty much get what he wanted, so due to this smooth talker, many unsuspecting people had been conned out of their hard-earned money.

My drinking mate and friend Finley was sceptical of my seeking treatment from Samaita and dismissed him as a charlatan from the very outset. "For fuck's sake, Fari! A man of your stature? Don't tell me you've fallen for this hogwash from a low life Mbare charlatan. Why put your fragile health under perilous conditions anymore? Why not relocate to England? After all, you have the queen's citizenship. You could just return to England, and, boom, you are treated."

A fellow *Gunner* like myself, as we called our Arsenal football club, my friendship with Finley had been borne in Fife Avenue's Montagu pub one evening. He was part of the crowd watching the big match of the day, Arsenal v Chelsea, so that evening started our inimitable friendship, as we went on to thrash voluble Jose Mourinho's hapless Chelsea 3:1 in that high stakes English premier league match, which saw us go top of the table with that epic win. "We are Arsenal, we get the job done," I drunkenly bellowed loudly in the pub, drawing the attention of a heavily- built fella I later learnt was Finley.

"True, my brother, we don't hang around Finley here," he'd spoken stretching out his broad arms and strong handshake amid a wide grin which somehow reminded me of Tony Blair's trademark perpetual grin.

"Fari Mupawaenda, how do you do, mate?" I had replied reciprocating his friendly gesture with a firm handshake for one so happy at witnessing Arsenal's win. From that circumstance, that moment, Finley and I became drinking mates at the usual watering holes in Harare, though Montagu pub remained our favourite. The fact that we shared a similar totem, *Gwai Gumbi*, was a bonus in cementing our amity, as I playfully called Finley my *munin'ina* or *Bambomunini*.

Usually, if there was a big English premier league match, Finley and I would meet at the pub for a football galore hullabaloo guzzling ice cold beer and devouring Montagu braised steaks from their famed kitchen. Besides, as our friendship evolved, Finley started visiting me at home frequently, and his missus, Mainini Nyemudzai as I called her, became good buddies with my own Liz. And today Finley was here to fight from my corner as he cajoled me to consider returning to England, a place I'd turned my back on. I wasn't sure I liked what Finley was saying, but there were three of them against me. The balance of power was heavily tilted against me here.

And so Finley carried on his new role as my assumed keeper, as he sought to convince me otherwise. "You know what, Fari, it's not a sign of weakness to raise your hands and admit, 'I got it wrong folks coming back to Zim, leaving behind my cushy life in England.'

"Much as you denigrate England, I think you are better off returning there, mate. Once back, you can access the national health service, the famed NHS we all hear of. I get it you can't afford the $30k medical fees needed for your treatment plan and surgery, but equally don't take leave of your brains! Use them dear! What's an academic like you doing being duped by a semi-literate Mbare thug Samaita? I'm sorry, but the joke is on you, mate, if you can't see it. You are being played here. Where on earth have you heard prostate cancer being treated by herbs?"

"We will see, mate," I said uneasily and with a sense of dread, mainly because part of me agreed with Fin's scepticism. I couldn't say that so openly to him in case I encouraged him further to see through my insecurities and uneasiness. Mainly, I had gone along with Liz's traditional herbal treatment because of desperation. There was no way I could have raised $30 thousand US needed by Avenues Clinic to commence on my treatment. I am not laying any blame on Liz; I would never do that. Goodness knows, Liz always had my back, that woman, the woman I refused to openly commit to, though I knew inwardly I felt something for her. I had seen the good side of Liz throughout my illness thus far. Liz had been my rock and anchor. Dearest Liz had loyally and had diligently stood by me without fail.

I found it easier; I could easily open up and chat to Liz. Because of the way I am, I tended to be private about my business, and in those rare instances during the course of my illness, I surprised myself by opening up. I intimately shared with her how I hated the looks people gave me each time I opened up about my prostate cancer diagnosis.

"There is something troubling and unsettling about the odd looks and stares I got from all and sundry each time I reveal my cancer diagnosis," I said, sharing my discomfort and uneasiness with Liz one evening, in the comfort of our bed.

"Are you just not being overly sensitive in your reaction, or reading people's interaction with you, Fari?"

"Far from it, honey. How can I express it to you, this disconcerting look I get? Each time I mention my cancer is clearly blatant, like I'm an object of pity. Henceforth, I'll just keep things to myself in my way of dealing with the situation. Many atimes I've felt like screaming at people, *'Don't give me that godamm awful "oh you're going to die" look! I don't need your sympathies folks.'* Death is inevitable to all of us at some point, the only difference being the manner in which we leave this planet. We all have to die, but how that happens is bound to differ for each one of us."

"I hear you; I empathise. It's a difficult one, love. I get it, it's your man way of clamming up on issues as a coping mechanism, but rest assured, you can always talk to me. You and I can always talk without fear of being judged."

"I know, sweetie, and thanks for that," I remarked as I kissed her on the forehead. "Goodnight sweetheart, tomorrow will be another day," she said as she kissed me back as we drifted off to sleep in each other's arms.

Chapter 11

Rubicon Moment

As if emerging from a nightmare, I could hear distant voices speaking, "He's coming round, he's coming round, thank heavens!"

My eyes felt hazy and numb. Gradually the voices became distinct. I strained my eyes and could barely make silhouettes of various people peering at me. I could just about make out my nephew Chabuya's with his unusual craggy face. Liz also, and then Finley and his wife, Nyemudzai.

Why are they all crowding around me? Confused thoughts coursed through my dazed brain.

"Why are you all peering at me?" I found my voice at last, as I recognised Dr. Bvirakare in his unmistakable white coat, trademark stethoscope dangling down his shoulders. "Can someone please explain what's happening to me? Do you hear me good people?" I asked accusingly.

"Good old Fari, always a fighter," remarked Dr. Bvirakare smiling. "There's nothing wrong. You had what appeared to be an epileptic seizure, and Liz wisely got you whisked in an ambulance. We've done some further tests on you to investigate what triggered your seizure, but I'm afraid we'll have to keep you in hospital for a few days under observation. It's just precautionary measures. Meanwhile, this will give me time to review your bloods and other results from the lab."

"Did I hear you right, Doctor? You just said I had a seizure, but that's not possible. Samaita's herbs are supposed to cure me of this cancer..." I blurted out without thinking.

"Samaita's herbs? Who is Samaita?" calmly inquired the doctor. "Is this the infamous Mbare herbalist you are referring to, Fari?"

"Yes, what's wrong with him? Why call him infamous? Surely what's good for the goose is good for the gander, if he's treated presidents, cured them from prostate cancer, then why should I be an exception? Now, don't you start on me, Doctor, I've just about had enough of this excruciating pain."

It was at that point I noticed the contorted weird look on Dr. Bvirakare's face. He looked like he was watching a horror show with every word I said about Samaita. Clearing his throat, he requested everyone else to leave the ward except Liz.

"What's wrong Doctor?" I inquired, searching his nonplussed face for answers; he gave nothing away until he had firmly closed the door behind the others.

"Please Liz, don't tell me it's true you've been consulting a herbalist with the belief that would cure your partner's prostate cancer? Whatever faith you may have in Samaita, I'm afraid it's misplaced."

"But, Dr. Bvirakare, Samaita is renowned in Harare and beyond for assisting cancer sufferers, some whom the medical fraternity would have given up on," said Liz, who seemed to have found her voice at last.

The doctor had an uncomfortable cough, after which he spoke in a pensive tone. "Forget about the so-called miraculous success stories of curing cancer you've heard about Samaita. For years the Health Professions Council - HPC in this country have been lobbying to have him prosecuted for malpractice and manslaughter charges he has incurred exploiting vulnerable, infirm people, some of whom were on end-of-life care, or terminally ill, through misrepresenting the claim he could cure their illnesses.

"But because Samaita is politically connected in the highest echelons and corridors of power in this country, authorities have turned a blind eye to his devious machinations and malpractice. He gets away as an advocate of traditional medicines at the forefront of arguing these should be promoted and protected under the indigenous empowerment laws, as championed by Zinatha organisation, for which he is the secretary general. So, we're talking of a formidable figure with political clout and gravitas here, a kind of an untouchable Goliath, if I may put it that way."

The doctor continued, "But speaking to you off the record, for a lot of my former patients he attended to, things didn't end well. I'm not trying to scare you, but I have a duty of care to you as my patient, Fari. Now, as you've been taking his herbal treatment, I hope by jove you haven't in anyway been ingesting his notorious herbal tea, *Mufandichimuka*?

"The more acute side effects of Samaita's noxious *Mufandichimuka* brew have had terrible consequences for some clients who, because of extensive damage to their kidneys, ended up developing renal failure. So you see Fari, this Samaita chap should not be allowed anywhere near human patients if I had my way. But who am I in the grand scheme of things?" He spoke as he shrugged his shoulders in despondency, but even as he spoke, I felt a cold shiver which went down my body and made me sit up and take this man's words seriously, even though part of me felt whatever was in Samaita's awful brew may have exacerbated my illness, judging by the persistent throbbing pain and frequent dizziness spells I had felt in the last couple of days.

"Of course, my heart goes out to those unsuspecting cancer patients unashamedly exploited as guinea pigs by Samaita," carried on Dr. Bvirakare, "which is why, despite my low traction and at the risk of drawing the ire of the establishment, I continue to vociferously advocate that this charlatan be barred from practicing any form of medicine, traditional or modern science."

My heart skipped at hearing that familiar word, *Mufandichimuka*, Samaita's brutal herbal brew and realising Dr. Bvirakare may be onto something here. Liz and I exchanged knowing glances at the mention of the herbal tea. How could we not, given that I had been religiously taking this hideous brew.

Sensing our unease, Dr. Bvirakare proceeded with more urgency in his voice. "Many of our patients have reacted badly to this *Mufandichimuka* herbal brew and developed problems with their kidneys, which resulted in dialysis for them. I am not taking any chances and am having additional tests done on you right away, Fari. I will want to see you here first thing tomorrow morning, Liz, so I debrief you both on the results to all these tests. Now, you will have to excuse Fari as he needs additional time to rest following his seizure." With that, Liz had to leave me in the care of Dr. Bvirakare and one of his nurses, Sister Bettina.

Chapter 12

Moment of Reckoning

In typical time-keeping fashion, by ten o'clock the next morning Liz and I we were sitting before a stern looking Dr. Bvirakare in his Baines Avenues medical practice. In scenes reminiscent of Abba's *Fernando*© tune, there was something in the air that morning as the "good doctor," as I usually called him, did not waste time on pleasantries or small talk with us. He cut straight to the crux of the matter.

"I have to say to you both I have some grim news to share with you," he began.

"We are listening, please enlighten us," I said softly, as I was keen to get to the bottom of this, here and now. I hadn't slept a wink the previous night. It had been a wretched sleep in which I had turned and tossed on the hospital bed. The excruciating pains in my body had only served to escalate my ordeal. Perhaps being in hospital hadn't helped things either, though Sister Bettina had been exceedingly kind with her relentless supply of pain killers to ward off the endemic pain.

"Given my longevity of service in the medical field, I always believe in levelling with my patients, and today is one of those moments," the doctor said.

"I wasn't particularly reassured the moment you mentioned you'd consulted Samaita, as I'm privy to the damage his unorthodox methods of cancer treatment have caused suffering in many fellow Zimbabweans. I may have to speak off record in some instances, but in all, I urge you to follow my medical advice to the letter."

Next, he said, "If I had my way, Samaita would be locked up and the cell keys thrown away to dungeons guarded by marauding lions, never to be let out again! I am sorry to say Fari, but your prostate cancer has metastasised to stage 3, and here are the x-rays of your kidneys; one kidney has been gravely damaged as I feared, the inimical effects of *Mufandichimuka* herbal tea, which, in reality, is poison to the human body. Some of our past patients, recipients of *Mufandichimuka*, have ended up on dialysis, so we're talking serious health concerns here, Fari.

"We will now need to do your surgery as soon as possible, without further delay as advised previously, or else we're running out of time and we cannot afford to waste further time."

I sat through all this, dazed like I was in a trance. It was then that Liz's quiet sobbing jolted me out of my fantasy bubble.

"But what about the $30k Doctor? Is that still a precondition to surgery?" I almost shouted at him.

"Yes," he said. "I'm afraid that's the correct position as you've stated. I feel for you, but this is Baines Avenues Hospital policy as a private hospital. I could refer you to other government hospitals like Parirenyatwa, Wilkins or Harare hospitals but without a medical aid, as in your case, the picture is dim. In addition, they're only hospitals in name, there are no running facilities to talk of in these quasi-hospitals, not even paracetamol to stave off pain." He continued, "Either way, an urgent decision has to be made in respect of your surgery, Fari."

It was then that I lost it big time and started hurling insults at Dr. Bvirakare. "How dare you patronise us like this Doctor, with your sad little talk putting yourself on a high horse pedestal?

You have the nerve to diss a decent human being who has tried to medically help me, however unpalatable his methods are to you and your snooty world of science, but tell you what, Samaita has not asked for any payment from me. Now flip the coin over, there you are, on your high horse, demanding 30 thousand US dollars from a terminally ill man. Where is your sense of right and wrong Doctor, huh?

"That Hippocratic Oath you swore to uphold, was that merely rhetoric? Why not treat patients, save lives first, and ask for money later?" I countered."

Liz interrupted me halfway through my salvos, "Fari, please stop, will you? What's come over you? This is not the doctor's fault. Stop it! Will you, please?" She then apologised profusely to Dr. Bvirakare, "Doctor, I'm sorry about this unwarranted outburst. I thank you on behalf of Fari. Please give us a few days to sort ourselves out, then we will be in touch in relation to Fari's treatment. We really need to get going on his treatment as you've implored on us."

"That's all-right, Liz, thank you for your understanding," replied the visibly shaken doctor. "I am happy to discharge Fari, though I want him back as soon as possible. I cannot overemphasise this enough to you both; time is now of the greatest essence for want of a better word."

"I was still going to dismiss myself Doctor, with or without your consent," I rudely butted in. I certainly had an axe to grind with the doctor. "Come on Liz, off we go," I said grabbing her arm. "As a general rule of thumb, always know where we are not needed; in this instance, this is one such moment we are unwelcome."

Liz politely bid farewell, going overboard with her over the top apologies for my "out-of-the-norm" behaviour as she termed it. Dr. Bvirakare replied, "That's all-right Liz, I understand Fari is in a volatile space, and we all need to play our part to help him. You will notice in days to come; his emotions will be all over the place. That's because of the inner turmoil his body is undergoing. Please get back to me as soon as possible. I'm sorry I have to keep reiterating this." With those words we made good our escape.

"That was really uncalled for behaviour, Fari," Liz reprimanded me as she drove home, "for you to come out guns blazing on a man who has been trying to help you is certainly a massive overreaction, if I may say." She continued chiding me, but I was in no mood for these false pleasantries and immediately jumped down Liz's throat, "Aaah, I see, so now I'm not allowed to vent my anger and frustration, am I? Woman, you really need to ask yourself this question: whose side you are on, mine or Dr. Bvirakare's?"

"It's not about taking sides, Fari. After you've taken your new medication, we really need to sit down and chart an immediate way forward. Emotions aside, we should both agree in taking on board what the doctor has said."

"But where are we going to get $30 thousand US dollars in this shambolic economy and god forsaken country? We've walked this road before, Liz. I don't think I can do this anymore, and what was that all about, casting aspersions on Samaita? Did you fall for that?"

"It's difficult terrain to navigate, the Samaita issue," Liz replied. "I know Sekuru is a somewhat controversial and divisive figure because of what some term his unconventional herbal therapy, but I wouldn't have recommended you to him if I knew he had a darker side to him, would I Fari? Now that there's new information at hand regarding Sekuru's unorthodox treatment plans, it would be foolhardy for us to continue on this path and you taking a herbal brew which, as the doctor said, has done extensive damage to one of your kidneys."

"Look, I am really sorry this is happening to you, Fari, and wish I could do more to show my support. Perhaps I will phone your daughter Yeukai in England this evening and see if she can assist, you know, three brains are better than one, and since you say your relationship with your son is estranged, we can't reach out to him, can we?"

"I haven't been in touch with both children; they would rather see me dead first, especially my son. Things were okay with my daughter until she dropped out of university, and she didn't take kindly to my reaction to that, but like you say, perhaps anything is worth a try, though I hate to be beholden to people, that's just me, Liz."

"I know all about your pride, and manly ego Fari, you forget I'm your alter ego," chuckled Liz. I could see she was trying to make light of the sombre situation, bless her heart.

"But listen," she said. "This is no time to be pigheaded. Swallow your pride and let me reach out to your kids."

As Liz kept driving around Five Avenues looking for a vacant parking bay, I could feel the excruciating, searing pain again in my groin area. Liz could tell from the wincing, grimaces and groans from me. "Five Avenue parking slots are always a nightmare; let me squeeze into that bay where the Mitsubishi car is reversing. I need to grab your new prescriptions. See you shortly," and with that she dashed out of the car.

"Hello sleepy head," I saw Finley beaming at me ear to ear through the passenger side window of my seat, with a backslapping pat on my shoulders.

"Hello *Samusha*, how are you mate?" I returned his jovial greeting. "I see you and Liz bumped into each other in Five Avenue shops."

Finley continued, "It's you we should be asking how you are after we left you in hospital yesterday. Liz tells me it's not looking good. Tell you what, let me pick Nyemudzai from her Montagu Zumba classes, then we meet at your place. She texted me a while ago she should be done, so it will literally be a few minutes and we meet at yours, right?"

"Sounds like a great idea," remarked Liz, who'd been enjoying my surprise at bumping into Finley. "Well, he saw me first as I exited the pharmacy, it was actually hilarious as he kept on shouting, excuse me *ambuya* and as I turned around looking for an old hag *ambuya* I thought the message was meant for someone else, only for him to shout my name. That's when good old Finley got my attention," remarked Liz amid chuckles.

"Looks like your Liz doesn't take kindly to being called *ambuya*!"

"Of course not, I'm not that old! I'm a lady!" remonstrated Liz with some feigned annoyance.

"That's women for you, typical vanity stuff," I butted in. "Far from it, the term *ambuya* is not derogatory Liz, neither does it denote you're getting on a bit as you wrongly think. On the contrary, it's an honorific term I'm sure my good friend Finley was using as a mark of respect to his chum's partner. Anyway, it's all-in order Finley, see you shortly at ours with Mainini Nyemudzai." With that Liz drove off, still protesting her youthfulness and why she found the term *ambuya* demeaning to women. With my egregious pain coming back, I let her win the battle as I drifted off to my intermittent sleeping pattern.

I could hear voices coming from downstair. It sounded like Mainini Nyemudzai, Finley's wife, speaking in what were meant to be hushed tones, but I could barely make out the gist of what was being said. "We really have to encourage Babamukuru Fari to return to England. We can't delay any longer, if the situation is dire, as Dr. Bvirakare confirmed this morning."

"How is he? Is he still asleep?" That was unmistakably Finley's voice. "Let me check on him. He's intermittently slipping in and out of sleep. He harps on persistent pain around the groin area." Liz's footsteps were audible enough as she came to retrieve me.

"How are you feeling, handsome? The Magadzires are here, you must have slept for over three hours, it's nearly 8 pm evening time."

94

"Three hours, gosh, I'm sorry Liz, now I remember Finley promised to drop by, but I needed the sleep *wena*, my throbbing pain has subsided. You will have to support me to navigate the stairs, love."

"No worries. I have your cocktail of tablets for your consumption first. The doctor's orders, tablets first. I insist."

"Well, I am as well a walking pharmacy the way Bvirakare has encumbered me with all these different drugs. I hate them though; they make me nauseous Liz."

"Better to err on the side of caution as you always say, so take them you will, I'm afraid." With that Liz waited over me until I had gulped down the entire cocktail of tablets.

After what seemed an eternity, I managed with Liz's assistance to navigate her stairs which was now an arduous task for me. I used to do two at a time but climbing up and down was now a chore for me, with this omnipresent pain in my body. What was happening to me? Perhaps I had underplayed my illness and thought of myself as invincible, but this was prostate cancer slowly ravaging my now delicate constitution.

"Maswerasei Gwai, Gumbi Mukuruvambwa," Finley's voice jolted me to present reality.

"I am doing well, I am doing well, mate, the pain aside. How is Mainini Nyemudzai doing?" I said, addressing Finley's wife.

"Equally well, Babamukuru, how's the prognosis?"

"Aaah it's not looking good," Liz cut in before I could say a word. "I am relieved you're here today, both of you. We do need to put our heads together and chart a way forward as a family."

"Sure, sure, go on," Finley said, nodding his head. "Why don't you give us an overview of Bvirakare's prognosis this time around, so we have several brains dissecting this together," he chipped in.

"I won't sugar coat anything, given the gravity of the matter now. Bvirakare gave us the bombshell this morning. The cancer has metastasized to stage 3 prostate cancer, and as we've delayed on commencing surgical treatment, we can't afford to waste any additional time, again, his words. Fari needs to be operated on, but then we have that small matter of $30,000 US needed by Avenues Clinic!"

"The bastards, $30,000k! Do they think it's on parity with their worthless Zimbabwean dollar?" quipped Mainini Nyemudzai.

"Well said, Mainini," I echoed my agreement with her.

"So, what's your plan Maiguru? We know we can't raise that astronomical figure, given the current hardships in this god-forsaken country! Government hospitals, Parirenyatwa, Harare hospitals are a non-starter."

"Aaah, those gas chambers, why would I want to go there when they don't have even paracetamol to dispense? I would rather die in my house," I remonstrated.

"Fari, will you stop, please?" implored Liz.

"In a way, he's right. The Zanu Mafia have ruined the health delivery system of this nation. People are left to fend for themselves in the dirty corridors. The doctors and nurses don't even have gloves to put on with this Covid pandemic rife! The other day I saw nurses at Harare hospital donning blankets, torn bed sheets and plastic bags on their hands as PPEs to fight Covid. My heart went out to them, overworked and underpaid, the unsung heroes of our times. I tell you the Zanu Mafia is a cult, out to get citizens' blood."

"Anyway, enough of politics, but we do have to make a snap decision now. The other day Fari had unexplained seizures, and now it's this pervasive pain, now the constant blackouts. Next time, who knows what it will be? I could feel okay if we make a definitive decision now, on the way forward," remarked a worried looking Liz.

"Yes, Maiguru, I agree with you, decision time is now. I would say, Fari my friend, you need to quickly get on the plane back to England and see what the National Health Service will do for you, mate. Time is of the essence here."

"'I'm all for that as well, sweetheart," quipped Liz. "I spoke with your daughter Yeukai whilst you were asleep..."

"You spoke with Yeukai?" I sprang into my animated self now, reinvigorated at the mention of Yeukai's name. "Yeukai, Yeukai my lovely, my little flower, how is she?" I couldn't hide my obvious excitement now.

"All right, actually; we had a good chat and she's booked a flight for you for the day after tomorrow."

"Day after tomorrow, but that's too soon," I protested.

"Too soon, as if you have the luxury of choice, Fari. Remember we haven't got the time anymore as Bvirakare admonished."

"What do you need more time for *Babamukuru, chiitai semunhu mukuru?* Take it on your chin. The English health care system may well serve you in your hour of need. I would jump on this now, immediately in fact," chipped in Mainini Nyemudzai.

Not to be outdone, Finley butted in, "Listen, mate, now is not the time to put pride ahead of common sense. Whatever happened between you and your family back in England has already happened; there will be time for that. Time to fix it if it can be fixed." He emphasised, "Now it's 'me' time for you, for heaven's sake Fari, look out after yourself, numero uno, number one, and just get on that fucking plane so you can access treatment."

I could detect mounting frustration in Finley's voice at my lingering obstinacy and obduracy.

"It's a British Airways overnight flight via South Africa," Liz said, "so you leave Friday afternoon have a brief stopover at Johannesburg Airport, and by Saturday morning you should touch down at Terminal 5. Yeukai will pick you up at Heathrow."

Mainini Nyemudzai said, *"Aaah ndookubaraka uku Babamukuru,* you should be proud of your daughter Yeukai for throwing you a much-needed lifeline at this eleventh hour. Not many kids are like that, I tell you." I could see she was trying to make light of the dreary situation, but I put on a brave face nonetheless.

"Aiwa, ndizvozvo Mainini, I fully concur with you; it's always great when children do not forget their parents, though I have to say, I'm not sure my relationship is there between my eldest child Muchadei and me. I haven't heard from him for all the years I've been here."

'That's for another time, like Finley said earlier on. Children are always bound to be different in terms of how they relate to their parents, but there will be time enough for that kind of conversation with your son, certainly now is not the time, if I may also weigh in my sentiments."

"Haaa, you're telling me, Mainini Nyemu," I acquiesced with a big sigh.

I only had one and half days to pack my little belongings and make a return journey to the England I had secretly vowed to myself I would never do, but ill health had other plans for me. I couldn't help but reflect at the vicissitudes of life, that you plan this in life, but then something else happens to torpedo your plans spectacularly! Talk of best laid plans gone awry! What a life we live as mere mortals. There were so many emotions going through my being during that one and half days before I left Liz, my consort, a woman who had nursed me throughout my prostate cancer diagnosis, the fluctuating phases of the illness, the numerous ups and downs, highs and lows, the persistent excruciating pain, my irascible tantrums and outbursts. Liz had borne all of those with her quiet dignity and effortless grace. In the face of my erratic outbursts, her valiant efforts were to save me through her referral to Samaita, even though things had turned out the other way with Samaita's unconventional treatment methods. Still, I did not blame my Liz for this; I perfectly understood her gesture of love, forbearance and fortitude which had made her offer me anything to cling to dear life. "Hang in there, Fari," she was wont to say.

Liz, I loved her, but would I ever see her again? Then there was also the small matter of my first lawful wife, Maidei, from whom I had drifted apart in the eight years I'd been away. How was I going to re-establish any contact with her lost in my eight-year absentia? Was it at all conceivable to talk of there ever being a re-connection with Maidei? Our initial long-distance phone calls had gradually dwindled to silence as she came to terms with my foolhardy decision to leave England, and as I consolidated my relationship with Liz. There was no room for looking back.

I don't do sympathy or sentiments, and I wasn't expecting any from Maidei. Eight years is a long time to be apart in a marriage and still hope the smouldering embers of your vows and marriage bonds remained intact. I am a terribly ill man and now have to fight with every ounce in my body, this prostate cancer. Then and only then will I attend to the Maidei issue and my estranged children, although I had been moved by my daughter Yeukai 's kindness, which prompted her to buy me the airline ticket for my return journey. That is a good sign for possible reconciliation with my little flower Yeu, notwithstanding our previous falling out.

Then there was my so-called business empire or what remained of it, my *gonyeti* transport truck business, in addition to the *kombi mushika-shika* passengers ferry transport, both of which had spectacularly floundered. Turns out, my "return to the source" dream hadn't worked out well.

Harare International Airport on my departure day, late Friday afternoon, was a bundle of raw, fragile emotions on full display, an eclectic mix for what constituted my Zim kith and kin, my inner circle I had come to rely on during my stay in Zimbabwe. They came to see me off that Friday afternoon. As we all huddled in the departure lounge, Finley, Mainini Nyemudzai and my other half, it was exceedingly hard for Liz. She had steadfastly refused to discuss the future with me, our future. "You are unwell, Fari, and what matters now is getting you fit as a fiddle. Our future, the future we so desire, will eventually come, and then we can savour it together."

"But, but ..." I struggled for words, as I stammered to speak. Part of me was filled with the regret of yesteryear, the regret of a man who realises his fading sun, a man coming to terms with his mortality. "Perhaps we should have got married as you always wanted and insisted, love. I'm sorry for being headstrong and difficult," I blurted out.

Liz could see I was hurting inside, that I was falling into delicate, minute pieces. "Fari, if it's meant to be, we will have a future together dearest, now be a good lad for me like you've been these eight years and go kick this illness in the teeth. Yes, you can do this Fari, a kick in the bollocks is all this horrid cancer needs!"

Did she honestly believe we had a future together after Bvirakare's bleak prognosis of my cancer? As she hugged me goodbye in front of the immigration exit point, we looked each other in the eyes and perhaps both knew the unwritten future but couldn't say it.

"*Mufambe mushe Gumbi, Gwai yangu yiyi,*" she said brushing away her tears. "You are the man *Gumbi*, whatever happens, I love you. *Ndimi mune yese, Gumbi.*" And with that she gave me a peck on the lips, and I started walking towards the immigration entry point, blinking away my tears. *Get a grip,* I silently muttered to myself as I struggled to strengthen myself at this painful parting.

"Bon voyage *Sekuru*," shouted my nephew Gumisai, who'd surprised me by making it to the airport. I waved back at them all as I walked rapidly towards the immigration entry point; I didn't want them to see my tears. I turned for the last time before I handed my passport to the immigration checkpoint, waved at Liz and everyone else, the lump in my throat growing bigger by the minute.

"Make sure you keep taking your tablets Fari, till you're seen by your UK doctors," Liz had quietly admonished in my ear in our last embrace just before the first immigration passport check point. Lovely woman, how was I going to manage without her pampering me as I had grown accustomed to it? Inwardly, I felt grateful to have had her by my side throughout my cancer ordeal. Yet now, here I was, leaving her behind with an uncertain future ahead of us. Already the huge sense of personal loss and a foreboding grief descended on me like a blanket of thick, dense fog. I turned away from her, waving at her whilst struggling with my moist eyes of the strong emotions I felt at this parting.

As I sat in the Harare International Airport departure lounge, after going through immigration formalities, my mind couldn't help but wander again at my now uncertain future. There was an air of resignation within me at what fate would throw at me going forward, but part of me still wanted to live, to live and be with Liz. The past few months battling this cancer had shown me Liz in a totally new light. If I could fight this cancer thing, then perhaps there was a future between us after all. Going back to England would give me the chance to sort out my mess with Maidei, possibly work on a quickie divorce. Then I would sort out something with Liz, perhaps even applying for a spouse visa for her. Who knows? I was full of hope for a bright future of Liz and me.

My mind replayed the numerous occasions Liz had covered my back in my tumultuous battle against my illness. Those incessant times when I had one of my innumerable, periodic meltdowns during cancer. It had been Liz who took over the reins in the house, assuming, leadership and responsibility. She'd nursed me and shooshed me around when I grumbled about taking my medication, when I was broody, irritable, sulky. And I had been a right dick, hating everyone and the world, at times blaming Bvirakare for the cancer diagnosis in the first place. I contemplated *Why did he have to make the bloody diagnosis? Why couldn't he have lied to me? Some things are better left unsaid!* Many atimes I would throw these verbal missiles at Liz in an accusatory tone, as if it was her fault and she was Bvirakare. But she had stood firm, resolute, un-yielding, and well-nigh rock steady and tight, ever exuding kindness and al-ways her charming, reassuring smile. 'Toot...toot...toot...it will be well Fari," she would often remark in her cheerful, pleasant disposition. I would be fib-bing if I said I ever saw Liz cross or heard an angry word escape her lips. Liz had this aura of calmness and pervasive, quiet confidence imbued within her; she just kept things going, and it is an accolade to her character. She had been my rock in my darkest days, and now I was leaving her...

"May passengers for the 628 British Airways flight to Johannesburg, South Africa, prepare to board, please. Gate M308 South terminal," came the voice from the intercom, breaking my daydream musings. I rose to trudge to the boarding gate.

Chapter 13

Letitia Happened

I met Letitia!

I met this Thailand lassie at Hillside Residential Care Home in Aylesbury, where I was discharged from hospital, following six gruelling months of intensive prostate cancer treatment. I say "lassie" for that's how I would like to remember her.

Truth was, Letitia was an attractive, super slim, middle-aged Thai woman with olive oil skin, which suited her tall, voluptuous physique, accentuated by firm pointed breasts. Letitia was my companion and live-in caregiver during those touch and go six months when, at times, I could see the NHS physicians and consultants huddled in a corner. They spoke in hushed tones after doing their morning rounds in the big Stoke Mandeville hospital. When they thought I was asleep or sedated, I could still make out the gist of their conversations.

"His breathing has been laboured and coming in short, raggedy gasps. We've had to put him on a ventilator to aid breathing."

"The next few days are touch and go, he's reacting to the treatment though..."

"Why don't we switch treatment and try him on an experimental drug?"

"The benefits far outweigh the collateral damage to his recovery chances..."

"Perhaps we ought to move him to a hospice and commence end-of-life care; that will give him time to come to terms with this and spend time with his loved ones."

I tell you, it was nigh hard and excruciatingly traumatic hearing medical professionals talking over you, about your life being written off like that, whilst you are still alive, and it was much more bizarre to hear them conferring about it. That was the half a year I stayed at Stoke Mandeville hospital Gutman Centre wing battling for my life, fighting the prostate cancer in my body. Some of my memories during this period are increasingly blurred, though there are some bits which tend to come back in seeming flashback episodes. There were times I felt a deep sense of déjà vu, as if I dreamed some of these things. I can say, without equivocation, cancer is a horrible thing to have. I certainly wouldn't wish it on anyone, not even my nemesis.

They had been difficult, dark, dreary morbid months for me, going through the excruciating pain of chemotherapy, radiotherapy, and all the attendant marathon treatment plans. For the second time in my personal battle against the cancer, yet another lovely woman besides Liz had been at my side, supporting, nurturing, rallying me against this monster that prostate cancer is. At the thought of cancer as a monster, I found my mind wandering to the flamboyant, gregarious Samaita the Harare herbalist, for had he not equally called cancer, *mhuka*, i.e., an animal? *"Cancer is an animal,"* my mind wandered back to the maiden visit with Liz to Samaita and I could picture his larger-than-life build and persona as he uttered those words.

Letitia, Leti, as I liked to call her, nursed me to my miraculous full recovery. She was my specialist, one-on-one carer assigned to me throughout my physiotherapy sessions. I had to learn to walk again, under her austere tutelage as I had lost my mobility, having been bed-ridden and catheterised the greater part of that six-month hospital sojourn. A trained physiotherapist back home in Thailand, Leti used to push me during those gruelling, daily back to walk sessions. And she was a tough cookie who brooked no nonsense from me.

"You have to constantly push yourself Fari, you can do this," she would studiously encourage me.

"But, the pain in my legs, it's like they aren't my legs anymore, they've become logs."

"Aaah, you see, but pain is a state of mind Fari, it's all in your head see, one foot ahead at a time and we will make that phenomenal progress," she would say, playfully poking me in the head.

We were on it for a couple of weeks and in time Leti had given me my mobility back. "Thank you so much Leti. I can't thank you enough! You've restored my mobility."

But so modest was Leti, she wouldn't hear my declarations of gratitude. "You are exceedingly kind, Fari, but I was only doing my job, glad we got there, my god! What a difficult patient you could be Fari," and with that, she'd break into her trademark high pitched laughter that I found contagious.

It had been a rough road to recovery for me, for one who had flirted closely with death when I arrived from Zimbabwe, and inwardly, I felt I owed part of my recovery to Leti's exuberance, and charming personality; she was somehow egging me on, keeping me going in the face of mounting adversity. Was I also determined to live and had a zest for life? I don't know. How else could I explain my near-death recovery, when some people were on the verge of reading my last rites? So many questions, so few answers, and a befuddled mind to cap it all.

"You had unfinished business, Fari. The Man Above, as you call him, certainly gave you a lease of life for a reason. So, use your new lease of life wisely," Leti would later remark to me.

"Tell you what, you are likely to be discharged early next week after the resident Doctor Peel signs you off. Normally I wouldn't do this, but we have become very close over your stay here. I wouldn't mind touching base with you outside of this place. I apologise if it may appear too full on for you, or inappropriate, but I thought we've got along so well the time you've been here," she said, eying me timidly as if she expected me to jump down her throat for even daring to mention it.

She need not have tried to explain herself. The chemistry and pull between us had been all too evident during our myriad interactions. I am not a kid anymore, I may be getting on a bit, but I know how these things work. I am wiser to the ways of the world and know when I can pull a woman, even though I may be getting on a bit as a grumpy old git. I told this to myself, amid knowing chuckles of someone au fait with the dating game, a game of wits, as I've always called it.

"Nothing would make me happier to catch up with you at some point, Leti. Please oblige me with your number," and with that our future meeting was sealed. I didn't feel any qualms at this, even though I still thought of Liz, good old Liz! I hadn't heard from her throughout the illness, direct contact that is. She must have tried to make contact through Yeukai. "Your Zim friend has been asking after you, Dad. I've tried to give her the lowdown throughout your illness. In fact, I've kept her informed of your progress," my daughter Yeukai had remarked to me on numerous occasions.

"Thank you," I acknowledged Yeukai uncomfortably, as I didn't seem to know how to broach my relationship with Liz to my daughter. *Perhaps time will come for me to come clean,* I kept reassuring myself. But seriously, it's not exactly an easy subject. How do you talk to your daughter about the woman in your life, other than their mother, when the woman has been your consort, friend, lover, confidante and concubine all these years?

Time will come, and I will come clean, put my cards on the table. For now, let me celebrate my conquering prostate cancer, I kept reassuring myself.

Within days, I was discharged from Hillside Residential Care Home and part of me felt sad at parting with my lovely friend, Leti, my physiotherapist.

Thus on my day of release from hospital, I thanked her profusely. "You've been such a wonderful blessing to me Leti, thank you for all you've done for me," I gushed in praise of her as I prepared to take my leave.

"Thank you for looking after Dad," Yeukai chirped in, as she prepared to drive me off to her home. I didn't dare ask about Maidei, as I had only seen her on a few occasions during my sojourn at Stoke Mandeville Hospital. I may have been very ill, but I was smart enough to realise that things were not the same anymore between Maidei and me. How could they be, given our eight-year hiatus with my stay in Zim? Her hospital visits had been awkward, if not frosty. I knew we needed to have that proverbial, "We need to talk" moment, especially now that I'd been discharged from hospital. As Yeukai's car charged down the dual carriageway, she seemed to have read my mind, for she remarked, "I don't mean to intrude, Dad, but I guess you and Mama will need some clear the air talks pretty soon."

"Clear the air talks, you're telling me! Let me have a few days to sort out my head before I have this duel with your mother."

"It doesn't have to be a fight, Dad; you can still amicably differ and thrash out any issues between you two. I'm just saying, I'm not taking any sides," she remarked, raising her eyebrows in a remonstrative fashion.

106

I stayed at Yeukai's place for a few days as I psyched myself up, planning, plotting in my mind, girding my loins for my imminent tussle with Maidei. Things weren't great between Yeukai and me, even though, to her credit, she'd facilitated my return to England at that eleventh hour when I needed help the most. The bad blood had been mostly engendered by her university pregnancies, which had prompted her dropping out of uni, much to my horror and huge disappointment.

"But you can't throw away your future life just like that, Yeu, over some boy, you hardly know," I had remonstrated with her at the news of her stopping uni because of her first pregnancy.

"You just don't get it, Dad, I'm in love, and this is Jeff Willmore we're talking of here. He's a great lad, in a league of his own."

"League of his own, my foot! You forget I was once your age also, and at one point thought I was in love, with all the litany of platonic relationships I got into and the subsequent heartaches, they brought me. Why do you think I'm so cynical about relationships and human nature?"

"But we're different, Dad, different life experiences. What is true of you may not necessarily be replicated in my life.

"Toot, toot...toot..." I remarked impatiently, as I struggled to conceal my frustration at my daughter's fantasies about love and her Prince Charming Jeff. "Fair point, Yeukai, but see these eyes and ears, I've seen it all and heard it all. No wonder I'm the godfather of scepticism love."

It didn't take long for my mistrust and deep-rooted scepticism to be vindicated, as Yeukai was soon to change tack, singing a different tune as her Romeo took off on his French leave. Then what was only meant to be a maternity break to help her deliver and return to uni, took on eternity and an indefinite fashion, or so I thought.

I was too enraged to deal with Jeff's disappearing act, leaving my daughter in the lurch, so I resigned from the whole matter and directed Maidei to deal with the mess. "You deal with this nonsense Maidei, woman to woman. You're the mother and may well have a better understanding of what's happened between Yeukai and this scoundrel, Jeff. Besides, it's happened under your watch. As Yeu's mother, you're to blame!" I had derisively hammered Maidei, scapegoating her on Yeukai's fall from grace.

To give credit to Maidei though, she must have worked some beautiful magic of some sort, as she was supportive to Yeu throughout the pregnancy and delivery, the cornerstone of her motivation being, "However this setback, Yeu has to return to university, and I'll help look after the baby, I want Yeu to complete her degree." It was more like a mother's mantra from Maidei, rooting for her only daughter, the only time I had seen Maidei being on the same page with Yeukai.

In time Yeu was blessed with baby boy, Steve, though I took offence and protested at her choice of name for my grandson. "Surely you must be out of your mind, Yeu. Why Steve and not the name of someone from the Mupawaenda family clan?"

"Whom did you have in mind, Dad?"

"My father's name, Enos, of course!" I'd remarked nonchalantly, but Maidei wouldn't hear of it, as she had a weird thing about giving children names of the long departed.

"Why don't you let bygones be bygones," Maidei cut in. "Maybe now is not the time for this kind of conversation, Fari. Now is a moment of celebration for the new addition to our family, the little one. Besides, you know my feelings very well about naming children after dead relatives. I don't like it in case you forgot."

'Okay, Maidei, you win," I grudgingly acquiesced to her peace overtures. As it was only in July and the university's academic terms commenced in early October, Maidei went into overdrive, looking after baby Steve, pampering him. "I have to look after him well, first grandson of the Mupawaenda's clan, and in any case, I want it to be a smooth transition when Yeu returns to uni in October." I could see that part of Maidei was visibly excited at having a baby in the household again. It reminded me of our early years of marriage in Harare, when Maidei used to religiously make her conception goals known: "You know Fari, God willing, I want to have five kids," she would remark, holding up her palm at me in emphasis.

"Five kids?" I would recoil in horror, as if it was a bad thing.

"Yes, five children. Don't look at me like that, as if you don't come from a big family yourself. I am aiming for five children, hopefully before I turn thirty-five, so my menopause will be problem free." Then she would chuckle after this. Those were the days. We were madly in love. Such was our affection at times, and we would exhibit it, walking down the streets of Harare, Belvedere then our hood, arms entwined in those amorous public displays of affection.

Then tragedy struck, which put laid to rest Maidei's dream for five children. Due to persistent high blood pressure, coupled with an abnormally heavy menstrual flow, her obstetrician/gynaecologist had recommended a hysterectomy as the only way to treat what he called her endometriosis.

"This is the only way to stave off this condition," Dr. McClean had said, much to Maidei's horror.

"But I still wanted to conceive, have more children Doctor," she had remonstrated with him.

"It's all about maintaining a delicate balance, Maidei. You've had this endometriosis for ages, then we have your abnormally excessive menstrual flow, so clearly you have some hormonal imbalance issues which needs fixing, which is where the hysterectomy will come in. I am really sorry; there doesn't seem to be any other way to address this problem. Your x-rays have shown a not very positive outlook if we delay surgery. I empathise about children, but you and Fari, can always discuss other options for having children, certainly adoption or fostering," he said, setting his training gaze on me.

I had felt for Maidei and squeezed her hand in support as we sat in Dr. McClean's Whitehill surgery. That had been many years ago when our relationship was super strong with what had happened then. My mind flickered on the ghost of time of yesteryear and the toll of lifetime's challenges, differences, and mundane events in marriage. The proverbial road we'd travelled had been rugged.

And now, fast forward to the present moment, looking at Maidei, doting on baby Steve, attending to his every whim and fancy, little cries, little cooing sounds, made me realise how maternal my wife was, that woman I had fallen in love with at Harare Sports Club, cricket match. *But where had we gone wrong then?* I remarked ruefully to myself. I couldn't really understand it, the vicissitudes of marriage. One minute you're in love but give it a few years and you degenerate into inveterate enemies. I mean the whole thing didn't make sense to me, this marriage thing!

And so Maidei had worked tirelessly, and she pushed Yeu to return to uni in October to resume her degree. She reassured Yeu, "Don't you worry about baby Steve. I will look after him like my own; he's in safe hands, believe me. When you talk of bringing up babies, I can assure you I have a bachelor's degree in that area," Maidei would say, shooshing away Yeu's anxiety-deflated face. Yeukai need not have worried, as day in, day out she'd seen how great the emotional bond was between nan and grandson. So, by autumn she had resumed her undergraduate degree at Birmingham City University again. A fresh start again, everyone deserves a second chance, don't we all?

Maidei stepped into the role brilliantly, introducing him to formula milk, putting him to bed at night, rousing him up in the morning, reading bedtime stories to him, singing his favourite bedtime lullaby songs, *Twinkle Twinkle Little Star*, *The Wheels on A Bus Go Round and Round*, among others.

By the time I left for Zimbabwe, the terrible twos, the tantrums, had started with baby Steve. It was such a sport, seeing Maidei taking a tough stance with poor Steve when he stepped out of line, although I could see Maidei's softer side getting the better of her as she doted on Steve, "Okay, that's you done with the naughty step today Steve, off you go to your Thomas the Tank engine, after we do some readings again, okay?"

"Okay, nana," remarked the adorable little Steve as he waddled away, with one leg of his baby romper suit trailing after him, in a funny spectacle. That had been when we'd both savoured the early memories of our grandson Steve growing up.

Fast-forward, several years later. I knew there was something big when Maidei sent me an urgent WhatsApp™ SMS message the time I had relocated to Zim: "We have to talk Fari, it's very urgent, reference your daughter." That was it. That was Maidei's message, cryptic and not giving much away.

"What do you think it could be Liz?"

"Unless I were a mind reader, how would I know Fari. Why don't you phone her as she says? Do a proper Zoom or Skype call. That way, you can get to see her facial features and work out whatever is up," Good old Liz had wisely admonished.

"But here is a woman who has spurned my previous overtures each time I've tried to check on the children," I'd replied to a bemused Liz.

"Forget about your petty squabbling, Fari, this is where you get it wrong. This may well be an emergency. It's neither here nor there how she's rebuffed you in the past. Don't conflate issues here. The fact that she's sent you a desperate *SOS* call means there's something big, so phone her as she requests. You can use the study upstairs for your Skype call. I won't be snooping around or eavesdropping your call, if that's what you fear," Liz had remarked amid chuckles.

"Of course not, nothing could be further from the truth. I will phone her then."

And that had been it. That evening, as I spoke with Maidei over Skype, the bombshell was about Yeukai's second pregnancy scandal, the gist of which entailed a married, illegal immigrant man who had thought impregnating her would earn him a visa and the right to stay in England. Of course, when Yeukai caught wind of this, she gave the poor sod his marching orders: "You can eff off to your country, mister. I may as well look after my own child than be with a person who is only marrying me for the visa."

Strangely, that shooting from the hip response seemed to have won her admiration from the mother, Maidei, who praised it. "Better to get into a relationship for the right reasons not this visa bullshit stuff. As much as it disappoints me, Yeukai has erred for the second time, but she has a point in terminating this unproductive relationship."

"I see, and since when have you and Yeu seen eye to eye, that you're now partners in crime?" I jeered sarcastically.

"I would cut the sarcasm, Fari. It is not very helpful and grown-up. Your daughter is pregnant out of wedlock for the second time in three years, which may well scupper her university studies, but with all due respect, now there's the need to show your mettle, not sarcasm. Has it even crossed your mind you may be partly to blame for this catalogue of mistakes, recurrent errors of judgement, whatever you call it?"

"Aaah, I see, now it's my fault, isn't it? Typical, vintage Maidei, playing the blame game as usual. And tell me, Maidei, how am I supposed to show my mettle to a silly daughter who doesn't seem to understand reproductive health and contraceptive use? Did she not study biology at school? You should shoulder the blame; you humoured her first time around by pampering her over Jeff. So, any talk of blame rests squarely on your shoulders," I stated emphatically, laying the blame on Maidei's doorstep, shoving it, pushing it back to her.

"I'm afraid you're out of line, Fari. To err is human. What was I supposed to do? Throw her out on the streets because she was pregnant? You seem to forget it takes two to tango. If I am to blame as her mother, then so are you as the dad. What have you done to support Yeu ever since she went off the rails? Tell me. Then there's your strange relationship with Much; even the hardest of hearts soften. What will it take for you to heal the wounds, reconcile, and have a normal father-son relationship with Much?"

"Don't talk about that young man! He's not my son anymore. I refuse to have anything to do with him. Do you hear me, Maidei? I excommunicated Much, long back from my mind. I cut him off. End of! I don't want to hear anything about that boy, do you hear me Maidei," and with that I rudely ended our Skype call because I was seething and fulminating at the mouth. *Much. Why would Maidei have the nerve to bring up Much's subject with me,* I wondered. Hadn't he done enough already to humiliate and wound me, bringing an indelible stain on the Mupawaenda clan and name?

But Maidei had other reasons; she was not going to let me get away with this. She phoned me back right away and I instinctively acknowledged her call, only to get an earful. "You may walk away Fari, end the call, that's all-cowardly stuff! All I'm saying is, forgiveness is at the core of humanity, let alone parents. To err is human. Show me a man who hasn't made a mistake and I'll show you a liar. And just so you know, those who live in glass houses shouldn't throw stones. Remember how you used to diss Ben and Taurai's twins for being married to white boys? I bet you should be hanging your head in shame, and eating your words now."

"Why should I?"

"Well, for someone who is appalled at your beloved daughter having kids out of wedlock, is it any wonder, having them in the sanctity of marriage, regardless of the father's ethnicity, would have served you well?"

I didn't respond to her taunts and made a hasty exit out of the room with, "I'm sorry, Maidei, I'm going to have to end the call again." And that was it. I needed some fresh air; this whole thing was stifling me.

That second pregnancy subsequently put Yeu's hopes to complete her degree at the point of just about severing my relationship with her; it was the proverbial last straw for me. That was it. I refused to engage with Yeukai at all, let alone have anything to do with her. I felt greatly let down and disappointed by her crass lack of judgement. No wonder I had been excited when Liz had mentioned she'd spoken with Yeukai over the phone, and equally surprised when I learned Yeukai had thrown me a lifeline by buying me a British Airways ticket to facilitate my return to England.

So, coming back from Zimbabwe, staying at Yeukai's place, there was all this prior history lurking in the background, thus, I didn't want to overstay my welcome at her place; it was really not ideal with her two children, Steve and Ewan. There wasn't much space to accommodate a fourth occupant in that dingy, box room flat. Perhaps, it was just me being hung up on the past and obsessing on my perceived "falling" out with Yeu. Perhaps, she'd forgiven me. What if she didn't mind my staying at her house? But then I am quite astute in my dealings with people and I didn't want to antagonise my daughter by overstaying my welcome.

Spending time with my grandchildren Steve and Ewan, however, had proved to be a priceless experience nonetheless.

"Tell us stories about Zimbabwe *Sekuru*," they would badger me, both scrambling in my lap, and I would revel in this and willingly put my spin on my hilarious tales which always left them rocking in unmitigated guffaws of laughter, much to Yeukai's delight.

"You do have a way with the lads, Dad, you know that?" she would say with a cheeky wink.

I loved that. In a way, the numerous games I played with my grandchildren gave meaning to my otherwise mundane, insipid life. For what is life, if a man can't enjoy and savour being among his family, let alone his grandchildren? Do I sound hypocritical now that I embraced my daughter's sons? Perhaps I had mellowed. If anything, my softer side, which had been underscored to me by my illness, had been to appreciate the meaning of life and family. I had now learnt to see life experiences in proper, holistic perspectives, not through half-measures anymore.

Through my protracted battle with cancer, I had come to realise family and good health are everything. In all this, part of me still thought of my Liz, "good old Liz." *I need to check on Liz,* I kept on saying to myself. I appreciated the difficulty of her trying to contact me through my daughter, and it was about time I made the effort to reconnect with my Liz, so I made a silent note of that to myself.

Chapter 14

Retracing Shadows

Upon my return to England, I had been detained in hospital for several weeks, convalescing from surgery on my prostate, which nearly took my life because I had failed to access Zim's prohibitive medical costs. Put differently, Zimbabwe's health delivery system had failed me. I am told my protracted battle with prostate cancer on my return to England was a close shave for me. It had been long and onerous weeks for me in Stoke Mandeville hospital's intensive care unit. Some of the timelines are blurry in my memory; there seem to be gaps, like I had amnesia. My daughter Yeukai was later to recount to me, filling me in on some of the hazy bits, "There were moments when it was touch and go, Daddy, times we thought we would lose you."

"Really, was it that bad, Yeu?"

"Don't even go there, Dad. I had to visit Mummy to try to knock some sense in her skull, so she would come visit you in hospital, and make peace with you."

"Is that it Mummy, so you would rather your very own husband dies in hospital, without you ever paying him a visit? Where is this hard heartedness coming from, from a woman who used to preach forgiveness and reconciliation each time I fought with Much? Do you ever not get tired being hypocritical, pretending to be this radiant paragon of virtue? It's utterly exhausting just watching you."

"Of course not, Yeu, don't be preposterous. I don't want Fari to die. If anything, I have always harboured positive thoughts about that man, that eventually we would work it out, get back to being friends again. Who are you to lecture me about my duties as a wife, coming from you, you have the bloody cheek? Tell you what, miss smarty pants, know-it-all mountebank, have you had a similar conversation with him about deserting his family, chasing his

116

so-called fantasy dream in Zimbabwe, whilst I held the fort for you and Much? Of course not, it doesn't matter does it, as long as it's good old Daddy Fari, he can do no wrong by you. Can he? It's always my fault, isn't it?"

"For once in your life, Mummy, why can't you have the grace and humility to raise your hands and accept it when you've got it wrong. A 60-year-old woman, really, holding onto petty grudges to a husband you bore two children with? How petty and mean can you be, Mum? Why not attend to the pressing matter of Dad's illness first, then restoration can come later."

"You're one to talk," and with that she left the room in a huff, banging the door after her tantrums.

"Whatever Mum, so long as you've heard me! This needs to be called out for what it is, your hypocrisy is eye-watering," Yeu shouted gleefully after her as she stomped off.

I said to Yeu, "Your mother visited me twice though. Must have been after you spoke with her, but on both occasions, they were awkward if not frosty encounters. There wasn't much going on by way of conversation between your mother and me."

"So, if you can't strike a conversation, then why are you here, Maidei?"

"Well, I'm here to see you, ain't I? After your pesky daughter poked her nose in my affairs again, telling me about my so-called marital duties in relation to you?"

"So, you are telling me you are here because Yeukai arm-twisted you to pay me a sympathy visit?"

"Not really. Look, you are unwell, Fari, and I wish you well and a full recovery regardless of what happened between us. Once you beat this, which I'm sure you will, you and I will need our moment of clarity to sit down and talk about our marriage."

"Talk about our marriage?" I asked incredulously as if she'd proposed something weird.

"Yes, you heard me correctly, talk about our marriage and way forward, even though we've had an eight years hiatus of some sort."

"Whatever, be my guest Maidei. One thing for sure though, I don't need your sympathy, I don't do pity," and that had been it. The next time I sat again with Maidei was three months following my discharge from Hillside nursing care home where I'd been recovering after my long hospital stint.

On being discharged from hospital, I made the shocking discovery that Maidei had defaulted on paying the mortgage on our marital house within the last two years prior to my return to England, although she had constantly assured me, she took charge of our matrimonial home expenses and didn't need my money, as she put it. Yet I had a damning shock waiting for me when I came back. Perhaps it was mostly shocking because throughout our marriage, Maidei was the sensible one with money matters in the house. A stickler for financial prudence, Maidei was the one who always got things done, i.e., in terms of ensuring household bills were paid on time, be it council tax, water, gas and electricity bills. With Maidei, household bills were always considered topmost priority and therefore had to be paid first. So perhaps part of me may have inwardly taken for granted that the mortgage would still be sorted or paid for by her, even though I had gone AWOL for my eight and half year jaunt in Zimbabwe. Besides, had she not bawled over the phone to me, "I don't really need your money Fari. If you don't want to contribute your share of the mortgage, I can go it alone." So, what part of "go-it-alone" did she mean, if the last two years the mortgage payments were in arrears?

When I felt brave enough to confront the elephant, I called her for a sit down together meeting as I tried to establish having a grip on this and other matters pertaining to our "marriage" and possible way forward. Inwardly, this seemingly imminent duel was not something I was looking forward to, no wonder my misgivings at even seeing Maidei face-to-face. To her credit, good old Maidei had the guts to turn up for our meeting at the Red Lion pub and was able to look me in the eye, even as she dished the shit to me, big time. Always an attention-seeker, my wife had a flair for the dramatic as she proceeded to give it to me then.

"So, why don't we get to the bottom of this, Maidei, and try to reach an understanding of how we extricate ourselves from this invidious situation in which we find ourselves," I said, clearing my hoarse throat and somewhat surprised in the first place that she's turned up for the meeting. "In the mean-time, shall I order something? Drinks maybe? what will you have?" But her curt response showed me she was in no mood for pleasantries with me that day.

"Why don't you save that for another day, Fari, and we speedily get to the crux of the matter?"

"Well, I get it, I may not be your favourite person anymore, Maidei, but surely we can still talk over a drink, for old time's sake, can't we? I'm only trying to be polite and adult here about things..."

"Let me save you the hassle Fari," she rudely interposed. "I wouldn't dare use the word 'we.' Are you delusional? How long have we been apart since your ill-fated Zim misadventure, nearly nine years if I can clue you in," she said this raising two fingers at me as if to drive home her point. "So cut out this 'we' business; we're no longer an item anymore."

"I didn't say we're an item. Did I, Maidei? Are you missing something here?" I remarked, turning my head sideways in utter, contemptuous disbelief glancing at her askance.

"Don't interrupt me, Fari! You hear me, I was still speaking, so you...you...you... don't get to interrupt me ever again, you hear me! It's been some time, true, and I'm a changed girl. In those eight and half years of absentia, a lot has happened. Time moves pretty fast. There are a lot of things you don't know about me, Fari. I haven't been merely resting on my laurels, moping over your self-destruct decision to go to the back of beyond. I have moved on, managed to get myself into a new relationship with Mudiwa, and we don't really have anything to talk about other than the matrimonial house which, as it's in your name, you're pretty much screwed with the mortgage company. As for me, I can easily walk away with nothing to lose from all this shambles. The children are grown up, so I don't see any problem in that regard," she went on babbling, looking at me intently.

I was tongue-tied for a few minutes before I finally found my voice and bravado to speak again. "So after over two score years of marriage, this is how you want to end, Maidei?" I remarked to her, the contempt and loathing unmistakable in my quivering voice.

"Suit yourself, Fari. Spare yourself the self-pity and take this setback head on like the man you used to say you were those years of your foolhardy actions. The mortgage is not really my concern as a liability. As I said earlier, it's all in your name, in case you're forgetting, so, you're legally liable to the lenders.

As they say in ghetto parlance, you're screwed, mate!

"Unlike you, mister perfecto, I am willing to take responsibility for my fair share in our failed marriage. For so long, I indulged you so much in this marriage, allowing you to do as you pleased, carte-blanche freedom, so to speak. And you were happy to play along with your Gumbi patriarchy, Jindwi bullshit crap! Stifling me, denying me freedom of thought, action, and what have you. I was far too timid to challenge your toxic masculinity baloney. But we've been apart for too long to even talk of a subsisting marriage anymore. This is reality, Fari. You can't always get what you want in life, you know. For far too long, you've been a lazy wastrel, fleecing me of my resources. I wish you could get out of my sight, Fari."

"Listen to you, Maidei, your voice. Do you even believe that yourself? But who is here to talk of a subsisting marriage as you put it? I just wanted some closure with you and for us to sort out our tangled finances in relation to the end of our matrimonial house! Do you think I care so much about the house? What's the worst that can happen, huh? Tell me, Maidei, what's the worst that could possibly happen? A repossession by the bank? And so what! Life goes on. Who says life grinds to a standstill because the fucking bank has repossessed their house? You really don't get it Maidei, do you? This is a futile exercise. You're throwing stones at windows here. For whatever reason, when the writing is clearly on the wall for all to see, you've lost this one. It's only a fucking house at the end of the day, Maidei! Bricks and mortar, so what?"

"Spare me the melodramatics. Then of course, there's the small matter of the divorce, if I may also remind you, Fari," she spoke softly. Having waited for the last word, so she could cruelly twist the knife in my back.

"Whatever, Maidei," I interrupted as I got up to leave. "I had wanted us to part on an amicable note for old time's sake, but it appears one of us needs to do some serious growing up. Enjoy the house." And with those words I left, never to cross paths with Maidei again.

Chapter 15

Infinite Possibilities

I returned to my daughter's residence, Wendover village, after my domestic brawl with Maidei. Inwardly, I was still fretting about my continued stay at my daughter's cramped apartment. Perhaps I was imagining it, but I felt Yeu was being polite to have me as her guest, but really the scenario was not conducive to house all of us, me, Yeu and her little boys, Steve and Ewan, much as the lads adored me. Being astute and wise in the ways of the world, I didn't want to overstay my welcome and so these feelings of uneasiness kept nibbling at me, gnawing on my heart.

I could see my phone flashing Leti's name on the screen as it buzzed. Perhaps Leti's phone call was the very antidote I needed to cheer me up following my earlier spat with Maidei.

"Hello, Fari, is this a good time to talk?" came Leti's upbeat, cheery, lovely voice over the phone.

"Aaah, couldn't be happier to talk to you, Leti. All these weeks I was thinking of phoning you, and you beat me to it."

"Haaa, you lie," I could hear her chuckling over the other end.

"Seriously, I meant to phone you all along. Can we meet? I could do with some feminine company."

"Why don't you come over to my place, then I can cook you some Thai dish for you, Fari, a chance to savour my culinary skills," and with that she broke into her trademark infectious laughter. That was Leti for you, always genial and bubbly. I'm sure it would have taken a gargantuan earthquake to knock her over.

"Perfect, Leti, I like the sound of that, count me in and thank you."

And that was how the new friendship developed and blossomed between

Leti and me. Leti, my physiotherapist who had nursed me from my early days after hospital discharge, as I learnt to walk again like a toddler.

"I'm delighted to see you looking brilliant, Fari," quipped Leti, after she gave me a smothering hug which left me a tad overwhelmed.

"Welcome to my den of iniquity, and how are you feeling now, Fari?" she remarked, flashing me her trademark wide grin.

"Couldn't be better. I'm on the mend, thanks, Leti," I replied, beaming from ear to ear.

"You're on the mend, sweetheart, I can see that, so what's been happening to you in the meantime? Why don't you fill me in, Fari? How's your wife?" the avalanche of questions kept raining loose and fast from Leti, who seemed oblivious that I needed time to respond.

"Well, where do I even start? I'm glad I'm making good recovery progress as you can see. I thank The Man Above for looking after me and giving me another lease of life. I don't know what you believe in, in Thailand, but I believe in the supreme deity, The Man Above, as I call him," I remarked, training my eyes up to the skies, as if to acknowledge my divine beliefs.

The interior of Leti's house was well-furnished with finesse-looking furniture and nicely carpeted; my bare feet comfortably sank in the fluffy carpet as I walked. The woman certainly had taste.

"Look at me, Leti, I was on the brink of death, but once more I seem to have been spared. Now if that doesn't make you believe, I don't know what will. By the time I left Zimbabwe, I was actually flirting with death, I can tell you this. I swear, I had one foot in the grave."

"How's your wife?" my heart skipped as Leti reiterated her earlier question, which I thought I had tactfully dodged.

"I don't know! I don't know what to say, Leti, about my wife, or ex-wife, if I may say. It's, it's complicated. I've been away living in Zimbabwe these past eight years, and I come back to a person supposedly meant to be my wife. Maybe I was too naive to think there would still be a relationship to talk of, especially as we rarely kept in touch in my absentia."

"So, are you still together or not?"

"Technically not together anymore. I've been staying at my daughter's two-bedroom apartment, but it's about time I think of moving out, methinks. What about you, Leti? Tell me about yourself. I'm curious and want to know more about you."

"Just ask, I have no secrets. For want of a cliche, my life is an open book."

"But...but... Why me? Why the interest in a patient under your care? Is that not against your care rules or medical ethics, whatever you call them?"

"Don't you like to be loved, Fari?" she sniggered under her breath, her forthrightness catching me off guard. I must admit, there was something alluring I found in Leti's carefree, lackadaisical attitude, that carefree demeanour which saw her asking me what, with any other person, I would have been offended and considered private, personal, intrusive questions to ask on a first date, assuming we were on a date, that is. Perhaps that was me being presumptuous already, but in a disarming way, this avalanche of questions coming from Leti hadn't fazed me at all. I found my tongue loose, talking to her as if I had known her in a long time. It was just natural talking, spontaneity, conversing with Leti, my tongue felt like a tap of water left running and free to overflow.

"Of course, I'm flattered by your attention, given the medical challenges I've been going through. I have a lot of baggage with my health issues for anyone to want to be remotely interested in me."

"Not really, Fari, people are different. I speak for myself; I would never let a health condition stand in the way of someone I like. I warmed up to you early on during my first physiotherapy sessions. I found your stubbornness appealing as you argued with me non-stop." She mimicked, "I tell you, I'm tired, Leti, we are skipping today's training session because I say so."

"Where's your fella?" I said, nonchalantly ignoring her awkward impressions of me doing our physiotherapy session.

"Did you see anyone when you came in?"

"Nope."

"So, there you are. Why would I agree to host you in my house if there was someone else in the fray?"

That was all the clear signal I needed from Leti. Without hesitation, I stood up and kissed her luscious lips. "Easy tiger, easy tiger," she remarked as she kissed me back, slowly and hungrily, and I knew we were in business. I closed my eyes to the sweet tingling of her long tongue ramming down my throat looking for other orifices.

In no time, I was savouring her beauty, and what a delightful spectacle it was. Leti had full round breasts like ripening apples. The nipples were still and erect as she hungrily kissed me back. Just looking at them teasing my chest exacerbated my hard on.

She was a patient and masterful lover, as she skilfully unbuttoned my shirt whilst kissing me at the same time, her other hand guiding me to pleasure her. What an absolute queen at multi-tasking Leti was. An excited moan escaped from her, as our passionate foreplay reached the crescendo. As I snuggled into her warm bosom, I was suddenly lost in the vortex of her unbridled passion. She slid her thighs apart, allowing me to get into her, thrusting in and out, in and out, in a ceaseless rhythmic movement, till we both came at the same time and our spent, content bodies sprawled on the settee.

"Gosh, you're beautiful Leti, thank you," I remarked as she rested her head on my hairy chest.

"You're welcome. That was awesome, Fari."

The feeling was mutual. It had been a while. My body had been aching for a woman, but then Liz was far away in Zimbabwe. The last time I had done it had been with Liz, before my cancer woes escalated.

"You're a generous lover, Fari," remarked Liz as she playfully poked me in my ribs, her mouth nibbling on my neck and ear lobes.

"Aaah, thank you, muffin. I'm surprised I still have my mojo. I thought the cancer had ruined it."

"You still have it; I give you that, young man. Now for that promised Thai dish," she said, gliding off the settee, revealing her voluptuous figure, which further gave me a hard on.

"What are you preparing for dinner then, this much touted Thai dish?"

"Well, just you be patient, will you, Fari?"

To cap our lovemaking that evening, Leti served what she termed a traditional Thai meal which had five flavours.

"Well, make yourself at home, Fari," she said as she beckoned me to the long oblong shaped table where she had put an array of steaming hot dishes, flanked with glowing purple candles. Sensing the utmost surprise on my bewildered face, she offered an explanation. "No need to have that expression on your face, Fari. Here, wash your hands so we have dinner together. I've prepared here some of our Thailand popular dishes, fried noodles, what we call Pad Thai, chicken in coconut soup, Tom Kha Kai, and best of all, spicy shrimp soup, i.e., Tom Yum Goong," she explained as she beckoned me to this eclectic mix of dishes. Even then, my mouth was already salivating.

"Here, Fari, let me have your dinner plate near so you can try our fried rice, we call it Khao Pad." My plate was already overflowing with different types of succulent Thai dishes. I had to protest with her as I felt it was a lot of food for only the two of us. Quietly playing in the background was some soft, serene Sam Cooke's music which resonated well with our candlelit Thai dinner. The track, *Darling You Send Me,* kept on auto-replay much to my delight!

"Oh my god, you're a connoisseur, Leti. Where did you ever learn to cook such succulent dishes? Why don't you open your own restaurant? I would sure be your number one supporter," I gushed effusively as I stood up to replenish my dinner plate, yet barely a few minutes earlier I had been moaning, "It's too much."

"Thank you, Fari. I got it from Dhegu, my culinary skills, Dhegu, my mother, she is one in a family of four boys and being the only girl, mother's cooking prowess is legendary. I tell you, all the other children in our Bangkok hood would usually throng to our house because of Dhegu's cooking finesse." Leti spoke as she darted into her kitchen and came back armed with what looked like more food, encompassing both her arms.

"Are you out of your mind, Leti?" I quietly remonstrated. "Surely that can't be more food. Are you trying to give me bellyache? Is that your plan?"

"Far from it, Fari, you are my guest tonight. Allow me to pamper you, ad infinitum and show you Thai traditional hospitality in its greatest entirety. Now I hereby introduce you to Thai dessert," and she curtsied with an exaggerated bow and flourish of the hand as she put the bowls of dessert next to me.

"What is this dessert called? What do you have for me?"

"Aha, this is mango sticky rice, one of the most popular Thai desserts, followed by coconut rice dumplings, and since you're complaining, I would recommend the first option, mango sticky rice. I've got more options in the fridge. If you fancy sticky rice in bamboo or Sweet Thai Crepe, be my guest. I'm all yours, Fari."

"Aww, thank you, this will do me fine," I remarked, between mouthfuls. I thrust my spoon into the mango sticky rice, shovelled it into my mouth in one fell swoop, and boy, I whistled in utter delight as the succulent mango hit my palette, much to Leti's delight and amusement.

"See, Fari, never say never, as cliched as it sounds." She was chuckling as I shovelled more mango delight into my mouth. *This is no time for behavioural decorum,* I inwardly remarked to myself.

When we were finally done, which was quite some eternity, we both washed down our meals with a glass each of Bailey's wine. This was certainly a redletter evening for me. I was all smiles as Leti eventually drove me home. But that was before we did it again, this time in the kitchen on top of her Beko washing machine. I knew I was pleasing her, when I heard her purring with unmitigated pleasure, responding to my fingertips stroking her now erect nipples. Now, for the second time that night, I knew I was on solid ground once again with Leti, as she cried for it relentlessly and I rammed my stiff, erect cock into her, in-out-in-out, much to my delight as her fingernails dug into me. After what seemed like an eternity, we were both spent and had that contented glow which comes from mind blowing sex. I scrambled off her as she wiped off the semen from my organ, amid chuckles between us.

"Good night and thank you for tonight," I remarked, giving Leti a smack on her lips, as we stood outside my daughter's flat. 'Likewise, Fari, goodnight," and then she drove off into the misty darkness. I waited till I couldn't see the red lights of her car in the distance anymore.

There was a springy step in my gait that evening as I unlocked the door into my daughter's place, quite a swagger of my once boyhood confidence rejuvenated. Two rounds within one evening given my age, not to mention my febrile health, was certainly a feat for me. Had I not been at death's door only a few months back? Yet now, once again, my fortunes had somehow changed. I was on another level that night. Never underestimate the rejuvenating power of sex. Perhaps I just needed to be inside a woman to get me going again, and Leti had been my medicine in that respect. I had got my mojo back. I smiled with contentment that evening as I retired to bed. I even had a beautiful dream to cap it all. Can you believe it when things turn right, then one has an avalanche of good fortunes.

Did I feel guilty about Liz? The honest answer is, I didn't, not that I didn't love Liz or had any sense of disloyalty towards her, but I rationalised within myself: *I have physical needs and desires which need to be quenched every now and then, and being practical, how else would this be possible without me having to bed someone, and that someone happens to be my newfound flame, Leti, my muffin.*

I know this may sound disingenuous, but I had immense respect for Liz, for looking out after me during my cancer battle in Harare. I really do, I'm grateful to her for her selfless kindness, utmost love and devotion. Of late, something strange has been happening, by and by. There are moments when I feel like I talk to Liz, I have these telepathic conversations with her, like now. In such instances, her kind, ghostly persona fills and enlightens the room. She was cut out to be wife material. Liz had been there for me in my eleventh hour in Harare as I battled my first bout of prostate cancer. *For this Liz, you deserve more respect than I ever gave you, and more than you give yourself. Sometimes I have recurrent dreams about you, my true diamond.* I knew I can't bring myself to resume contact again with Liz, but I don't know why? Really, I do not know why. Or I am just deluding myself here, perhaps deep down in my inner persona I do know why. I can't summon the courage to re-ignite the spark with Liz.

Following a few weeks after our first night of sin with Leti, it didn't take long before Leti and I were consorting under the same roof. It sort of boosted my ego though, that this new arrangement came courtesy of Leti formally inviting me to move in with her. So, I felt loved as if I was a teenager, pining for love again.

"I say, Fari, seeing our relationship has evolved to another level, what would you say if I invite you to live with me at my place?" remarked Leti flashing her dazzling smile to me one evening.

"What would I say, you're asking me, love? Nothing would give me greater happiness than to be by your side 24/7, muffin, and of course it's a resounding affirmative to your invitation. I do, I do, sweetheart," I remarked stroking her head. That had been it, sealed with a passionate snog and in time I had moved into Leti's two bedroom Bicester house, located on the plush Kingsmere estate, near the posh, world-famous Bicester Village shopping mall.

It was difficult to tell whether my daughter Yeukai, was unhappy with this move, as all things considered, I still had unfinished business with her mother.

"I hope you know what you're doing, Dad. It's not my place to say, but I'm not sure you're ready to commit in a new relationship so soon."

"So soon? What's that supposed to mean, Yeu?"

"So soon after your illness. I am not equivocating here, am I? You barely know this woman, but I will respect your choice, Dad. You're an adult after all. Though, there's your friend in Zimbabwe, Auntie Liz, really Dad? I have no clue what's going on in your life with the comings and goings of different women seemingly in one go. Has your love life become a sliding, revolving doors moment?" There was no mistaking the clear tone of disapproval in Yeukai's voice as she spoke, making clear how she felt about my behaviour.

"What will be, will be, Yeu. I'm not one for sympathy as you know. I nearly lost my life and that has given me a new perspective: Live life to the full. Live everyday as if it's the last, as cliched as it may sound, but that's exactly how I am living my life now. So let me be with Leti as we carve a new chapter in our lives moving forward. As for Auntie Liz in Zim, I wouldn't go there if I were you." I dismissed Yeu peremptorily with a flourish of my arm, though inwardly I felt embarrassed at being called out by my daughter for my errant playboy love life. I had once chided over her out-of-wedlock pregnancies. Talk of role reversal, chickens coming home to roost, as legendary civil rights activist Malcolm X would have termed it.

"Your choice, Dad. I can only wish you well, though you need to sort out your mess with Mum as soon as possible."

Chapter 16

Letitia

White Cliffs of Dover Beckons

I have been living a lie for the twenty years or so I have been in England.

I have been living under an assumed name and identity. I've been living in the shadows, the labyrinthine maze that is the British underworld. Now they are closing in on me, the UK immigration border force authorities. My asylum application was on its last leg, so when I met Fari, a British citizen man, I couldn't believe my luck.

The man was a godsend. Talk of being in the right place in the right time, meeting Fari at Hillside nursing home, where I had recently taken up a new job. Perhaps Fari would be the solution to my long-standing immigration problems in this country. Or so I thought as I chuckled to myself those early weeks as I drew closer to him. My plan was clearly formulating in my head. I knew it needed time and precision to set the chain of events in motion that would eventually deliver UK legitimate legal status to me. And so, like a pawn, poor old Fari had unwittingly walked into my dark, spiderweb underworld. He had fallen for it in one fell swoop, hook, line, and sinker!

My real name is Pattama, though everyone back home called me Pat.

I came to England as a blooming teenager soon after turning seventeen, assisted by the notorious Thai human trafficking racketeering gang, The infamous Carbonaros secret society. The deal with them was, they would arrange one's illegal crossing into England, a treacherous, high stakes cat-and-mouse dalliance. It involved surreptitiously evading law enforcement agents' expeditions via porous borders, areas such as the white cliffs of Dover. Then it included moving through the French border port into England, smuggled in a heavy goods lorry, hidden amongst goods, or sometimes hiding perilously in refrigerated trucks. Thus, I made my maiden journey into England and was taken to the local opulent residence in West London belonging to burly Mario the Italian mobster.

Mario the Brute. How can I ever erase that monster from my memory and psyche, after he so violated me, a young, naive seventeen-year-old Thai girl? I was wet behind the ears, hungry to make a fortune and support the family back home, particularly my widowed mother Dhegu and my two little sisters, Busaba and Achara. All of them would be at the mercy of the Carbonaro gang if I failed to repay their £20,000 fee to them with exorbitant interest piled on top of it. The Carbonaros were not known for making empty threats; they followed them through with sadistic violence and gruesome murders. They perpetrated these horrors in the streets of Bangkok, Thailand upon families of perceived offenders, to serve as a chilling deterrent reminder of the consequences that would happen to would-be offenders, "…should you not pay back our UK entry facilitation fee," as the local Thai mobsters were wont to say to my fellow citizens.

"So, you will stay here with me for three weeks, till we finalise your papers and get you working in the system," Mario curtly said to me in his gruff voice, barely looking me, the contempt on his ugly scarred face evident, as if I was a piece of shit."

Yet in the dead of night, on my first night at West London, Brentside, the Carbonaro residence, burly, overweight Mario violently forced himself on me with his bulging belly, threatening untold maliciousness and extreme terror and reprisals on my family back home, if I dared reveal the unwanted sexual violence.

"I am not pissing about Leti," he growled under his stinking breath and to-bacco-stained teeth. He brandished a large knife which gleamed menacingly in the darkness as he pressed it on my naked boobs to drive home his point. He seemed oblivious to my terror and fright; he was far gone, consumed in an insane, sexual frenzy, during which he thrusted his manhood in me. He huffed and panted over his gruff voice, "I'm coming, I'm coming...oh yes, yes...Pattama!" And that was it, in no time the beast was done and resumed hurling threats to a pure blossom he had just unceremoniously deflowered. On my arrival in London, far away from home, it was all too surreal for me, coming to terms with this monstrous horror in sight. Such had been my austere initiation into the seedy side of London's underbelly, the criminal underworld. Cruelly ravished that fateful night, my bottom was sore, and blood spots trickled down my thighs from my undercarriage. This made no difference to the brute who somehow carried on wittering about, hurling his chilling threats at me.

"Do I make myself clear, Pat?" he barked at me menacingly. Cowering in fright, I could only nod my head to show I heard him loud and clear.

"Now, just so we are clear, in here you belong to me, Pat, and you will for the next few weeks until we place you in one of our employment establishments. You will remain beholden to me. Forget about the Thailand middlemen who organised your illegal entry here. That was then, now is now, and you belong to me. I own you, you're my property," he growled, exhibiting a hideous grimace and fiendish gritting of his teeth. With an exaggerated snarl, his last words to me were, "I own you," which exacerbated my fear and terror.

I have to say, for the duration of my stay at Brentside, his West London residence, each night was my reliving of that macabre horror at the behest of Mario's selfish passions and sexual guns misfiring. It was an indelible trauma which defined and gave me an inward steely resolve I was to need in subsequent years during my torrid life in England. I learnt to survive in the rough-and-tumble of the streets. That inward tenacity was to put me in good stead. Unbeknown to me, working in Mario's underground establishments was a far cry from the big lie we had been sold back home: "Life in England is a heaven on earth; the streets are paved with British pounds sterling. Come and join some of our young Thai professionals who are helping to transform and sustain their families back home," ran some of the typical adverts flighted in our local press. It was one such glowing advert that had prompted me to make enquiries and thus make arrangements with the local mobs who facilitated my illegal entry into England.

Dhegu, my mother, had scrimped and saved working long shifts in the local rice fields, doubling up also on the local Bangkok wildlife meat market. She toiled endlessly to supplement her meagre restaurant wages, just so her daughter would be able to pay the local mobster's part of the initial illegal entry facilitation fee. The difference was to be paid off by me once I secured successful entry into England. Yet, in barely a few weeks of trying to settle in

England, the reality so blatant on the austere streets of London was a far cry from the big lie they peddled home.

Within just a few months of my arrival in England, I came to realise human trafficking was a vibrant and thriving industry in Europe, targeting young vulnerable girls like me. It was a well-orchestrated, embedded criminal enterprise web spanning Europe's capitals: Berlin, Bucharest, Krakow, Paris, but somehow London tended to be the favoured destination for most undocumented immigrants like myself. In London, some of these unfortunate souls were thrown into the highly lucrative underground escort prostitution rings in London's seedy streets that they called the red-light district, analogous to Amsterdam's with a similar name.

Within a few months of still trying to find my feet in London, I later learned of the tragic deaths of thirty-nine Vietnamese immigrants. They sadly lost their lives in the back of a refrigerated lorry. I remember this mishap vividly, for there was a huge media storm and backlash to it, with the British establishment sanctimoniously professing, "We will work tirelessly with law enforcement to ensure this human evil is nipped in the bud once and for all." But talk is cheap; this empty rhetoric would soon dissipate as it had in the past, while more horrendous immigrants' deaths were recorded; sometimes, minors died, as in the case of four deaths of Kurdish-Iranian immigrants who sadly passed on in a dingy boat trying to cross into England; among the dead were two minors, one a 15-month-old baby.

With increasing frequency, bodies of drowned asylum-seekers on the beaches of the English Channel were becoming a horrendous norm in our mundane lives. Notwithstanding this unfolding human tragedy, the authorities continued to look the other way. Meanwhile, the burgeoning underground crime of human trafficking flourished in a 21st century world, where publicly we exhibited our outrage at the horrors of slave trade in yester-year, yet our hypocrisy will never address contemporary, systemic human trafficking, organised prostitution crime, and its attendant criminal atrocities of organ harvesting. Talk of double-dealing, duplicitous hypocrisy! Perhaps we need to save our misplaced public and moral outrage for another day, when society really means it. If my experiences in England, trying to survive under the underground economy are anything to go by, then we better walk the talk, or just shut up.

"Are you listening to me, Pat, do you hear me?" Mario's booming voice roused me from my momentary reverie.

"So, like I'm just telling you, young lady, in England we have vast opportunities for young Thai women and men, working in the hospitality industry and office work with good pay, accommodation provided. In no time, you will be placed amongst some of our people." That had been several months ago, when I had worked back-breaking jobs, working my ass off to pay the mob's entry fee supplementing Dhegu's efforts. Although I was now in England, my mind kept wandering back to the big lie peddled back home. Hadn't we seen it all in Thailand" In no time, most of the seemingly successful immigrants to England would lavishly transform the lives of their parents and siblings, as in Dhengu's friend's daughter, Maharaja. Mother would never cease to extol Maharaja's work ethic which had now catapulted her friend into instant stardom in downtown Bangkok.

"Do you realise Maharaja now moves around with the latest iPhone because of her daughter's exploits in London? Now, she doesn't even talk to me; she's now all high and mighty. Next, she'll be having tea with the Queen at Buckingham palace whilst I'm stuck in this hovel. Now that Maharaja has money, everyone kowtows to her. But you know what hurts me most, is that she has always been lower than me. But now, she lives like a queen, strutting around with airs, high and mighty, bossing everyone around to do her bidding."

My mother, Dhegu, would go on and on about this whining and whinging woefully herself, in her self-pitiful voice about her enduring poverty. In the end I succumbed to her subtle pressure and manipulation and that was how I approached the Bangkok criminal syndicate which facilitated my illegal entry into the UK. To her credit, though, Dhegu had joined me in the concerted effort in raising the gangsters' facilitation entry fee into England.

The journey from Thailand to England, crossing through European capitals, hiding in the back of heavy-duty vehicles, is surely an epic tale which deserves a significant chapter on its own. Possibly, it is a tale for another day, and that is all I am saying for now. Suffice it to say, it was nigh difficult, degrading, demeaning and excruciatingly painful being hauled under the cloak of darkness, shuttled around in shady secret locations during the dead of night, sometimes at dawn, as those were considered ideal times to evade the prying eyes of Interpol and local law enforcement agencies.

"Shut up, will you?" the raspy-voiced local mobsters would constantly shout to some of the timid ones amongst us, those who were now clearly wilting, their resolve tested, breaking under the pressure, and asking to go back home, or just to be left in these host countries. Sometimes these requests were met with violent brute force. Fast forward this onerous, death-infested journey to London, with the obtaining realities which awaited us on its streets. Then it had surely been an exercise in futility. If only we'd known, but then hindsight is always a wonderful thing in life, though belated insight is gained.

Working in Mario's establishments was a well couched euphemism which meant forced prostitution in the sleazy brothels of London's infamous red-light district, and getting your wages forfeited to your pimp who was Mario in my case. To ensure absolute compliance and double insurance immunity, the pimps like Mario ensured they kept your passport, so I was pretty much nameless, even though I had an official name – Pattama -- in name only.

I had it rough the first two years under Mario's well-orchestrated trafficking syndicate with Madame Dell'allio, his obsequiously loyal matriarch sidekick who oversaw the day-to-day running of the London prostitution syndicate. Other Thai girls and I had a torrid time at the hands of the ring. At times I contemplated suicide, but my inner resolve wouldn't allow that; *Why should I allow him Mario and his sadistic hoodlums to win, for if I give in, kill myself, they have won, haven't they?* So, I bided my time until an opportune moment presented itself through a punter foolish enough to fall in love with me, Odi Millikan. One of the cardinal rules of the game is you never do emotions; one does not cross the line and fall in love with clients, but then Odi was an oddball. Through Odi I was finally able to escape from Mario's clutches after I took advantage of an extended stay at Odi's posh Kensington London residence. Upon setting my eyes on Odi, seeing how weak he was in terms of his emotional make up, it hadn't been difficult for me to make the all-important, life changing decision on which my dream for freedom depended. Seeing how he doted on me, reduced to a mere weeping boy, I had already decided: Odi would be my meal ticket until my future looked more certain. I didn't have to wait for long before I struck, setting in motion my well-orchestrated freedom train plan.

I couldn't help resisting a chuckle as I reminisced how brilliantly I had played an old man. I was getting quite adroit at these games, as now I had my eyes trained on another old man, Fari, an old ex-patient of mine. And each time,

I kept repeating my mantra to myself: *Keep your eyes on the prize, on the prize, girl, always.*

The events of that breakthrough evening with Odi are pretty much seared in my memory as though they occurred yesterday. I remember very well how I steered the conversation with Odi in the particular way I wanted, and Odi fell for it. He decided to play ball.

"So, this is the story of my life, Odi," I'd said. "Are you able to help me escape the clutches of this horrid man? The stakes are high though." Pressing on and throwing my bait further, angling for my catch, I asked Odi, "Are you willing to take the risks?"

To give it a veneer of legitimacy, huge teardrops fell from my eyes, as I transfixed my gaze on Odi's face and emitted gut-wrenching sobs that I anticipated would tug at his manly heartstrings. The sound of Abba's *Chikitita*© playing in the background reflected the more sombre mood in the room, accentuated by the majestic looking chandeliers hanging over us with a dim glow.

"Of course, yes, honey bunches," Odi gushed. "You know how utterly devoted I am to you. I would get the stars for you if I had to, Pat. Besides, your freedom means you and I can have a future together." The gullible old man had kept on wittering about, believing in self-delusions that I was in love with him. Never underestimate an old man's ego and delusions of bedding a younger woman. They feel so virile and empowered, it goes to their head and clouds their judgement. I mean, what is it with men, that at times they can't think straight when it comes to matters of the heart? You see grown men like Odi reduced to whipping boys.

All men want sex at the end of the day. They become whipping boys, which was one of Odi's Achilles heels; no wonder it was easy peasy for me to manipulate him. Goodness knows, the innumerable times I had to fake multiple orgasms at his dreary, insipid, always one sex position and, boom! I knew I was in business with him, standing firmly on solid ground. Now wrapped around my little finger, Odi could pretty much do my bidding without so much as a whimper. Add to that, the "holy treatment" I gave him with surprise BJs, and I knew he was now my puppet ad infinitum; all I had to do was pull the strings whenever I needed to.

Once I gave him a blow job like there was no tomorrow. This was just about the time I was upping the ante for him to facilitate my escape from Mario's clutches. I could hear him breathing heavily, panting amid gasps, and in no time, he was totally blown over, coming fast and hard in my mouth, shouting my name in a vortex of fumbling and ecstasy not befitting such a pot-bellied old man.

If ever there is any wisdom I've gleaned over my ephemeral life, one "truth" remains uppermost: Men are the same. They just want their egos pampered, and hapless old man Odi was no exception. Always a first-rate schemer, I considered my dealings and liaisons with men as moves on a chessboard. Perhaps I shouldn't have seen that TV show, *The Queen's Gambit*. It was now messing with my head as I plotted and planned how to manipulate my meal ticket Odi to my freedom. I carefully and methodically crafted each move in my little head in the privacy of my squalid abode at Mario's lodgings.

Can't these geriatrics see it for what it is? Wilful manipulation. Why, in a normal set-up, would I be hanging out with a middle-aged, pot-bellied man close enough to my gramps's age, unless I had ulterior motives, as was the case with Odi? For heaven's sake, as the saying goes, "If it looks like a duck, walks like a duck, and quacks like a duck, then it's a duck!" Of course, it was wilful manipulation which enabled Odi not only to fall for my ruse, but thus pledge to assist me in earning my freedom.

"Leave it with me," he said. "Consider it done. Pat." Within weeks Odi had facilitated my escape from Mario's clutches under the guise of believing he would set up a happy family home with me.

Chapter 17

Under the Radar

Shaking off Odi was not difficult for me; he had served his purpose and was thus expendable. As I lived under the constant fear that Mario and his thugs might resurface, I didn't feel safe in London. Mario's tentacles were ubiquitous in London, especially within the criminal underworld. I wasn't taking any chances, nor did I have a false sense of illusion that Mario was bluffing if ever he got wind of where I was. That meant making my mind up wasn't difficult. I left Odi's place whilst he was away on one of his myriad business engagements abroad as a business executive. It was a shame I had to deceive a man as nice as Odi. Part of me felt guilty at leaving, but in the grand scheme of things, this was no time for sentiment and emotions that could derail my plans. Besides, what choice did I really have? It was either that, or I remained stuck in Mario's servitude. To allay my faltering conscience, I left behind a polite note on Odi's dressing table as a sweetener for my French leave.

Sorry, Odi, I had to leave. Thanks for everything you've done for me.

Infinite thanks.

Pat x

My fascination with Fari was no coincidence. I had rubbed shoulders before with Zimbabweans in the UK and somehow warmed up to them. There's a high-profile Zimbabwean community in Coventry's West Midlands. Thus, I stayed with some Zimbabwean immigrants in Coventry after my escape from London. That was how I met fast-talking, suave immigration lawyer Simbarashe Chatikobo.

I was referred to Chatikobo by friends, and the first consultation hour was free. Chatikobo was a wily looking, tall, skinny fella; it was hard to take him seriously from his Scooby do™ face, but I hung on to every word during our first meeting. "You see, as I am saying Pattama, shall I call you Pat?" he re-marked, exposing a gaping hole in his front teeth.

"Please do," I nodded, encouraging him to speak further.

"Because you have no passport, it compounds your problems as it means you are undocumented. As far as the British home office is concerned, you are nothing but a statistic, one of the oft cited avalanches of illegal immigrants flooding this country. But rest easy, you've come to someone who knows the system in and out. There are so many chinks your case will be easy peasy to me."

"So, do I have a chance?"

"Chance! Listen to you, my sister," he shot back incredulously, as if to signal his offence at my doubting him.

"Of course. You have multiple avenues we can pursue till we make you legal. I never fail my clients."

"What are my options then?" I asked impatiently, part of me quietly optimistic at the chance to redeem my legal status in England at last, if only it could be done. I was already in reverie mode, ruminating on how I would apply for visas for both my little sisters Busaba and Achara and possibly my mother Dhegu, so I could rescue them from Bangkok slums.

Chatikobo's raspy voice cut short my daydreaming session. "We need to make you legal first. I know people on the other side who can create a work-ing passport for you, just so you're able to work here, and also a working NI, national insurance number. Just so you know from the onset, you can never use the passport to leave the UK. Do you get me, Pat?"

Again, I nodded in affirmation.

"Good! Now we're talking. So, to restate, the passport is a dummy which allows you to work legally in this country; it's a means to an end, if I may say, but first we need to ditch that Pattama name of yours and give you a true English-sounding name, like Letitia. I once dated a Thai girl called Pattama," and with that, Chatikobo broke into raucous laughter, with tears streaming down his cheeks. It was just hilarious interacting with this dandy talker, Chatikobo.

"Switching your name to Letitia also guarantees you a double layer lock of protection from your criminal overlord Mario in London; you will remain undetected under your new, assumed identity as Leti, unlike if we retain your Pattama alter ego."

Even though Chatikobo was all confidence, guns blazing, and convincing, I had some inward turmoil and tussled with my inner demons. Part of me was unnerved. *Should I really trust this sod with my life?* But then he had come highly recommended as "the fixer" by my hub of friends. "I tell you Pat, if anyone can fix your dodgy immigration woes in England, look no further than Chatikobo," Emmy, my other Zimbabwean friend had insistently pressed on me.

And who am I to doubt Emmy's word? Hadn't she told me in her own words, "I was illegal for over ten years and Chatikobo got me my citizenship square and fine! Mine was a complicated case. I had overstayed my visa, failed asylum application, and throw in some domestic violence allegations from hubby. We had to go all the way to the AIT. Do you know the AIT Leti?" Emmy had asked condescendingly?

"No, what's AIT?" I asked, somewhat embarrassed at not knowing what she was on about.

"Aha, let me clue you in, mate. AIT is the Asylum and Immigration Tribunal body, the highest, if not supreme authority in the land to do with settling the long-standing immigration issues for underground ghosts like you, no offence meant Pat."

"None taken."

"So, we're in court in Birmingham immigration chambers and the Home Office lawyer kept shuffling through his bundle of legal paperwork, failing to string together a coherent argument after Chatikobo had done his dazzling, brilliant magic! The poor guy appears to have no body cues, he couldn't perceive that he had pissed-off the immigration judge. To cut a long story short, the Home Office appeal was thrown out unceremoniously with costs and I was given my long-desired reprieve, discretionary leave to remain in England. The rest, as they say, is history," Emmy had said gleefully waving her red British passport in my face.

"Okay, Emmy, I hear you loud and clear, I am happy to meet your legal counsel Chatikobo. What of the costs, is he reasonable?"

"Of course, immigration law is not cheap as he'll tell you, but look, Pat, we're in this together, Bangkok, Harare, we're all immigrants. I will have a word with Chatikobo; he's my brother by another mother. I'm sure something can be done to arrange something along the lines of a payment plan. Think of the bigger picture, my sister, not the charge. 'Eyes on the prize,' as Chatikobo will earnestly tell you."

And here I was in Chatikobo's offices in central Coventry, beholding this somewhat caricatured spectacle of a man I was meant to trust with the deepest secrets of my life.

"So, to recap, Leti, now, you better get used to your new identity and name, so I'm saying, we progress your case in phases. First, we do this pseudo-EU passport for you. Portugal or Poland, make your pick!"

"What do you mean?" I was thrown off by his question.

"I mean, pick your preferred citizenship for the bogus passport you'll henceforth have."

"O barmy, forgive me, Chatikobo, for being so slow. Portugal will do for me."

"Very well, Leti, my sister Emmy has alluded to your financial challenges but that can be sorted retrospectively once your Portugal passport starts earning you British pounds. You will do a payment plan with my assistant Lucia in the adjoining room that you passed through. So, for brevity's sake, be back here next Thursday afternoon to collect your new Portugal passport and national insurance number. Once you're armed with both documents, you're pretty much legal in the sense of escaping the shadowy economy."

"Henceforth your new name will be Letitia though, Letitia Johnson. Make sure you get that. Forget about you being Pattama, get that?"

I nodded to show my acquiescence to this seemingly dazzling man, though part of me felt sad and weird at ditching my real name. I realised, though, that it had to be done if I was to navigate my existence in England.

"See me if you encounter problems with hooking up a job. We sort everything, Leti, waterproof job references. Mind you, they don't call me *Mister*

Fixer for nothing, sorry for my immodesty, but I am the go-to guy with your immigration woes in England. I don't do modesty. Just take a few minutes to leave your details with my assistant Lucia and we will get the ball rolling for you." With that Chatikobo stood up and shook my hand vigorously, as if to dismiss me. Meanwhile, he was gushing as he congratulated me for exiting the "underground economy" as he termed it. "Your new identity, Letitia Johnson, is actually the passport to your life."

I have to give it to him; Chatikobo was more of a showman than a lawyer, if my first impressions of him were any litmus test to go by.

"Once more, congratulations, Leti my sister, a subject of Portugal your now-adopted country," he spoke with a bow, then he gave me an exaggerated, firm handshake, like I was on the threshold of something big.

Somehow, I found myself comparing Chatikobo to crooked, fast-talking law-yer, Saul Goodman of *Breaking Bad* ©TV show fame, who later made it big in another equally captivating TV show, *Better Call Saul* © as devious lawyer Jimmy McGill. Come to think of it, there was an uncanny resemblance in how both men were dandy talkers and theatrical in how each exhibited his persona as a crooked lawyer. But as I had thoroughly enjoyed the portrait of gregarious lawyer Saul Goodman in *Breaking Bad*©, I put it down as a good omen that I saw Chatikobo in a similar realm of this other lawyer's alter-ego.

"Obrigado," I sheepishly muttered. The only Portuguese phrase I remembered could be used to mean thank you as I bid Chatikobo farewell.

So that was it with Chatikobo, my fixer, Zimbabwean lawyer who, for the second time, initiated me into the criminal underworld apart from Mario. With my Portugal passport and UK national insurance number in hand within a week, true to Chatikobo's word, I was able to use the passport as my newfound currency, switching jobs willy-nilly and at ease. I had a long stint at Halifax plc financial institution where I worked as a mortgage broker. That job really elevated me, and I was able to pay off Chatikobo's nigh extortionate legal bill of £5000 for my assumed Portugal citizenship. Halifax, as an em-ployer, looked after me well. In no time, I was able to buy my two-bedroom apartment in upmarket Kingsmere area Bicester town. What could go wrong? I remember shedding tears of joy to my friend Emmy at the housewarming party I threw for her and our fellow immigrant community, who'd driven all the way from Coventry, some from Birmingham, to celebrate my being a homeowner.

"Emmy my sister, I can't thank you enough. Where would I be, were it not for your kindness that made you introduce me to your fellow Zimbabwean brother, Lawyer Chatikobo?"

"You know, you don't even have to say it, Leti. We're all family in here, like I always say to you. We look out after each other. Look at us, we are foreigners here; home is far away and what is friendship if we can't close ranks? This is nothing to me. I'm glad you got the new lease of life you needed, sister."

All had been fine and hunky-dory for me for six good years. I settled well, acclimatising in the British, mundane way of life and commercial world. In no time I developed greater friendships, mostly with the Zimbabwean community in Coventry. Perhaps I've always had a thing for Zimbabweans as Emmy used to tease me. "Why wouldn't I, my sister, your men are so loving, ain't they?" I cheekily retorted to her.

"Tell me how I seem to get all the jerks and douche bags then?" Emmy retorted.

"You're meeting the wrong ones; are you sure they're Zimbabwean men you're dating? Because I can tell you for sure, my experience has been different, my sister. Come to me for free consultation and tutelage. It's the only way I can repay you for your Chatikobo kindness. Besides, I don't want you missing out on our Zim men who are so well endowed." Both of us broke into a frenzy of laughter.

"O, are you sure you're not philandering with Chatikobo, Leti, the way you keep banging on about him?"

"Of course not. I keep the professional and personal boundaries clearly distinct. I don't want the lines to become blurred," I said with a feigned offended tone, which Emmy didn't fall for. I was thoroughly enjoying the cheeky banter here with Emmy. Such was the camaraderie and friendship I shared with her and other like-minded socialites within our friendship groups. Many times, we would meet in the Coventry social scene and get together parties, for Emmy was a social creature who had slowly initiated me into this new world. "Oh, come off it, Leti, why won't you come to this all-white party? Don't be a loser, wasting away your life and miserable in that flat. No more all by myself stuff. Besides, how will you pull a hunk if you don't go out?"

"Okay, then, see you there, Coventry socialite." I would give it back to Emmy in equal measure.

They are not wrong in saying, the proverbial storm comes after the lull. It was coming up to my sixth year when personal tragedy struck. My Portuguese passport expired at about the same time my employers started asking for papers from all employees. "Because HR needs to update our records," my human resources manager Nicola remarked to me one morning as I sweated inwardly, whilst trying to conceal my uneasiness from her. Talk of ill-suited timing. At about that very time, within England's political establishment saw odious Theresa May assuming the Home Secretary's post, whose remit oversaw immigration among other policing roles. Looking back, it appears suitability to this role must have required one of a mean and awful disposition, which personal attributes Theresa May seemed to embody and in no time under her watch as Home Secretary, the Tory party commenced what they dubbed, a hostile anti-immigrants policy, in simpler terms, let me call it out for what it was, *an all-out and out racist policy* to target ethnic minorities, particularly undocumented immigrants like myself, though the policy ended up extending to the Windrush generation, i.e. Caribbean immigrants who helped build Britain's reconstruction in the post second world war period were now dubbed, "illegal" aliens and many were arbitrarily stripped of their legal and medical rights, just like that at the drop of a hat. Some were illegally deported to their purported home countries like Jamaica or Barbados where they had hardly set foot. It is this callous hostile environment policy, which brought my hitherto settled immigration status into the fore, was further exacerbated when my employer Halifax started demanding to see copies of my passport. And how could I give them an expired passport? There was no way I could shoot myself in the foot that way.

"We are just following Home Office guidelines and protocols," Dawn the Human Resources Assistant had pointed out to me when I queried her relentless demands to see my passport. I was beginning to take it personal and perhaps I just wanted a perfect scapegoat to vent my frustrations and immigration woes on.

I went back to Chatikobo, but something must have happened in the intervening period I hadn't seen him, up until now for it was a different Chatikobo, I beheld. Sitting behind his now threadbare desk, he cut a lonely, sad figure from his former ebullient self; it appeared like something had hit him terribly hard this time around, like he had been a lucky survivor of a terrible inferno. Perhaps it was deliberate weight loss or maybe he'd recovered from a long illness, I inwardly surmised to myself as I kept staring at him, my mouth wide open agape in utter disbelief at the wretched spectacle he'd become. Either he was a good actor, or he was keen to conceal whatever was behind his dramatic weight loss, so he left me none the wiser by not shedding light to his new mystery appearance, let alone to acknowledge the palpable surprise registered on my face. "Great to see you my sister," he exclaimed, stretching his hand into mine. "So, what brings you here again, Leti?'

"Can't a sister visit her own people on a bona fide journey, without wanting anything in return?" I remarked back at him as my usual affable self.

"On point, on point, you're very much on point Leti, I know what you're on about," he interposed, switching on his yester-year charm and smile. I allowed time for some fine pleasantries and small talk, after which I eventually broached the passport expiry issue to him.

Notwithstanding his rustic look, he was still able to proffer me some help from his proverbial bag of legal armoury. This time, Chatikobo decided on a different brand of his magic wand, coming up with a change in strategy in fighting the British Home Office system. "I will arrange for you another set of "fraudulent" papers to get you some work, so you remain on your feet, just like last time. I understand your current predicament you don't want to be out of the system, without a job especially as you now have a mortgage to service. Welcome to British capitalism, where all the money you work for stays in the host country," he remarked amid chuckles.

"You do, my brother, I can't thank you enough for your timely intervention," I interposed.

So, in conformity with Chatikobo's new plan and "magic" wisdom, I ended up quitting my Halifax job as human resources escalated their call for checking my right to work in England, which had now become a weekly war of attrition. That was how I was forced to switch to working in a residential nursing care home as a physiotherapist, which was another gross lie again, as I had no professional training in physiotherapy. Yet Chatikobo was able to work his magic again, and threw me another lifeline, some more fake documents which served their purpose, attesting to my being a holder of a Bachelor of Science Honours degree in Physiotherapy from a Thai university.

Chatikobo's fraudulent papers served me well as in the last time. They got me the care home job, as a carer-cum physiotherapist; but there had been a cautionary caveat from Chatikobo as if to keep my relief at getting new papers and a job in check. "This time we have to put in an asylum application for you right away, Leti," Chatikobo had admonished.

"But how will that help me?" I asked him quizzically. Part of me subconsciously blamed him for not having a Plan B at hand to oversee that my Portuguese passport would eventually run out at some point. Otherwise, I wouldn't have been in this predicament.

"It's buying time, that we're doing with the Home Office. Once we put in your asylum application, the clock starts ticking, but the bottom line is, now they can't kick you out of the country. See what I mean?" He looked at me theatrically, as if he expected me to rejoice.

"And what if they reject the asylum application?" I had become so despondent; it was all too obvious in my quivering voice.

"And why would they reject your application? I've handled asylum immigration cases before and many atimes my clients always win, so you won't be an exception, Leti." He appeared exasperated by my seeming insouciance and scepticism.

"Technically, once you're claiming asylum, you won't be allowed to work, but count yourself lucky, my sister, the new set of papers I've sorted for you will enable you to get another job in the underground world. I have spoken with my contact at Hillside Residential Care nursing home in Aylesbury, and they expect you to start as a live-in carer/physiotherapist imminently. So do give them a buzz as soon as you can to discuss when you can commence work."

"So fast, thank you," I said, feeling better and relieved at hearing this bit of good news from Chatikobo.

"I will need to fix another lengthy meeting with you Leti, so I can go through your asylum application with you. I will need to coach you on what to say before an immigration judge when we go to court."

"Coach me? How? What do you mean?"

"The whole point is to create a heart-rending fictitious story in which we are trying to make a case to the immigration judge that your life is in danger if ever you return to Thailand. We may use either the Mario story, your pimp, or we may have to lie about your sexuality, and you say you are a lesbian. Thailand being a conservative country, you would be persecuted for having an alternative sexuality, if not stoned to death, should you return there."

"But that's blatant lying and a gross misrepresentation of facts. What if I'm caught in future?"

"Look, Leti, the die is cast, you're now past the 'what if' scenario. I thought you wanted to stay in England, ad infinitum, isn't it?"

"I do but..."

"Well, you do what you have to do then, no ifs, ands or buts. You can't be a pussy either, or you'll lose out." With that he rose as if to signal me that our meeting was over.

So, it was largely through Chatikobo's criminal underworld connections and carry-ons that I was able to get a reprieve yet again, a bridging job at Hillside nursing home, whilst on the other hand my asylum application was submitted. I was very nervous about this but had to feel allayed by my legal counsel's reassurance. Part of me, though, had inane misgivings. It was still fresh in my mind, this passport expiration furore. I kept asking myself, *why hadn't he anticipated that at some point, my passport would run out and thus have an alternative plan at hand?* These seeming oversights by Chatikobo were the genesis of my doubts and sense of unease, which lingered and kept festering like a lingering wound in my inner psyche.

Chapter 18

Connecting the Dots

My plan was simple, at least that's what I thought in my little head. Get hitched to Fari, possibly get married, and hopefully that would take care of my immigration problems, which were mounting by the day. The asylum application was dragging on with no end in sight, and I was constantly on the edge in case Hillside nursing home, my new employers, started to ask to see my papers again; that had happened previously with my Halifax employer. Ever since Chatikobo submitted the asylum application, I had been in immigration and asylum tribunal court twice in Birmingham. Not much progress had been registered in those two court appearances. In the last court appearance, the judge, a hard-nosed pensive man, looked mean and cruel as he adjourned the case to allow the Home Office lawyer to file more heads of arguments. They needed more time, to which the judge acquiesced. The judge had barely looked at me, other than when I stated my name, but even then, it was a cursory glance as if I didn't matter at all. Yet it struck me that I was the main player in this case, meant to determine my right to live in England. Part of me felt disgust and distaste at my treatment by the British moral economy. Even though I was deemed "illegal," had I not been contributing my taxes and national insurance contributions to the national fiscus and coffers for well over two decades? And are they saying that did not merit recognition, on account of a mere legal technicality that I am an "undocumented immigrant?" Is there a difference in national coffers in taxes paid by mere mortals like me, on account of my legal status, or is it still British pounds sterling remitted to the Exchequer, nonetheless? These and myriad other questions plagued my troubled psyche.

Then there was something strange happening to me. At first, I had dismissed it as stress and possibly the onset of menopause, I had been having daydreaming sessions. Of late, I started seeing flashes of Mario, my former tormentor, following me everywhere. When I went in my bathroom to take a pee, in my sleep, Mario's craggy face stalked me relentlessly. Mario haunted me, sometimes taunting me with maniacal laughter that sent chills down my spine. He then repeats his chilling words of yesteryear: "I own you, you know, you're my property now."

I have lost count of the numerous panic attacks I had each time I encountered Mario. At times, he would hurl his threats again, "I'm coming to get ya Pat, better keep running." Sometimes he would be smiling at me, with his ugly smile on that Y-scarred left cheek which was quite sinister and much more bizarre; the man doesn't do niceties as far as I remember him. Not one for superstitious thoughts, Mario's recurrent ghostly appearances unsettled me. They propelled me all the more to want to instigate my rescue plan with Fari.

In my scheming mind, I was well aware, there was the small matter of Fari's moribund and decadent marriage to his wife Maidei. That would need to be taken care of first. That didn't faze me. But first things first, I had to get Fari on board and our amorous last meeting had been a brilliant, if not promising start. I felt pleased with myself at having made those significant inroads, getting closer to Fari during his post-hospital recovery phase at Hillside nursing home, constantly waiting on his every need, pampering him with attention, like saying, "You really need to eat some decent portions Fari, if you're to make progress with your walking you know?"

"Why can't you treat a grown man like a grown man, Leti?" he grumbled, pushing aside his tray of rice, salmon and mushroom.

"But, I'm your carer, Fari, and part of my remit is to look after you, particularly your welfare," I politely reminded him, but increasingly I found his obstinance attractive.

"Don't you think if I want to eat then that's my choice," Fari began, "especially as I'm fully compos mentis? I'm not stupid; I know I wouldn't make a steady recovery if I starve myself, which is not the case in this instance."

"Okay, Fari, whatever you say," I reluctantly gave in.

The man was a tough cookie when he chose to be. The more I insisted on something he didn't want, the more he dug in his heels. I knew when to tactfully withdraw, as I didn't want to antagonise him. *Keep the man happy, so he's on your side. Equally keep the communication lines open so we can keep on liaising when he's discharged,* were my guiding principles in my constant liaison with

Fari.

He didn't seem to be attached so there was hope for me, I silently reassured myself. Yet part of me felt like a fraud and a predator preying on this man who was recovering from prostate cancer. But I quickly brushed these thoughts aside. No way would I make Fari out to be a victim, for he certainly wasn't one. He's a grown man. Whatever was going to happen between us, I had to tactfully engineer it in such a way that it appears things were consensual. Just like two consenting adults, I laughed out loud at the irony of this statement. It reminded me of Mario when he used to sexually gratify himself with me against my will, and as if to allay his conscience -- assuming he had one -- he would relentlessly say, "Pattama, you are an adult now. Don't tell me you're not enjoying it. We're two consenting adults here, which makes us even. Even-Steven." Then he would break out in those annoying guffaws of laughter. What was wrong with the man? Did he see laughter in everything? Was laughter a derisory way to deal with his monstrosity, and hence a convenient facade for him? I don't know. How could I work out people smugglers who had caused untold suffering and death to many immigrants who made that perilous journey through Eastern Europe, Turkey, Greece, France, and finally, the treacherous waters of the White Cliffs of Dover if at all they made it, that is. The poor souls escaped the vagaries of the austere English Channel's horrific storms and treacherous weather. So many immigrant families on the Channel had perished in dinghies, sometimes with small children. as they tried to illegally sneak into England. You had to wonder why human traffickers, like Mario and his underworld, had no conscience to be moved by such tragedies, a broken trail of destruction and loss of lives in families.

I have a chance with Fari, I reassured myself, starting way back during his days at Hillside nursing home. No one seemed to visit him, apart from his daughter, Yeukai. So possibly the man was unattached, which aligned well with my best laid plans. Hadn't he refused to commit himself that he was still in a relationship with his estranged wife or partner during our last intimate encounter? Possibly they had some issues reading between the lines, but these could be exploited. So Fari and I could become an item. *Keep your eyes on the prize girl!* I silently reassured myself with my now well-embedded mantra.

Chapter 19

Fari

Letitia, Leti, had appeared at an opportune moment in my life, coming as she did soon after my altercation with Maidei. That exchange had effectively rendered me homeless, not that it would have been viable living under the same roof with Maidei, given our acrimony and our eight-year hiatus. There was no way I could continue staying at my daughter's inadequate place. No disrespect to Yeukai, but her place couldn't house all of us together. *Sometimes, one has to show they have brains, so you leave before you are pushed out or before relations break down,* which is what I kept mulling in my head. And then, boom, Leti came on the scene with her offer: I could move in with her in exchange for what, really?

"Moving in with me will give you time to sort out and clear your head on what you want. In the meantime, we take each day as it comes between us and see where we go from here."

That sounded reasonable to me, so our cohabiting commenced, notwithstanding the objections from my daughter that things were moving exceedingly fast between Leti and me. "Are you sure, you've given it due time and consideration, Dad?" Yeu would ask, adding, "I mean, do you really know this woman quite well, to want to move in straightaway with her?"

Too many questions from Yeukai, but I brushed her aside. I knew I had a certain fatalistic headstrong streak. Once I put my mind onto something, the man was not for turning.

Leti was fun to be around. In the first few months of moving into her place, we consolidated our relationship as we got to know each other, seeing what made the other tick. And then Leti came up with the plan. She dropped the idea on me one Friday evening, "Hmmm, I've been thinking of taking our relationship up a notch further, Fari. Will you marry me?"

I was gobsmacked, of course. I hadn't seen this coming. There had been no tell-tale signals whatsoever.

"Aaah, aaah, I'm quite flattered, Leti. Is this some kind of joke?"

"Charming. What an absolute romantic you are, Fari, calling a woman a joke when she proposes to you."

"I'm so sorry, muffin, I didn't mean it that way," I said. I could see I had offended my happy-go- lucky woman, who wasn't easily ruffled, based on the several months we'd been together.

"Of course, I do want to be married to you, in fact, nothing would give me greater happiness, but..., but..." I stuttered as I struggled to speak.

"But what?"

"I... I have a lot of mess and baggage to navigate through first, and it's only fair I come clean with you first, love."

"Speaking of skeletons in the closet, hold your peace and hear me out first,' she'd said. And that had been it! The floodgates were turned on as Leti fed me her narrative, which threw me into a cacophony of chaos, unbridled emotions, and turbulence.

"To cut a long story short, I'm messed up, Fari, terribly sick in the head," she'd said, jabbing her head with two folded fingers as she spoke. Then, after tears galore had subsided, she said, "I've done terrible things, Fari. I am not asking for any sympathy from you."

She continued, "Now that you know, I feel vulnerable; I am now at your mercy. Everyone I get close to, they leave me. You can shop me to the British Border Force Immigration police if you want, but bear in mind, I'm telling you all this because I want a clean slate with you, Fari. A fresh start, so to speak." She looked at me intently, boring into my eyes, waiting for a response, but I had been emotionally rumbled, numbed by her tragi-personal story, the near perilous journey, the near brushes and misses with death from Thailand human traffic mobsters, across European borders at the back of refrigerated trucks and lorries, and the near-death experience, crossing the English Channel in a dingy which twice nearly capsized as she'd said.

Finally finding my voice, I gave her the reassurance she needed. It was her candour which had done it for me. Call me a simp, but that honest, unmitigated confession just made me fall into love with Leti, and boom! I realised I just wanted to be with her, to look after her, and to offer my protective arms around my muffin.

"I am so sorry once again, little flower, you've had to go through all this, such a shitty life experience." I squeezed her hand for support as I spoke.

"I so want to be with you Leti, and since you speak of openness, allow me to come clean with you, as well. I am no saint either, I can tell you this. Now that we have something in common in terms of a crooked past, perhaps that makes us most suited for each other.

"Do you remember the first time we did it here on your settee, you kept asking me about my wife or ex and all I could do was prevaricate with you?"

She nodded as a gesture to encourage me to speak.

"Actually, I am still married to Maidei, on paper that is, but to be honest with you, Leti, there's no marriage to talk of anymore. I will push for divorce with a view to us getting a legal union to stave off your immigration woes, but hear me out first, sweetie! Let's get this straight, honey. We are not doing this for the visa, are we?

"We have to start from the premise that we're getting married for the right reasons which, in this case are that we want to be together and share our lives as a couple." I spoke with an increased passion, my eyes transfixed on her.

She could only stare back at me vacantly, as if I wasn't making sense to her. I was far too gone in my explanations, so I carried on, unperturbed. "There is another woman," I said, directly fixated on her face. This time I got a response from her. Leti's face suddenly lit up at the mention of *another woman*. There must be truth in the adage, no woman tolerates a rival, and Leti's interest was about to prove she wasn't an exception to the dictum either.

"Another woman? Please enlighten me, Fari." It was almost a command from her.

"Like you, I've done some bad things also, in my time. During my first bout of cancer in Zimbabwe, I'd been with this woman, Liz. Lovely woman, Liz, nursed me throughout my stage 2 prostate cancer battle, but what have I done to her? Turned my back on her as soon as I arrived back in England. I tell you, perhaps I don't deserve you either. What an unfeeling, insensitive man I've become. At least I should have made restorative contact with Liz."

"You can't be hard on yourself, Fari," she said, patting my forehead as she spoke softly. "You were hospitalised for a considerably protracted time, and to be honest, you were totally out of it since then. And then there was your long recovery at Hillside nursing home. So, to counter your guilt trip, no, Fari, you've not been nasty. For heaven's sake, you've been through a train crash, prostate cancer, and survived. You've been backwards and forwards to hell if I'm to be crass. Now is not the time you should be beating yourself about past relationships."

Listening to her speak, her rationalisations seemed to make perfect sense to me, though I could never shake off the feelings of guilt at how, just like that, I had seemed to freeze Liz out of my life, as if she'd not been important to me at some point.

Feeling encouraged at Leti not condemning or judging me, I carried on with my confession. "I have kept in touch with Liz, here and there, a trickle of a text message, a WhatsApp™ audio note, the odd email, but gradually, communication has dried up between us. Perhaps we're both facing up to the futility of our long-distance relationship, impacted by this cancer, which necessitates my stay here. I am just telling you all this, so you realise I also have my baggage, Leti, and again, so we start our new relationship on an even keel. That's the best we can do, build our relationship on an honest platform. No one is clean here and can claim a moral pedestal over the other."

"As cliched as it may sound, Fari, things happen for a reason. Who knew our paths would cross, and so why don't we make the most of it? I'm sure we can build something unique between the two of us, regardless of our seemingly murky pasts."

That had been it, a firm foundation laid for a relationship in which we both pledged to be true to each other.

Chapter 20

Yeukai

I hated Mama with a passion. I reviled and loathed her for many reasons, not least for her constant put-downs of me, how I was an unwanted pregnancy, how she said, "I wanted to abort you," and how she would never cease to remind me, relentlessly going on and on about it, like it was a song on auto-repeat. Things came to a head when she started comparing me with her sisters' twin daughters in Harare, Tapuwa and Rufaro. Things were always framed like I was engaged in a life contest with them. "Hee, Tapuwa this, Rufaro this, Tapuwa has smashed her A Levels and she's going to study medicine. Why don't you pick on a more prestigious career choice like law or even engineering?" Mother would sarcastically sneer at me. But then, what she seemed to forget was, I was my own person, I wasn't Tapuwa, neither could I ever be Rufaro.

There was also the case of our next-door neighbours' twins, Mazvita and Makanaka, in whom mother tried valiantly to excite petty jealousies and rivalries amongst them and me. But fortunately, I had had the good sense to see through this shallow façade and was able to ignore Mum's bait. Besides, I got along well with the twins, both of whom I looked up to, since they were lovely, modest beings, though slightly older than me. The twins and I generally had a great vibe going. We bonded well during their high school days, and then, when they went off to uni, Dad and Ben, their dad, threw a befitting send-off bash for them, memorable not least because of Mother's making a blatant show that I should be like Makanaka and Mazvita. "See, Yeukai, better you hang out with your big sisters, the lazy bones you are, you may pick one or two useful titbits from them." I let it pass, as we were at a public gathering, and I didn't want to embarrass myself having a public spat with my mother.

Mother's relentless put-downs ensured I ended up highly distrusting her; and I kept my thoughts close to myself, particularly my university degree choices, and my personal relationships with boyfriends. Thus, it was only one dreary mid-morning on the eve of my university departure that I made known my degree choice in a bizarre way.

"I will be reading English at Birmingham City University, Mum, just so you know."

"English, why would you want to do that?" she asked contemptuously.

"Because that's my personal choice," I shot back at her defiantly.

"But that's limiting Yeu; what can you do with a degree in English other than be a mere teacher? You could have aspired for something much loftier and do better with your life."

"It's all a question of perspective, isn't it Mum? I see lots of potential in pursuing English. A degree is how you make use of it. In time, an English degree will help me launch my writing career."

This seemed to rile Mum further, and she looked at me horrified after my last remarks.

"Writing career? You're obviously out of your mind, and I need to sit down with you and your dad, so we exorcise this madness from your head. Where have you ever heard of one living on a writing career? About time we rid you of those fanciful notions, Yeu."

And so that evening over dinner, Mama broached the subject in a bid to rope Dad against me. "Fari, what's your take on this? All along, your daughter has been hiding her university choices only to spring a surprise on me this morning. She wants to pursue a degree in English. What for?"

"Well, it's her choice, isn't it, love? We have to respect Yeu's choices and give her that due respect for her agency as an adult individual. In addition, we have to offer her our support as our daughter."

"What!" Mum almost choked over her food. "Are you not even going to tell her off, so she elects for a better degree?"

"There's nothing like one better degree choice over another, Maidei. A degree is only a steppingstone to a future career. Allow Yeu to live her life. That way she can thrive and explore her untapped talent."

Poor old Mum, there was nothing else she could do as her own husband closed ranks with me. I remember looking at the anger in her bulging eyes for not getting her way, but then in time she accepted I was an adult and not one perpetually beholden to her.

Papa's response had just about put Mother in her place. That was vintage Dad for you, always his own man, perhaps that's why I got along well with him and had a soft spot for him. Unbeknown to Mum, I had secretly confided to Dad about my preferred degree choice, and he'd given me a thumbs up. "Your choice, love, go out and shine there, and the world is your oyster," he'd remarked, back slapping me on the shoulder.

One thing about me and Dad, we were tight, although our relationship tended to periodically fluctuate. Still, there was an unspoken alliance of some sort between Dad and me.

I am the product of a dysfunctional Mupawaenda family, my father Fari and mother Maidei's union. However, Mother demonised and vilified him, Dad was my rock, my absolute anchor. What a man for me. He will always be my first man, even though my ensuing stint at uni was shortly to test my robust relationship with Dad.

Chapter 21

The Birmingham City University Years

Leaving home for uni was a welcome relief for me. Perhaps, inwardly, I was happy to be going to university, as it somehow provided some sort of escapism from our unhappy household, the eventful Mupawaenda abode, never short of drama. The house of strife and acrimony. I had had enough of Mum's endless bickering and squabbles with Dad over what I clearly saw as petty issues. As a child, I should have been spared the vagaries of my parents' dysfunctional relationship, but hey ho, there were times things fell on my lean shoulder, yet I was only a child. How could grown-ups constantly bicker over trivia like staying or not to stay in England, yet they were firmly rooted in this country, at least for as long as I remembered. I had been born in England, which I clearly considered my home country, even though Dad constantly drummed his mantra into me: "Forget about England. Zimbabwe is your true home, your cradle, and one day you will return like me."

Yet for all I remember, we'd only been to Zimbabwe on a handful of times in summer holidays mostly, when I had six weeks off from school. Though to be fair to Dad, those trips were usually Dad, my brother Muchadei and myself; Mum made it clear she wasn't at all interested in these trips. She could never cease to demonise with unmitigated zeal and passion, as a complete and utter waste of money and resources. "Why not go to Spain, Malibu, or New York on holiday, rather than flipping Zimbabwe?" she would rage on unabated, as if someone had set her off. Dad would virulently give it back in equal measure, in his usual, cynical, sarcastic tone which somehow reminded me of Jane Austen's Mr Bennett's sardonic humour in *Pride and Prejudice*. Actually, I always saw Dad's persona in that Mr Bennett's perspective, given the nature of his acerbic humour and relationship with Mama.

"So much for you, Maidei. Dissing a country which made you what you are today. Only a few years in England and you are now more English than middle England itself, Aaah you should be proud of yourself," he said with his trademark derisory laughter.

I think Mother deliberately let it pass, for that day, as she walked out of the room shrugging her shoulders.

Truth be told, no word of a lie, Mama was a difficult human being to get along with. I take my hat off to Dad for his resilience in putting up with Mama's antics. Hard work is what I would call her, more like it, to be precise. She was physically and emotionally draining because she was a show girl, an attention seeker of the highest order, and everything had to be about her, perhaps more like she was power-crazed, as if she craved power as an aphrodisiac. No wonder Dad used to say of her, she was in the wrong profession, given her mundane job as a nurse. As Dad put it, "Seeing you crave so much attention, Maidei, nursing is not for you. You should retrain; in fact, you don't need to retrain at all. Just get into showbiz, your stage is beckoning, my dear."

Poor old Dad! I felt sorry for him sometimes, having a virago for a wife.

Many times I opined on why we couldn't be a normal, happy family like other people, or households where we saw the mum and dad regaling in gaiety and laughter as they went about their mundane, dog walking exercise at sunset, or holding hands on a Saturday or Sunday morning. *What's wrong with our family? Why can't we ever be normal? Are we jinxed?* These and a host of other questions tended to plague my psyche every now and then.

Dad came from a big family. He had four sisters, each of whom he insisted I call *Tete*, as an honorific title for Aunt. "*Ndoozvatinoita mu culture yedu.,*" he'd said. "That's what we do in our culture, you address them using their designated titles; it's a mark of respect, Yeukai."

There were Tete Maita, Tete Millicent, Tete Mavis and Tete Nyari. Of all my aunties, Tete Nyari was more colourful and gregarious in her personality and exuberance. I agreed with Dad on one thing about Zimbabwe: Though, it's a beautiful country with its varied landscape features, particularly in Mutare, where Dad grew up. I was always struck by the majestic, picturesque, mountainous areas, and the plush, green fauna of Vumba and Nyanga, where we used to go every time we were on holiday.

Once we visited the peak of Christmas Pass Mountain, a breathtaking view which overlooks the greater part of Mutare, a sprawling mountainous city quietly ensconced in a valley. It was a beautiful spectacle to savour, which has stayed with me to this day, and has been the subject of many creative writing projects in my writing pursuits. It was certainly a red-letter day family outing with my aunties' brood and harem of children running around, much to Dad's delight. I had never seen him that animated as he tended to exhibit when he was amongst his kith and kin. He was always fired up. Perhaps I have to give it to him; deep down, inwardly Dad was a real traditionalist, family man, though not without glaring contradictions, which always made me chuckle at them. He loved to be amongst his people, and it would fascinate me often to see him deep in conversation with his own sisters, laughing unguarded, something I hadn't seen him do back home in England. That afternoon, we all packed into Dad's rented 4 x 4 black Range Rover, which somehow reminded me of Obama's *Beast* presidential limousine vehicle, so I had nicknamed the Range Rover, *the Beast*, and *the Beast*, it became, Dad's holiday car.

What a blast we'd had that summer holiday, as the Beast crawled and chugged, negotiating and dominating the rugged, mountainous curves and paths of the picturesque eastern highlands. First, we made a stopover at Juliusdale Montclair hotel, where we had lunch and enjoyed their succulent trout, washed down with Malawi shanti and Tropical African drinks in the sweltering July heat. The icy cold drinks were a welcome relief to our dehydrated throats. It had been a beautiful spectacle seeing Aunties' different children, *wana muzaya*, as Dad called them, the little lads, Tawana, Tapiwa, Kadesh, and the lassies playing hide and seek, skipping and running around at Montclair's beautiful gazebo and adjacent thatched huts. Then there had been the usual perennial fights over food by the youngsters, with nonchalant screams of, "He's taken my drink, Mama, Kadesh has gulped all my drink, but it was only a dare," to the exhortation of the Aunties stepping in as arbiters to fight their children's petty squabbles and childish battles. "That's all what growing up is like Tawana, fight your own battles, without calling your mummy. When will you stop being a cry baby?" Auntie Maita had chipped in to a distraught, tearful Tawana, much to the mother, Auntie Millicent's scowls of disapproval at her sister Auntie Maita's remarks, which didn't go down well with Tawana's mother. Such petty squabbling was comical to savour, especially seeing the mothers getting sucked up in the little ones' games of "infamy."

In the end, beloved *Sekuru*, as they called Dad, had stepped in as the legendary knight to save the peace for the day. The neutral arbiter that he was, he stepped in, graciously buying Tawana another drink, at which juncture the other aunties had vehemently insisted in a chorus of unison, "Seeing Tawana gets to have another drink, then everyone deserves an additional drink also, so that we are all even!" What an explosive and delightful afternoon it was all in one. I savoured it amid regaling laughter and hearty chuckles as Dad took it in his stride, relenting to his sisters' wishes, spoiling his nieces and nephews with more beverages and additional ice-cream desserts and fruits to top it all. After this colourful Montclair stopover, with domestic peace re-established and everyone satisfied, we'd resumed our excursion in the Nyanga Eastern highlands drive. Then Beast, Dad's 4x4 Range Rover had chugged down the meandering curves, twists, and turns of the Nyanga main road as we headed to Troutbeck Inn hotel, down in the deep valley of beautiful Nyanga, Eastern highlands Manicaland. In all those journeys and the accompanying sightseeing, it was gaiety and unmitigated laughter, with the children screaming and laughing, cheerily waving their tiny hands from within the big Beast. Inwardly, part of me felt for Dad, as I saw him making up excuses for Mum's absence each time his sisters enquired at Mother's no show. "Aah, Mai Muchi has exams for her Public Health England Master's degree; she sends her apologies, she couldn't make it, but she would have loved to be here," Dad glibly told a white lie with a straight face. I could only exchange knowing glances with my exceedingly reticent brother Muchi, who mostly chose a low profile during these Zim visits. At times he opted to stay at the Greenside home immersed on his PlayStation™ console. Perhaps, I imagined it, but I could swear I saw, Tete Millicent wink at Tete Nyari, after which they both let out exaggerated laughter following Dad's public relations makeover about his elusive wife, who was hardly ever with us on these family Zim holidays.

One other thing, I noted Zimbabweans were a friendly, polite lot, with a laid-back way of life. Perhaps that's why Dad always talked up going back there sometime to set up base again. I could see his face beaming, his eyes animated, each time we were at Greenside homestead where he grew up, as he chatted with his sisters and his aged mother, affable Mbuya Mupawaenda, the family matriarch. The man loved his sisters dearly, including his aged mother nan Mupawaenda; that I can give to Dad. I got along with my nieces, particularly Tete Nyari's daughters, Tawana and Chenai, though they somehow treated me as strange in our interactions. This always made me feel uncomfortable. I struggled to communicate with them in Shona, their mother tongue and they thought it was funny to mimic my cute British accent, much to my annoyance. I had to call them out once, "Why do you do it?" I snapped, my gripe with them so obvious.

"But it's cool; you speak funny, Yeukai."

"I don't speak funny, it's my natural way of speaking," I replied, much to their delight as they kept giggling at me.

Then there were the dietary challenges for me as I struggled with eating their mealie meal *sadza* staple diet, and Tete Nyari wasn't amused with me when I constantly requested to have rice, noodles and pasta instead of *sadza*.

"Do you think you're white Yeukai," she would rile at me. "Why can't you eat *sadza* like everyone else here? What would it do to you? I tell you, if I had my way, you would just have sadza and our traditional meals here. I wouldn't humour you with your silly fancies one bit," went on Tete Nyari, wagging her index finger at me.

"Oh, come of it, Nyari, give it a break, let the poor girl have whatever meal she wants; she's on holiday for heaven's sake," good old Dad, butted in, leaping to my defence. I flashed him a grateful smile at sticking up for me.

Tete Nyari relented, and we lived to fight another day.

I remember vividly one other summer holiday that sticks out to me like a sore thumb, only because Dad's sisters' young children, among them my nephews and nieces, called me *munose wefake, musalad,* which I could only suspect were derogatory terms and pejorative titles, given what happened that Saturday evening as we all crowded in Mbuya Mupawaenda's Greenside house, huddled around the glowing fireplace, some watching television or pretending to do so, as I was lazing around on my I-Pad.

"*Aaah, vana Yeu masalad chii chamunoziva?*" and there was a whole household bellowing raucous laughter following this, much to my chagrin of course; I didn't quite comprehend bits of their Shona language.

"What is she saying Thabo," I pleaded one of my cousins, to which she'd remarked, "Surely, you don't want to know what Ruu has just said about you?"

"Oh go on, just spill the beans, who cares?" I shrugged it off, encouraging her.

"Don't say I didn't warn you though," Thabo had remarked shrugging her own shoulders defensively. "Ruu is actually being mean to you Yeukai, by calling you *a salad, munose wefake* she means you're a cultural outcast, one who is steeped so much into the Western way of life and has no regard for their cultural norms and traditions."

"Really? And how has Ruu managed to reach that rich estimation of me only within the four weeks I've been here?" I had countered incredulously, my sarcasm all too unmistakeable to all.

They could only exchange knowing glances as I turned the heat on them both. In the end, I decided to flip the banter on its head back at them and started taking ownership and pride in these myriad identities and badges they bestowed on me. "Good morning, Thabo, good morning Ruu, *greetings from munose wefake, musalad* from the Mupawaenda clan."

They had been speechless. It took them by surprise, but in the end, seeing the humour as the penny dropped on them, we'd all regaled in boundless laughter, rolling on the ground. "Look at Thabo's tiny face, with tears of laughter streaming down her cheeks."

"Gosh, that was fun Yeu, *Yeu munose wefake,*" quipped a giggly Thabo, but that only further ignited the frenzy of laughter amongst all of us. From then on, relations with my kith and kin had greatly improved; we'd bonded in our own strange ways, them poking fun at me, and my revelling in this, not taking offence at every little whim and pot shots. Dad appeared to have been pleased with this turn out of events. He later privately remarked to me, 'Well done, you, Yeu, for turning things around with your nephews and nieces. Way to go. I like your diplomacy and tact, young lady,"

"Oh, it's nothing Dad," I had modestly brushed him off. "I would rather we get along as a family than spend needless time on petty squabbling and differences."

Besides, the old matriarch Mbuya Mupawaenda would not have it, people keeping grudges in her home. There were many times when she would rise to the occasion, settling out any furore amongst my nieces and nephews, with me drawing on her copious lectures to put us right. "*Aaah, garai zvakanaka wazukuru,* i.e., learn to peacefully co-exist." That was vintage mbuya for you, always preaching conciliation, even in the face of extreme provocation. If you dared disrespect her, mbuya would draw on her lectures galore, reprimanding one of our errant siblings on how lost we were as kids. Mbuya certainly loved to lecture as she did on that evening I was dressed down as a cultural outcast. All mbuya needed was a stage and she would spout pearls of wisdom from her inimitable fountain of knowledge.

This was just one of many of my experiences in Zimbabwe on my usual trips with Dad. Looking back as I do now, in retrospect, perhaps my nephews and nieces were not being mean as such. We had grown up in two diametrically opposed environs, to which they just couldn't relate in the same way. I failed to get some of their peculiar idiosyncrasies, as well. This had been one of these whirlwind, six-week summer holidays when the weeks just flew. Each time in Zim with Dad meant many days out trips sightseeing in the comfort of this luxurious vehicle, the Beast. At times, I felt for Mama, that had she been with us, perhaps she would also savour the joyous family moments.

Before long, we had to return to England as the summer holidays came to an end, and university was beckoning to me.

***

I arrived at Birmingham City University on a fine, sunny September morning to commence my undergraduate degree in English. My lodgings comprised a shared, 4-bedroom house with three other students: Maya, from up north Leeds, Tami from Scotland, and the inimitable Kundai from South Africa. Although we shared the house, it was mainly the kitchen which was a communal area; we each had our own private bedroom with two bathrooms and toilets per two of us. University life was a surreal experience for us, especially our fresher's week, the hallmark of university arrival where we drank ourselves till we dropped dead as was the norm with university students. I had certainly been looking forward to it. For, hadn't we heard that fresher's week was the week to look forward to for any university student? That's when all the booze, sex and partying thrived, as the saying went, and boom, we arrive at BCU. Freshers' week was revelatory in many respects. I learnt many things about my roommates, not least that Kundai drank like a fish. What a guzzler she was. Many times, we'd playfully reproach her, "Surely, you don't want to die of liver cirrhosis the way you are going on about it, this alcohol thing Kundai?"

"Whatever. Everyone dies at some point," she'd say, grudgingly dismissing our concerns as misplaced and an overreaction.

Within several months, however, we had settled into our new routine as university students. I enjoyed a vibrant life with my "mad" three housemates, "the Three Musketeers," as we cheekily called ourselves. We had our moments of fun as we settled down to university life, coming to grips with my new life, finding out more about the beautiful holiday resort town that Birmingham was, and also the exciting and vibrant life I shared with my roommates, particularly Tami, "the Civil Engineer," as I later nicknamed her on account of her degree course. Tami, from Aberdeen, Scotland. She'd initiated me into adulthood with her relentless matchmaking, for it was through Tami that I met my first serious boyfriend: the disaster later known as Jeff, and something I prefer not to talk about. The trauma I endured was catastrophic and immense. All I can say is, so bad were things that it was only about the time Dad was prepared to break his self-imposed hiatus in Harare and had to fly from Zimbabwe to attend to the Jeff fiasco. But I digress; perhaps the Jeff experience is a subject for another day, when I have the energy and bravery, when I feel I'm ready to open up about it. The scars, the trauma of that twisted relationship, were permanently etched on my inner psyche; it left indelible marks. I will acknowledge Steve though, for he's only a little boy and he didn't ask to be in this world, did he? The sins of fathers shouldn't be visited on children, as some say.

Then there had been my bizarre and acrimonious relationship with Mama, only exacerbated when she started her cheating game with her toy boy lover Mudiwa. At 52, she was still unashamedly hurtling along like a rolling stone, chasing a toy boy lover like a bitch in heat. How despicable, even though she was my mother. Her moral turpitude grated on me... that constant, frolicking and running around like she was a teenager, spraying on the latest Christian Dior fragrances for those evenings she sneaked away. She unashamedly tried to look sexy in the latest protruding thong lingerie. And add to that, her breath-taking arrogance, which made her think she was the only smart one in town and the whole thing was a secret affair conducted with military precision and discretion. Only, it wasn't, of course! I was thoroughly mortified and embarrassed for Mama as Mudiwa was a few years older than me.

Besides, it's not like Mama had split from Dad; they were still legally married, even though at the time Dad had taken off to Zimbabwe on his so-called second coming sojourn as he termed it. Mother's illicit relationship with Mudiwa thoroughly disgusted me on account of its disloyalty. I hate disloyal people. I had to call her out for this sordid conduct, "Surely, Mum, you can do better than this, twisting the knife in your husband's back, running around, sneaking around with your toy boy lover. The whole thing makes me sick!"

Mum had been livid with me for daring to step on her toes, as she called it, and she gave me a blazing dressing down. "Aaah I see, now you're a marriage counsellor Yeukai, are you?" She laughed sarcastically, but she was not yet done with me. "Just for the record, let this be the first and last, you try to step in my lane and tell me how to run my life, Yeukai, do you follow? How dare you come in here, insinuating you can tell me how to run my marriage? Hearken then, my marriage to your father is a no-go area, not only for you, but for Muchi, as well, and it will stay that way."

But I gave it back in equal measure, defiantly standing my ground. I wasn't going to let her cow me into submission. "Whatever, Mum, it's disgusting. A woman of your stature, at your age, cuckolding your husband, and for your own information, I refuse to be denied my voice."

There had been no clear winner in this verbal altercation; both of us refused to concede ground. How could we? We were both fiery, headstrong people, each completely beholden to their position in which we were convinced we were both right and entitled to uphold.

Mama was a bit of an oddball and tended mostly to shoot from the hip in her dealings with people, particularly her own husband. I felt for Dad that things had regrettably floundered to this level of marital hiccups and dishonesty.

My first year at Birmingham City University was somehow hampered by the Jeff fiasco, as I had to temporarily withdraw from uni due to pregnancy, which resulted in the birth of my first son Steve. For all my differences with Mama, she really stepped up and supported me during navigating the difficult patch of having my son and dealing with his abusive father, Jeff. I have to grudgingly give Mama credit, as we've not always been the best of people who get along, but during the Jeff mishap, she had my back, and in no time, I returned to uni and resumed my second year in residence, having carried over some first-year courses in an arrangement to catch up on the disrupted last semester I had missed.

My second coming at Birmingham City University flew about in a somewhat lightning mode, and before we knew it, we were now in our third year, and it was around mid-second semester that I met Alex Okoja, the self-styled software engineer, my seemingly second serious boyfriend after the Jeff car crash romance of yester-year.

Chapter 22

Meeting Alex

I met Alex at our Afro-Caribbean group fortnightly meetups we usually had at BCU students' union. The Afro-Caribbean group at Birmingham City University is an inter-grouping of diverse nationalities from African and Caribbean countries, which serves as a networking portal and also opens up career opportunities through the cultural capital created via relationships spawned. Exceedingly tall, handsome, and very dark-skinned, there was no way, I couldn't have fallen for this Prince Charming, with his gruff, chocolate voice that somehow reminded me of legendary Hollywood actor Sean Connery. That was Alex's charisma for you. He had an uncanny way of standing out in a crowd, like he did that evening as I caught his gaze and sharp eye. Alex was certainly captivating with his seemingly boyish handsome looks; there was no way one could ignore him. He commanded instant attention. It is fair to say I was quite smitten by Alex. At the time, I thought Alex was a BCU student like me, and things became much clearer a few months into our relationship. Alex wasn't a student per se, but one of the Afro-Caribbean Society's external patrons from the local Birmingham community. They came in to express their solidarity with the Afro-Caribbean university community every now and then when we had our get-together gatherings.

"So, what's your story, handsome?" I remarked to him one Friday afternoon. I snuggled on his hairy chest, having skipped an afternoon tutorial at uni. Goodness knows what my prim and proper father would say if he knew I had taken to bunking lectures and tutorials, picking and choosing when to attend, at will.

"What do you mean, what's my story, Yeu?" he remarked, stroking my forehead.

"I mean, I don't really know you Alex, do I? It's been eight months we've been together but you're still a bit of a dark horse to me, love, yet you know almost everything about me, inside out, I would say."

"Well, there's isn't much to my story as you call it. I'm one of the high-profile patrons of the Afro-Caribbean society at your university, and when I'm not tied up with that, I run my own things. I have a private consulting company as a software engineer specialist."

"Hmmm... Software engineer, that sounds posh and clever Alex."

"Not really. It's a question of perspective, I guess. There's nothing glamorous about software engineering. Believe me, it can be a damp squib. It has its moments though."

"From afar, it looks all cool and brings in an air of sophistication. At least that's what I think from a layman's view," I remarked, the unmistakeable admiration in my voice clearly palpable.

"It's all perspective, like I'm saying, which is relative. Look at me, I look at you in utter awe, studying English and Classical Studies, devoting your time to Dante and Homer, studying *The Iliad, The Odyssey,* Oh my god! My woman is super clever."

"Tell me about your family Alex?" I deflected his compliments with a totally different question masking my unassuming air.

"What exactly do you want to know, duchess? It's a long story."

"For starters, do you have brothers and sisters?"

"I come from a big family, we're from a distinguished family in Eastern Nigeria, Umuofia. I am from the Igbo family, royal descendants of the Igwebu clan. So, one day, when I am fed up with all the shit in England, I will retire home to reclaim my chieftainship," chuckled Alex as he gave me a smacker on the forehead.

"Oh Alex! You are royalty personified!" I squealed in delight. "I love you for your subtlety."

That was me with my Alex. I was so much in love with this burly hunk of a man, what could go wrong? Alex was my soulmate, alter ego, very understanding about my sordid past, which had left me with a son, Steve. And when I told him about Jeff and how he couldn't care any less about his son,

Alex was horrified and wouldn't hear of it. Mostly, he had no kind words for Jeff as he was wont to say, "What kind of a man turns his back on his own son, flesh and blood? I have no respect either for a man who bashes a woman," he remarked in apparent disgust at hearing of Jeff's previous physical assault on me.

"Well, you say so, you're a rare gem, Alex. I love you so much, handsome. How did I earn such luck to have you in my life? Glad you came into my life," I remarked as I gave him a smacker on the lips.

When I decided to open up to Mother about my new love Alex in a rare moment of intimacy, Mother didn't disappoint in her negativity. She was very dismissive and sceptical, poking holes at our age difference.

"There's something off about your Alex fella, Yeu!"

"That's unfair and blatantly unkind Mum, you haven't even met him. How are you going to be objective when you're this negative already? We are so excited and happy together, and so should you!"

"I don't need to see him to make an honest, correct assessment of character."

"Aaah, I see, now you are psychic, you can assess people's inner worth and persona without even setting eyes on them. I didn't know, until now, that I had a mother who has supernatural abilities. Congratulations, Mother of the Year," I remarked sarcastically while clapping my hands mockingly at her In-wardly, I wished Dad wasn't in Zimbabwe. I knew I could have confided in him in person about my newfound love, Alex.

"You can be sarcastic for all you want, Yeukai, but reading between the lines from what you've told me about this phantom lover of yours, Alex, you hardly know him at all, if I may say. And you know what? Your 15-year age difference is a gaping hole for me, a massive red flag, if I may say! Something tells me, things don't add up with this fella. What if he has a wife back home in his Nigerian homeland?"

"Oh sod off, Mum!" I reacted angrily exasperated by her needless nit-picking. *How could she be so negative? Such a party pooper! No wonder, I always strove to hide my personal business from her.*

"Really, are you that sad Mum? Why can't you ever be happy for me, just for once? This is Alex Okoja from Umuofia, Eastern Nigeria, son of a chief; for all you know, I will soon be marrying into royalty," I remarked derisively as she rolled her eyes at me.

"It's called hindsight and age-old wisdom, my daughter. Add to that scepticism and a whiff of a mother's cynical intuition, my gut-feeling, then, boom! There you have a cocktail of a so-called darker Prince Charming out to philander and play my daughter. It's already happened before with Jeff and you had to take time off uni, I surely don't want a recurrence of this with this dark horse!"

"I don't know where you get your scepticism, Mum. Just because things didn't work out between you and Dad, doesn't mean all men are douchebags. Alex is different, that's what you have to understand. He's in a league of his own. Do you know he has promised to adopt Steve? Now, tell me, what kind of man does that if he's not genuine?"

"Of course, any man would say that if he wants to get in your knickers, dummy! Don't you realise it yet! Talk is cheap, but action is something else! A man can say anything if his dick is hard and he is horny as hell, and it's only woollies like you who fall for it, hook, line and sinker. Pathetic and sad all in one fell swoop! Are you so impressionable as if you're a teenage girl still wet behind the ears?" She sighed in resignation with these words.

And then the verbal avalanche resumed with Mum giving it back to me just when I thought it couldn't get any worse with her toxic vibes. "Aaah, I see a girl so much in love, a hopeless romantic, if I may say so. You love him, don't you? I bet your love is an unrequited fantasy though. Forget it, it's not gonna happen between you and him, Yeu. I know these old timers like Alex. Half-the time, they have a sordid past they are hiding, which they cover up by being so goody-goody; it's usually all over the top affection, a well-choreographed charade just to suck you in, but in time you will see yourself, I'm vindicated. Just give it time, love."

"Well, that's it, Mum, thanks for your support, what a cheerful mother you are," I said, mockingly as her full-on character assassination avalanche of my boyfriend Alex had just about got to me. And I took it badly. Coming from my mother, it hurt. Part of me wished I had kept things to myself as I usually did, I don't know why Alex had been an exception for me to lower my guard with Mama. Perhaps I had wanted to carve a new chapter with Mama, give her a chance, seeing she had helped me out with childcare during my first ordeal with Jeff. But it appears my overtures of peace had spectacularly floundered.

"Truth be said, Mum, I find your supercilious attitude annoying. Does it ever occur to you that children are a mirror image of what their parents do? An apple doesn't fall far from the tree. Where have I got this so-called wayward behaviour from, I wonder?"

"Eeh, what exactly are you trying to say, Yeu? I don't think I like the tone and direction this conversation is taking, Miss Lippy," she'd protested to me.

"Well, then you shouldn't be throwing stones, Mum, seeing you live in glass houses like mere mortals like me."

"Arrogant sod! That's always been you, Yeu, personified and stinks to high heavens," and with that she'd stomped off in an exaggerated huff.

It gave me a curling smile on my lips knowing I had had the last word and defeated her in one more of our epic titan duels! *Bravo!* I remarked to myself. I couldn't help reflecting, *here we go again, the very woman purporting piety was, by night shagging a man close enough to my age, yet now she wanted to preach to me about decorum.* The bloody cheek! She was such a dandy talker! Thank goodness, I had put her in her place. I guess I had a bit of Dad's irascible temper in me.

My heart drifted to Papa. I couldn't help reflecting, "Papa Fari, where are you when I need you most?" It's been a while and he's been away in Zimbabwe; gossip being peddled is, he's consorting with another woman. Mother refuses to entertain this talk, choosing instead to dismiss it contemptuously, "I have no time for trivia, you hear me," not that she's a saint herself, given her amorous, clandestine shenanigans with her toy boy Mudiwa.

"If Fari sees fit to be with another woman, when on paper we're still married, then fine, that's his choice. After all, it was his fanciful, silly idea to relocate to Zim; it's not like there was ever any collective consensus there."

But here is the thing, I found Mama's hypocrisy revolting here. How did she reconcile her over-the-top piety with her secret liaisons with Mudiwa? Mother would never cease to amaze me; the very same woman would preach forgiveness and yet act to the contrary in her mundane life. One minute she could be demonising and vilifying Dad for his alleged infidelity, but then I always wondered within myself, *how does she rationalise her own "secret" relationship with her young lover?* Did it not embarrass her that there were people like me or Taurai, our longstanding neighbour, the twins' mother, whom I am sure does know and disapproves.

Part of me could never really understand this strange relationship or marriage between my parents. Can we even call it a marriage still subsisting? I mean, Dad had long been gone in a huff, nearly eight and half years ago, now living his so-called awakening dream in Zimbabwe again, but no one really knew what was happening there, other than through titbits and snippets of gossip trickling in from that end.

Mine was a weird, twisted, oddball family. Talk of a marriage which was not a marriage in every sense between Mother and Papa, with this strange arrangement of Dad being in Zim whilst Mum continued to reside here. For as long as I can remember, our family has always been shaped by inflection points. Always, it had to be one thing after the other.

Then there was Muchadei, Muchi my elder brother. Ever since he came out as gay, that had severed his relationship with Dad. He wouldn't hear of his son "batting for the other team," as he called it. We hardly saw Muchi since he mostly lived with his partner Fredo in London. Fredo was a Bohemian Scottish musician who had run away from his wife after finally coming to terms with his repressed sexuality as a closet homosexual. Fredo also doubled as a television broadcaster on one of the leading UK channels, which meant his coming out, leaving his wife and three grown daughters for Muchi, was news fodder for the tabloids, all of whom went into a hysterical frenzy in the coverage of this, according to the tabloids, salacious story.

The sum total of this intense media scrutiny was the law of unintended consequences, which meant Muchadei was caught up in it, with some glaring newspaper headlines, screaming:

"Milton Keynes rent boy, home wrecker ends Fredo's sham marriage of twenty seven years."

Looking back, this media circus and its unwanted attention on our family from the vagaries of the British media must have taken a severe knock on both Mother and Papa, so much harder for Papa, that self-styled custodian of African Shona culture and values.

There is something insidious about the British media when they think they're onto something, particularly a purported scandal about a high profile celebrity, as was the case with Fredo here, the darling of the nation, UK's leading breakfast television host Fredo, who had been living a lie with his poor wife, Marina, the victim and their three daughters for close to a generation, but now his facade and sham marriage had come crashing down because of a thirty-something, "rent boy" as the tabloid media conceptualised my brother, Muchi.

Mother tried to put on a brave face, but behind her charade, I could see, the whole ordeal wore her right to her inner psyche and bones. Once I overhead her pouring her heart out to Taurai, the twins' mother, "*Shuwa here mai Mazvita*, there has to be a semblance of proportionality to human ordeal. I hate self-sympathy and neither do I consider myself to be a victim, but what have I done to deserve this social opprobrium of my family? Honestly, I'm increasingly beginning to think the Mupawaenda family are cursed."

"Pull yourself together, Maidei, will you," Taurai said, "and shoosh away this bullshit cursed talk. Hang in there, love. I'm speaking to you here as a friend, fellow sister and mother. Children always turn out differently as they enter adulthood and there is no way you can talk of policing them or blaming yourself for their choices. Muchi is a grown man now. At over 30, he is an adult who has chosen his own path, however unpalatable to his father, but that is something you cannot continue to beat yourself about. You, I, we're not responsible for the choices our kids make. You have to get that, Maidei."

"I hear you, Taurai, so says a mother, whose twins have done you brilliantly, and served you well and Ben as proud parents. You must have done something right by your children."

"Yes, I get that, but still people are different. Let's not get into the trap of comparing families or kids here, lest we get into a perpetual cycle of frustration. What is true of me may not be the case with someone else. We all need to bear and carry our own cross, as my late father used to say."

Taurai's wise counsel appeared to have quietened Mother and soothed her into a quiet acceptance of her situation, particularly Muchi's coming out and subsequent volatile falling out with Dad. And so, the family returned to a gradual slumber of normalcy, albeit Muchi moving out of the home altogether. Meanwhile, my relationship with Alex was growing in leaps and bounds. What could possibly go wrong?

Chapter 23

Ewan

It was accidental how I discovered I was three months pregnant.

I had been totally oblivious of this. For someone who's had irregular periods as the norm in my cycle, how could I have known, let alone suspected, until it came from Dr. Jenkins' remarks? "Your symptoms and personal recounts fit very well with early pregnancy, Yeukai, so I have done a rapid pregnancy scan among other tests with your samples. Have you been trying for a baby?" remarked Dr. Jenkins to my bemused self.

"Aaah, not really," I stammered, a bit befuddled as I struggled to gather my thoughts. It had been completely out of the blue, this pregnancy scare story. Of course, I'd been feeling stomach cramps, nausea and fatigue in the last few weeks, but had put it down to general tiredness and uni pressure work, especially because I had been spending long hours working on my dissertation. Besides, I had a very demanding and pedantic supervisor with whom I was increasingly finding it difficult to work, so I put all this down to stress associated with the daily rigours of life. And now here I was, my doctor alluding to my possible pregnancy. And true to his prognosis, my pregnancy scan returned positive.

"So, congratulations, Yeukai." Dr. Jenkins' voice roused me from my midmorning reverie. "I'm sure your partner will be pleased," he continued to ramble.

"Of course, he will, Alex has always told me how he so much wants to be a dad," I politely remarked as the penny finally dropped. For the second time whilst I was at uni, I had become pregnant. A flurry of thoughts coursed through my mind as I played out various possible scenarios of how both my parents would react to this news, given the cataclysmic, seismic shifts of yesteryear when it happened with Jeff.

But, this time, it'll be different, I spoke inwardly to myself, as if trying to reassure myself. *It's Alex isn't it? This time it's my tall, dark, handsome Mister Right.*

Everything else will fall into place, possibly a lavish marriage and wedding. Who knows, maybe a honeymoon in eastern Nigeria, Umuofia, my boyfriend's birthplace. I was already fantasising a glowing future together with my other half.

"That will be it, Yeukai, once more, accept my warm wishes and congratulations." That was Dr. Jenkins' voice, again rousing me from my momentary trance. I thanked him politely and left with a sense of subdued excitement and anticipation for my meeting with Alex that evening. As was the norm in our relationship, we tended to spend most evenings at Alex's flat in Central Birmingham, which was not far from uni, and thus made things handy for me in the instances I had morning lectures.

Chapter 24

The Other Side

"**G**uess what, Alex, we're expecting a baby in spring."

"A baby in spring? Is this for real, Yeukai?"

"Of course it is, dummy, why would I joke over something like that? I heard confirmation from the horse's mouth, Dr. Jenkins."

Alex went deadpan quiet for a good few minutes, as if reflecting over the baby news. My heart skipped a bit as I let his body language sink in. Somehow, I had an uneasy sense of deja vu I could only connect to my ex-boyfriend Jeff, when he started playing up after I got pregnant the first time.

Clearing my throat seemed to have jolted Alex out of his serene silence into speaking, "Well I am not so sure it's a great idea having a baby, considering..."

"Considering what?" I interrupted his seemingly insipid monologue "Well, the thing is, it's, it's, complicated, Yeu..."

"What's so complicated about having a child? It's either you want it, or you don't. I know it's something which has happened when we haven't planned it, but where do you stand, Alex Okoja? May the men stand up and be counted from the boys!"

"Aaah, aaah...," Alex was behaving strangely that evening. Suddenly, he was struggling to speak, as if he had a speech impediment, something I had never witnessed before, and he carried on with his theatrics, quietly dropping the first bombshell of the evening, "The thing is, Yeu, I haven't been entirely clear with you..."

"What do you mean you haven't been entirely clear with me, when we've been going out all these months? A rock-solid couple, if ever there was one!

I get it, the baby news may have come as a shock, but that's why we're having this conversation, Alex. Isn't it?"

"Well, hear me out. Allow me to put my cards on the table, Yeu. I have too many complications in my life at the moment. I can't afford to have another child."

Second bombshell of the evening...boom!

"Alex, why don't you stop this unashamed hide and seek game, and just come clean with me. 'Another child,' what's that supposed to mean, for a man who told me, he's never had any children previously?"

"I'm sorry Yeu, forgive me. It's not what it looks like. Let me explain fully, I have three children and a wife back home in Nigeria. I don't love her; it's been a stale relationship over the years, and then my UK student's visa ran out ages ago. All these years, I've been fighting deportation from the Home Office, but perhaps if you wait for me to finalise my divorce, perhaps... perhaps, we could get married and then, you could assist in regularising my stay in the country."

Third bombshell of the evening...Boom!

"I have three children and a wife," those words, delivered just like that, were the final arrow through my heart. Delivered, served cold, just like that, in an un-flinching mode, as if Alex was an automaton.

Hearing those words, I had that sinking feeling in the pit of my stomach. I never let him finish. I exploded into unbridled anger and let rip into him, guns blazing.

"Aaaah, I see, you lying, cheating bastard! So, all this time, you've been living a lie, and now you have the nerve to utter such hogwash to me? So, you only want me for the visa, huh?"

I was just getting started and flung at him, "Then it's not gonna happen Alex! On account of my principles, I would rather be with a man who is true to me and loves me, than a lying, cheating weasel like you! No, it's not happening Alex, not now, never, and certainly not in my name."

"I can explain myself further..."

"There's nothing to explain yourself further here, Alex. We're done. So, without tiptoeing to protect me, as you insinuate, as well as dressing things up, you could have come clean with me. Shown me you had balls. I would have respected you as a man of mettle, with depth and substance. Then we could have had a viable future together. All I wanted from you was genuine, unadulterated love, as you well know from my prior experiences. I never asked for your pity. You know me well enough; I wouldn't stoop for that shit! Equally, I never asked for your betrayal," and with those words I exited his Birmingham flat and life for good.

My sense of pride, good judgement, and personal value system would never allow me to be with a person who fell short of genuine, unadulterated love. The catastrophic mistake that had been the Jeff relationship of yester-year, had schooled me and taught me well. Never again, kowtow to an abusive, lying man under the guise of love. I was done with that Stockholm syndrome shit. I refuse to be used as a door mat.

Hindsight is such a wonderful thing. Grudgingly, I found myself reflecting, perhaps Mother was right after all in her seemingly austere estimation of Alex. Those fiery exchanges I had had with Mama suddenly came back to haunt me. For me, Alex had failed the litmus test the moment he mentioned his well-choreographed subterfuge, concealing his marriage and children.

Integrity in relationships was sacrosanct for me. These were the very core tenets of a relationship. You fail on them, there is no relationship to talk of, no ifs, no buts, no compromise. How dare he cross the line! The intensity of his insults was to dare to float an idea around that I was merely a cog in the wheel to facilitate his visa application and ensure he gets right-of-stay in England. That, to me, was a cardinal breach of trust to which there was no atonement, no second chances, nor going back. I had to face my setbacks headlong, alone. I knew the fall out with both my parents would largely be a bruising encounter, especially as something like this had happened before. As I trudged into my uni digs that evening, I couldn't tell whether I was ready for the subsequent duel and fall out with my parents.

Inwardly, I quickly came to terms with Alex's treachery. Given my near-miss, death, traumatic experiences with psycho Jeff, I rationalised within myself that Alex was a closed chapter for me. The only saving grace was his disclosure to me. He had another family back home in Africa, albeit it came at a price, termination of our relationship. Still, I accepted it. Some things one just has to let go for their sanity's sake and to enable them to forge ahead with life. You gotta take it. Some battles leave no victor, only a trail of destruction and broken hearts. I had long wisened up to that.

Can the ends ever justify such wretched means? Preying on fellow human beings so you benefit through subterfuge as Alex had sought to do? I wager to the contrary, but who am I to proffer an opinion?

Chapter 25

Taking Stock

"Twice this has happened, I am utterly disappointed with you Yeu," Dad waggled his two fingers at me as he spoke with me over the Zoom call, as I had braved it to arrange a teleconference call with him. Now that I had been decisive enough to boldly end my relationship with Alex, there was no way I could keep things to myself anymore. It would be a difficult phone conversation; I knew that for sure. I'm smart enough to realise Dad had a soft spot for me, and yet, for the second time in my life, I had hugely let Dad down.

"Are you listening to me, Yeukai?" Dad's high-pitched, exasperated voice on the other end of the computer screen roused me to the present moment.

"Yes, Dad, I'm sorry, but it is what it is, and I had to talk to you, so I keep you in the loop."

"First, it was that dodgy Jeff Willmore, the brute, then now it's this married man, all because he wanted a visa to bring his real family from Nigeria. Oh, let me clue you in on this, Yeukai. All the guy had to do is, aha...let me hook up with a jackass black British girl, a nitwit, with silly, fanciful notions of love, impregnate her, then get a visa to England. Boom! I can then get my Nigerian wife and three children into England! Easy peasy, job done!"

'Dad continued, "And you know what sucks, Yeukai? You fell for that con, hook line and sinker! Utterly unbelievable. And to think you fell for that bullshit!"

The sarcasm in Dad's voice grated over my skin. Still, I let him carry on, if only, so he could vent his steam.

"Whatever happened to your brains since you went to uni? Have you taken leave of your brains, daughter? How did you mess up big time like this? What a toss-up! You've played fast and loose with your life, young lady. That's your

191

choice, but a poor and foolish choice for that matter."

It was a barrage of invectives from Dad, left, right and centre, with no let-up in sight. I struggled to compose myself to give a coherent response, other than, "What can I say? Things happened the way they did Dad, and now we're here," which seemed to rile him further.

"Don't say, 'we're here' as if it's a pleasantry. About time you accept responsibility young lady! You're on your own in the mess you've created for yourself this time. How dare you try to drag everyone else in it? Don't you know how to keep your legs closed!"

"What do you have to say for yourself? That doesn't cut it, your explanations. Forgive me for being such a straight shooter, but you've got to steer clear of a snake pit like these dodgy men you seem to attract. How did you mess up big time like this?"

Dad wasn't pulling any punches with me that day. He let rip his blizzard of pent-up anger, and went banging on about how I had let him down as a daughter.

"I thought you'd learnt from the twins, Mazvita and Makanaka, that one completes their university course first, before you think of becoming a mother, pre-empting your degree as you've done."

I had been far too quiet all along in this phone conversation which was increasingly degenerating into a farcical monologue. It was a complex situation, and I was not going to let anyone lecture me on morality. As human beings, we all have our own foibles to navigate.

I finally erupted, laying into Dad big time, giving it back in equal measure. "Aaah, Aaah I see Dad, so when it suits you, the twins have done well and are supposed to be quintessential role models," I remarked sarcastically.

"Of course, they are positive role models, you know that yourself! What's sarcasm got to do with it?"

"Well Dad, I seem to remember your harsh, parochial worldview when they both got married to their white partners. You went berserk, banging on about how disgraceful this whole thing was, marrying outside one's ethnicity."

"Er...er, different scenarios, Yeu," he stammered as he struggled to speak, and I could see I had got him where I wanted him. Then he charged on, speaking as if he'd just found his voice again, "You're full of inane, incoherent bullshit, you know that? And that's a rhetorical question by the way. I don't want your smarty pants tittle-twaddle back." I could see Dad was seething, bristling with limitless anger, both hands quivering as he spoke with me as if he had advanced tremors.

I could see him through his MacBook Pro screen, nibbling his lower lip, as if going through his mind, reflecting on what I had just said to him. Finally, clearing his throat, he found his voice and he sounded surprisingly conciliatory. "I love you, Yeukai, it's all been out of good intentions. If I've appeared harsh on you, it's because I want you to do right by me, so you have a brilliant future, love.

"I say it as it is, daughter, you should know me by now. Mark Anthony once said, 'I came here to bury Caesar, not to praise Caesar.' Don't take it personally, if this boot doesn't fit, don't put it on then. I'm not attacking you. It's not a personal attack on you, Yeukai, but I speak out of love, a father's love, which seeks the best for you, my love."

He went on, "Look at your brother, Muchi. I've lost him. A boy needs his father, but I'm not sure about Muchadei. He's gone full scale oddball and all these years, I thought we would find each other, possibly meet halfway, a compromise arrangement of some sort. But now I'm resigned it's not gonna happen. And then, my little flower, you decide to mess up big time, with a married man of all people!

"I was keen to end this rancour and recrimination with your brother Muchi, but boy, did he give me a chance? Before I knew it, he was out, consorting with his gay lover. To strike such unmitigated shame and depravity to me and my family..." Dad appeared increasingly unhinged and delirious as he said the last statement with exaggerated emphasis, pointing his index finger into his inner bosom.

Inwardly, I felt for him. I understood his pain and sense of social opprobrium for one who had grown up in a sheltered conservative Shona culture, back in Zimbabwe, where things like sexual freedom and alternative sexuality were frowned upon. I remember seeing a news article on how homosexuality was outlawed in his country of birth, so perhaps, it made sense, his failure to come to terms with Muchi's coming out. Add to that, my two out-of-wedlock pregnancies, which had inadvertently called time on my uni course. Looking at Dad, I saw a broken man staring back at me. Part of me felt sorry for him, at the hand life had dealt him. I say this thinking of his difficult relationship with Mama on top of this. "I'm sorry, Dad, I can only promise to do better in future," I found myself mumbling under my breath. I really felt sorry for Pops, I equally loved him as many times, he'd always fought in my corner. He had always been there when I needed him most.

"Can't you see, your promises don't stack up? You're full of bluff and bluster, Yeu," and with that I could see Dad's shoulders drooping as he looked like a cornered and defeated animal.

I could see the extreme anguish he was in, the poor man, the self-styled Zimbabwe cultural icon and custodian of *Shona* culture as he put it. I could see how I had let him down. 'Bye, Dad, speak soon," and that was it as I politely ended our zoom call. Inwardly, following my falling out with my father, I knew I had to figure out how to be his daughter again, make atonement to a man who meant a lot to me, someone I had always looked up to, whom I could count on in my dark days. Truth be said, Dad had always been an unwavering pillar of strength to me. Later I found myself in reflective mode, as my mind wandered to Mother's previous words, the first time my mishap with men had happened.

"Your father had high hopes you would one day marry well, in the fullness of time, Yeukai," Mama had earlier admonished me when I got pregnant the first time.

And now, I had disappointed my father for the second time in a row. It was now nigh imperative for me to be in his good books again. That mattered so much to me, it was important that I make amends with my childhood hero, Dad. I knew it wasn't going to be easy, considering the high stakes involved with my dropping uni to go and deliver and look after my soon-to-be child. And then things were compounded by Dad being in Zimbabwe. Perhaps things would have been easier to navigate had Dad been here in person. In my heart of hearts, I knew Dad had a kind heart and I was certain he would clearly come around in time.

It took me a considerable amount of time to get sorted within myself, picking up the pieces as I came to terms with my personal challenges. A fresh start was what I needed more than anything else. I had to contemplate my future now that the king and castles had been knocked off the chessboard. My set-backs merited a paradigm shift of some sort. Being a Mupawaenda, of the *Gwai Gumbi* clan, as Dad used to inculcate in me, I found myself, ironically revelling in some of dad's usual refrains to me in earlier years as we grew up in Milton Keynes, my brother Muchi and I. "We never give up, Yeu, in the face of adversity. Likewise, you mustn't give up ever, you two. Pick yourselves up and keep moving. I didn't raise you to sit at the back of a bus." Dad used to drum this mantra relentlessly into us.

I eventually triumphed over my adversities by taking up full-time employ-ment as I strove to raise the apples of my eye, my two boys, Steve and Ewan. Over a short space of time, I was able to bounce back. I worked exceedingly hard though, and managed to buy myself a two-bedroom house in pictur-esque Wendover Village, ensconced in the Chiltern mountains of Bucking-hamshire, and it was round about that time I received a seismic phone call from a certain Liz, in relation to Dad, which phone call left me jarred, numb and in utter shock as I leant Dad was seriously ill in Zimbabwe with stage 3 cancer which was turning out badly.

"I know this is all awkward Yeukai, we've never met, and here I am, a stranger informing you of your father's prostate cancer and unwellness..."the soft-spoken woman's voice had said on the other end of the line, as I remained tongue-tied for a good few minutes trying to process the jaw dropping news I had received, just like that, out of the blue, with no prior warnings this was coming.

"But I have to be upfront with you, your father's situation is dire, and I'm imploring you as his beloved daughter, please do what you can, so he's able to travel back to England forthwith to enable him to access medical care pronto. We have failed him here, with our cut-throat Zim medical fees, which prises out the ordinary man and woman from accessing healthcare delivery systems."

It had all been surreal to me as I spoke with this Liz over the phone. She spoke very well. I could tell she was cultured and refined, definitely an intel-lectual from her demeanour and lyrical, groomed voice over the phone. After my initial shock, I quickly pulled myself together as I threw back at Liz, a barrage of questions, trying to gather much information and knowledge about Dad's prostate cancer diagnosis and why it had been kept quiet from his UK family.

"Thank you, Liz, I appreciate your phoning me with this shocking news, I know now is not the time for this, but I would have wanted to know why we've been kept in the dark throughout Dad's battle with cancer. Surely, we could have done something, and stepped in much earlier, had we been kept abreast."

"I perfectly understand you, Yeukai, and appreciate where you're coming from with your concerns, but like you, I fully concur, now is not the time for recriminations. Errors have been made, that's not in question. I'm sure we both share the same sentiments here, the priority being to have your dad back in England, ASAP. Then, when this is done and dusted, there will be time to revisit our oversights and atone for them."

"On point, Liz, thank you again. I am buying Dad an air-ticket right away for a British Airways overnight flight through South Africa, so if you could just furnish me with your email address, I will shortly email you Dad's e-ticket and travel itinerary, thanks."

"Will certainly do, and I can't thank you enough for facilitating your dad's travel arrangements at the eleventh hour. Bye and lovely to speak with you."

"Bye Liz, likewise."

That had been it, and I had done what had to be done, my filial duty as a daughter. After my telephone chat with Liz, I immediately went online and bought Dad's airline ticket, promptly passing the details to Liz. I was happy to do this act of selflessness for Dad; perhaps part of me felt it was my way of atonement for how I had let him down in the not-so-distant past.

Chapter 26

Muchadei

As fate would have it, I happen to be the only son in this charade of a marriage between Papa and Mama. Perhaps Mama had a point; I could never understand why Papa's family failed to shoulder their responsibilities without constantly asking for money from him, as if he was a financial messiah. Gosh! Surely being related is not a crime. Or is it?

Guilt-tripping was another technique they used on Papa. He was a sucker for this, hook, line, and sinker. Papa's overindulging relationship with his family tended to typify most of my earlier bones of contention and squabbling with Papa, and I dare say, I found Mama's approach to matters more palatable.

"But you are not Father Christmas," Mama many times chided Dad, for his overbearing generosity, which at times extended to his own undoing, as he ended up relying on credit cards or loans to foot other people's business.

What disturbed me was how they, Dad's family, felt entitled to the money and perennial hand of assistance from him. So, when Papa decided to leave for Zimbabwe, I shed no tear for him; he seemed to have his family priorities skewed in a terribly wrong direction.

Dad tried to impose his Zimbabwean identity on me full on, but I rejected it outright. I did! That's where our falling out emanated from, as he threatened to disown me or send me back to Zim to be properly schooled in the art of respecting your elders, as he puts it. "I will not have you disrespecting me in my house, Muchi, do you hear me, boy? You got a smart mouth for someone so young!"

But I squared up to him, many times, refusing to do as I was told. I had had enough of his bullshit talk: "I am a custodian of the very indigenous Zimbabwean culture and values; where we come from; the Gumbi clan, deep down from the valleys of Honde Manyika, we the Mupawaenda are a revered and distinguished family. In time so shall you be, Muchadei. I have high hopes and dreams for you, son. One day, when I'm no longer there, you'll be the head of the family. Samusha."

But this was all mumbo jumbo bullshit to me. Looking clearly, I had no affinity or memories of Zimbabwe, having been born in upmarket London's Queen Charlotte's and Chelsea Hospital, and having grown up in opulent Milton Keynes town in Buckinghamshire County. Tell that mumbo jumbo to an English-born lad and you expect him to grasp it? Not a chance! I grimaced as I shook my head in disgust.

"Why don't you stop bullying your only son, Fari, and for once engage and build a relationship with him?" That was vintage Mum, always fighting in my corner.

"Your son is an idiot and should learn to respect his elders, and do as he's told on first request," Dad had barked at me, as was the norm in our relationship.

In the end, I sucked my teeth at this stalemate and gave up. I shut him out of my life as my father completely. I wasn't going to accept these brazen acts of bullying from a man who was meant to be my father and look out for me.

There should be a special place in hell reserved for people like my father for the anguish he caused me and Mama due to his constant vacillation about wanting a life in Zimbabwe, yet we were already settled here as a family. I could never understand why a grown man would have such an indecisive mind. Once, I asked Mother, 'What's on with Dad and his constant Zim fetish? I just don't get it. Can somebody explain to me why someone in their right senses would board a plane and consider going back to Zimbabwe, given the chaos and turmoil obtaining there?"

"Oi, watch your mouth boy, I heard ya," Dad interjected. I was mortified he'd heard me; I had thought he was out of the house.

A boy needs his father, they say, but I guess it wasn't meant to happen between me and Dad. How could it be, especially since I made him "sick" following my coming out on my eighteenth birthday Christmas mid-morning, before the entire family. Uncle Ben and his wife Taurai, our neighbours of many years, the twins' parents, happened to be present on that fateful day.

Dad went berserk and he came after me, guns blazing. "How dare you insult me like this, Muchi? I will not have it in my household, a child who has decided to take that twisted perverted path," he was literally screaming the house down as if he was high on some substance.

"But it's my freedom of choice, Dad, and surely I have every reason to feel insulted by your homophobic views," I countered, defiantly squaring up to him with my newfound bravado.

That seemed to rile him further. He went apoplectic with rage, "Get out of my house! I say get out of my house, Muchi! Do you hear me? What a puffed-up misanthrope you are! I will not have you disrespecting me like this, before my wife and neighbours, telling me you've gone out of your head. If your mother humours you and encourages these silly, twisted thoughts in your head, then that's both of you out of here!"

"Eeh excuse me, but sorry, Fari, why are you dragging me into this?" shouted Mother, visibly annoyed for being singled out in my furore with Dad.

I could see the Christmas dinner was not going to materialise that day, as quite an atmosphere engulfed the Mupawaenda residence, Dad kicking and screaming, as he paced up and down the living room threatening to kick me out, as Uncle Ben tried to quieten him down, saying, "You need to calm down *Babamunini* Fari, and give your son a chance, please, I earnestly implore you."

"Aaah, I see, you're in on this too as well Ben. I should have known better, coming from you who has allowed your daughters to be married by white men, and now you're telling me to calm down to this nonsense? And just roll over and accept that my son has become a faggot? Tell me, would you accept it, if your son tells you this bullshit? Certainly not, I'm sure you wouldn't put up with this hogwash Ben, and yet you expect me to? Unbelievable stuff!"

There was something nasty, horrid, and unpleasant in the way, Dad hissed the word *faggot,* through his anger-induced gritted teeth. There was a curl of my lips, accompanied by a victorious smirk. I'd finally got under dad's skin. How the mighty had fallen, that seemingly thick-skinned man had crumbled with my bombshell revelation. I can tell you, I was inwardly gloating and celebrating, even though this was a far too serious occasion.

Somehow, I remained calm and composed, as part of me was hugely relieved I had eventually chosen to reveal my hitherto clandestine sexual identity.

"Well, if anything, I was expecting some tolerance and understanding from you folks, not least my dad, the so-called custodian of *Shona* culture. I've been a closet homosexual all these years, and you know what? Today, Christmas day, I am free. Yay! Who will embrace me and acknowledge me amongst you here?"

I cheekily dared them as I surveyed the room, goading them contemptuously, scanning the different emotions registered on different people's faces, ranging from confusion on Mother's face, then what seemed like amusement on my baby sister Yeukai's face, the bewilderment on Mother's face juxtaposed by the bristling, stony face of Dad as he tried to come to terms with my revelations that fateful Christmas day. These were all a classic spectacle to behold which will certainly live with me in years to come. Only Uncle Ben and his wife Auntie Taurai seemed to exhibit a calm response at all this spectacle.

"You are a despicable slimeball, you know that?" Dad shot back at me, wringing his hands in utter frustration."

And then, out of the blue, the unthinkable happened. Dad lunged into me full steam ahead, pummelling me to the ground in one fell swoop, hitting me hard on the head with his clenched fists, which sounded like a sledgehammer as I slumped down heavily. I fell to the floor with a loud thud as it had all happened too quickly and was something, I hadn't anticipated at all. I screamed in agony, as Uncle Ben and Mother scrambled to restrain Dad in a tight embrace and headlock. All the while, Uncle Ben was still pleading with Dad to not be an idiot, as I suddenly blacked out into unconsciousness.

Chapter 27

Wrath of the British Tabloids

Fredo

Following Dad's humiliating dressing down and our blazing row over my coming out, things pretty much escalated downhill, as I decided to move in with my hitherto secret partner of several years, Fredo.

The only setback though, was the small matter of Fredo's marriage of several years that he had to sever, not to mention breaking the news to his grown-up daughters, Roxy, Amiee and Velma. What compounded matters was that my lover Fredo was no ordinary person; he was a household UK television personality, a bigwig powerhouse broadcasting host on one of the mainstream free view channels, which, in itself had presented challenges in keeping our relationship concealed all these years.

Now that Dad had blown his top off on me, things pretty much came to a head when Fredo's dithering and vacillation to come clean with his wife and children was spectacularly wrested out of his hands by an additional, unforeseen development, a flurry of newspaper journalists who got wind of our hitherto clandestine relationship. When they sought right of reply and confirmation from Fredo over the veracity of our relationship and were threatening to run an expose story on us in one of the Sunday papers, we knew the die was cast one way or the other. "I am going to have to come clean with Marina this evening before the Sunday papers break the story and feast on our carcasses, Muchi," Fredo coyly remarked to me that Saturday evening at our hideout rendezvous London flat.

"Goodluck, hunk, about time, though it'll sure be worth it and all right in the grand scheme of things," I replied reassuringly, as the weight of Fredo's herculean action that day played on my mind and weighed heavily on my shoulders. That brooding, fateful evening, Fredo crossed the Rubicon as attested next morning by the screaming, screeching, over-the-top epithets from the tabloids as they went into frenzied overdrive, excoriating our relationship. Words and phrases such as "broadcaster's sleaze, rent boy, double dipping," among others, were the currency of the day that Sunday morning, as these colourful, homophobic, hate-filled phrases were bandied around the generality of the rabid British tabloid press. I felt for Fredo. Why wouldn't I, seeing he was under this barrage of relentless attacks, left, right and centre, with no reprieve in sight? I need not have worried. Fredo's damage limitation exercise meant to cynically stave off the Sunday papers' expose appeared to have worked, as there he appeared the next morning, in front of me and other UK households, on the various morning TV channels' screens, openly admitting to our until now secret affair, and how he'd had to come clean with his wife of many years, Marina and his three daughters, with a quivering, at times, breaking, trembling, choking voice, Fredo gave it all for our relationship:

"Fellow Britons, I have a statement to make before you all this morning. For the past few years, I have been involved in a genuine, consensual affair with my partner, Muchadei. I am aware, I have failed my wife of many years, Marina and our three girls, Roxy, Aimee and Velma. Earlier, today, I made the bravest decision of my life, opening up to Marina and the girls about my repressed sexuality all these years, my duplicity. I will not seek to lie or sugar coat this extraordinary development, it's not been easy for Marina, and as of today, we have decided to split, as I want to concentrate on my new relationship with Muchadei, Muchi, my rock. At this difficult moment of our lives, I earnestly ask that the media respect my privacy and that of Marina and our girls, as they painfully come to terms with the new order, and I will not be commenting further or take any questions from the media..."

There was the whirring sound of the non-stop constant clicks of television cameras as the paparazzi jostled to get a vantage shot of one of Britain's most popular television host's spectacular fall from grace. That didn't faze me at all. It didn't matter in the grand scheme of things. I didn't wait to hear more of Fredo's admission speech. I was visibly elated that, at last, I could openly consummate my relationship together with Fredo. This 'come clean TV confession' was one such Fredo's kiss-and-tell all telly "confession" which pretty much did it for me that morning. My hands felt for the TV remote control as I gleefully switched off the telly a huge smile lighting my face. Shouting "Bravo Fredo! Fredo, good old Fredo!" I squealed in delight as I made an ecstatic run around our shared private London flat. The future certainly appeared bright, even though, as I drew the curtains, cold shouldering the hordes and barrage of journalists and TV crew members besieging our Belgravia London flat hideout. I checked the flashing text message on my iPhone with a widening smile, realising it was Fredo's name lighting up the screen; "all done for us love," was all I needed to see. The rest of the text message would wait until another time, now was not the time. Today was the day of celebrating the new beginnings of our relationship, not under the wraps this time. Never again would we have to conceal our relationship.

Chapter 28

Bluebell

One summer evening in early July was all it took; it was just about the tipping point for me. I'd had enough of this dysfunctional Mupawaenda family's crassness, I mean, for how long can one go pretending to put on a brave face, trudging along with that hard, austere façade that one is an unbreakable superwoman and doesn't care? Of course, deep down, we do care as mothers. I did care about my family, notwithstanding my differences, run-ins with Fari, and our car crash family relations. There's only so much one can take. I guess I'd been feeling pretty much rough, overwhelmed, and under the weather, with a lot of things on my plate, not least Fari's dramatic return from Zimbabwe ill; the guilt-tripping from Yeukai, and now Halifax bank were pressing on with abrasive repossession proceedings to take over the matrimonial home due to continual mortgage arrears.

How did Fari expect me to fund the mortgage payments on one salary alone during the time he'd been away on his French leave in Zimbabwe? It couldn't be done. Had we not taken over a huge mortgage monthly payments commitment, that time when we switched over from interest only to capital repayments mortgage? And yet in his typical, selfish ways, Fari hadn't paused to reflect whether a single salary would be able to fund and sustain this huge monthly commitment.

Of course, I had tried putting on a brave face the first few months following Fari's departure, saying, "I can manage. Who needs a man? I don't need Fari at all," but it was all a brave, false stunt. The truth is, I'd been struggling financially to manage on one income. Eventually, I threw in the towel. Gradually, I started missing mortgage payments, as I struggled to keep on top of other household bills and priority debts, council tax, electricity, gas bills, what have you.

Perhaps a culmination of these diverse pressures triggered my meltdown, as my hitherto secret partner, Mudiwa, found me sobbing uncontrollably one summer evening. I was slumped in a heap on the bathroom floor in my nightie. Goodness knows how long I'd been like that. I felt a firm hand on my shoulders, and I could barely make out Mudiwa's medium height frame silhouette as I was partly dazed and shivering violently. It was in that moment it somehow hit me that I was sitting on an overflowed bathroom floor and felt the cold, biting dampness on my night dress, and also the water on my bum and outstretched legs.

"For the love of Mike, Maidei, what on earth are you doing on the floor? Sitting in cold water like that. Are you trying to drown yourself? Are you unwell, honeypot?" Mudiwa's barrage of questions rained fast and loose as he approached me, now the alarm on his face dawning on me as his entrance seemed to rouse me from my slumber. Part of his strong masculine hands were concurrently turning off the bathroom tap as he kept talking to me.

"I can't do this anymore, Boo, I can't do it, I swear."

"Can't do what, love? Talk to me, Maidei, you know I have a listening ear, always for you."

"It's too much Boo..."

"What are you on about? You're not making sense, Maidei. Pull yourself together. What is it, what has tipped you over the edge?"

'It's everything; my damn twisted family, the flipping mortgage repossession, now Fari is back with his cancer and Yeukai and her car crash love life. I can't deal with this shit anymore. I want out."

"Shoosh, Maidei, pull yourself together, honey," Mudiwa spoke as he briefly retreated from the bathroom and reappeared later, armed with a glass of a cold fizzy drink and two small blue looking pills which he literally, thrust into my mouth.

"What's this?"

"Magic pills, LA wonder, the hottest thing in town, you'll love them I promise you, Snuggles."

And that had been it, it's still blurry and hazy how Boo transported me to bed that fateful evening. All I remember was the swirling and spinning of the room, non-stop as I was laughing deliriously, incessantly calling out to Boo. But there was another pleasant side to this fine madness. Within a split second, I could feel it, that long-sought-after euphoria which had been elusive all along was right here in this room, within my persona. I was suddenly teleported, transported into an orgy of non-stop ecstasy, a vortex of sensual fulfilment I had never felt before, a cacophony of mind-blowing sensations which were far better than sex, as I felt myself having multiple orgasms. I vaguely remember screaming to Boo, "Yes, yes toy boy, take me to high heavens, boy," and with that memory I drifted off to sleep, spent and contended. Whatever Boo had put in my fizzy drink was a wonder drug. For the first time in many months, I slept well without interruption and in subsequent days, Boo would give me the magic blue tingling pills and I would sleep flat out. My insomnia became an increasingly blurred memory.

The next morning following my maiden blue pills delicatessen, I woke up light-headed but feeling upbeat, quite a feat, considering I hadn't felt like this in the many months I had struggled with insomnia and persistent migraine, as I lay turning and tossing on the bed.

"Geez, you look fabulous this morning, Snuggles," Boo had remarked as I lazily ambled into the kitchen, my night dress hugging the floor as I joined him for the steaming mugs of hot coffee, he'd prepared for both of us.

"Of course, I do, thanks to you Boo. Whatever was in those blue pills you gave me last night, they did work wonders, I give you that my Boo. Here, let me put some marmalade on your toast. After last night, my man deserves some credit and recognition."

"Oh, bluebell from LA, that's for another day, honeypot. Anytime you feel low again, just holler at me. Boo will sort you out, I've got your back covered, Snuggles."

And so as stealthily as it started, I became gradually hooked on the magic pills; bluebell was our code name with Mudiwa, but it was our closely guarded secret. It had to be, given my vocation as a staff nurse at Milton Keynes NHS Trust Hospital, the ramifications would have been ghastly and dire, had my dirty little secret ever been found out. Not to mention our clandestine drug-fuelled jaunts with Mudiwa and like-minded sods in the dark underworld. *At some point, everyone has a darker side*, I quietly rationalised my hideous duplicity.

Perhaps, knowing there was now more to my relationship with Mudiwa, in which he was the conduit to my salvation, in a way consolidated our bond and I must say, it helped me cope with my issues.

Epilogue

Bangkok

Hello Fari,

Trust this email finds you well. It's me, Leti, hollering from Bangkok. I am trying to pick up the pieces. It's not exactly easy is it, having been jettisoned out of England against my will, a country I had come to regard as my other home these two score years past. But, what happened, happened. I'm not one for sympathy as you well know. I haven't had any response from you to my last email. Please email back, Fari. It's no one's fault things ended the way they did. Stuff happens, as you taught me well to understand and appreciate during our stay together. The silver lining, bittersweet irony, is the Home Office Relocation Repatriation fee has provided some sort of steppingstone for me to get started on Thai soil again, after all these years in the wilderness.

Did I tell you I lost my mother Dhegu, a few weeks after my arrival? It's a bit surreal, her going, as if she was waiting, hanging in there for me to arrive so we could both say our last goodbyes. They say, she had been on and off seriously ill. One minute they would think she won't last the day, only to bounce back! Dhegu, she was a tough cookie that one. I guess she was hanging on for me, to say her last goodbye to me. It will take time for me to acclimatise to life and things here, I will be honest. Nonetheless, I am awestruck at the resilience of the human spirit, that wise saying from you keeps me going, when the chips are down. My two sisters, Busaba and Achara, are happily married as they like to bang on about this, flaunting it in my face, all the time as if they begrudge all those years of separation when I was away, yet I used to look out well after them.

Keep well my lovely.

Yours Leti x

Fading Sun

Leti my love,

Thank you for your email and kind words, Leti. I haven't heard from you in relation to the said email you alluded to in your last email. It probably got lost in cyberspace, or somewhere in the dark web. Who knows how these things work.

Firstly, allow me to extend my heartfelt condolences at the loss of your mother Dhegu. I knew how very close you were to her. You always talked about her, extolling what a towering influence she'd been on you, a "luminary" as you called her. That was the word you constantly used to describe her. I'm really sorry at your loss Leti. Losing a loved one, grief is always a difficult terrain to navigate. In time, I pray for the strength of fortitude and resilience from The Man Above to guide you through healing, my love.

In equal measure, word filtering in from Yeukai this morning is the untimely death of Maidei over a drug binge overdose in upmarket Kensington London, last Saturday. Bizarrely, she is said to have passed on in a swimming pool drug orgy at a party of some sort. Talk of not knowing someone Leti; substance abuse is not something I would have put past Maidei by any wildest stretch of my imagination. Poor Yeu is undoubtedly distraught and heartbroken as she has to arrange the funeral on top of fitting in her hospital visits to me. It's certainly a weird world we live in, but I thought you had to know about this piece of tragic news, Maidei's passing on, just received. I am in shock.

The cancer has been back for a while now, my CT scans confirmed the worst. I'm living in an Aylesbury hospice with some lovely end of life, palliative care nurses and other support staff. There's no respite now, as it's come back virulent and has almost spread throughout my body, particularly my spinal cord. Radiotherapy won't be any good now.

"The treatment hasn't worked," the doctor has said.

Thanks to Abiraterone acetate, the new wonder drug, it's bought me extra, precious time to come this far. Everyone has been exceedingly kind at the hospice; the nurses have especially prepared me well to come to terms with my mortality. Two months max, that's what they've told me, that's what I'm looking at, but between you and me, I am ready, my love. Yeukai visits me, here and there with her two boys, Steve and Ewan, though Muchi has remained pretty much reclusive and adrift. No hope there, Leti. That ship long sailed.

I feel saddened, at times, and unbridled anger over the heavy handedness in which the UK immigration border force police executed your deportation warrant order, meting out such disproportionate, brute force and callousness to a decent woman of your nature. Never have I felt so powerless and woefully out of my depth. I couldn't do more to stave off the deportation. Incandescent with rage at the way it had to end, can't even cut it enough.

But at times I reflect and sink more into the depths and abyss of despondency, at what could have been, and what I couldn't achieve then. Reflecting, reminiscing, holding onto the memories, the years, musing on the road we've travelled.

But who am I?

I'm just a little grain of salt in an ocean that is the convoluted maze of the labyrinth that British immigration is, and its pitfalls. Brexit bullshit, British jingoism and misplaced, so-called world beating British exceptionalism, whatever hogwash the British establishment spouts. Most likely their misguided sense of nationalism sees themselves in the mould of the anachronistic British Empire. They just don't get it, don't they just, "the Little Britain brigade!" The world has moved on now, and we are a global village, whatever their separatist, divisive politics of hate!

Once more I apologise the UK system failed you, their failure to provide a safe haven and sanctuary to one who has endured and suffered exceedingly, as in your case, Letitia! Whatever happened to British values of tolerance, diversity and acceptance? Perhaps it's the poisoned chalice of Brexit after all, which has turned fellow humans against each under the banner of xenophobia, bigotry and parochialism, couched as patriotism, and taking our borders back mantra, whatever the latter means. All this toxic culture fanned and promoted by a British right-wing press, a whining cesspit of misplaced outrage which only further serves to divide the nation along ethnic and race lines.

God, haven't we seen it all, the toxic xenophobia! I am terribly ashamed of politicians who would rather let refugees drown in the English Channel instead of rescuing them, meanwhile taking pot shots at lifesaving charities like The Royal National Lifeboat Institution (RNLI). By Jove! How did we end up like this as a nation?

The lunatics have taken over the asylum and now they have bungled this Covid pandemic with spectacular ineptitude at gross human cost. I am sickened by this lot, Leti. Everything they touch, they flounder under their so-called banner of British exceptionalism, more of parochialism, I should say. We are being set up as canaries in the coal mine by this lot's crassness and world class ineptitude. My anger towards this government is off the scale right now.

This Brexit shit will be a powder keg of explosives, I tell you. And now I hear the Kent Road is clogged in a gridlock of heavy truckers' vehicles, rushing to stockpile supplies before the Brexit deadline. I grimace at the folly of mankind in the Brexit subterfuge that it is, which will wreak more havoc on this nation. Brexit subterfuge, the big lie, just like Trumpism across the transatlantic. But, again, who am I to pontificate about these car crash political fau pax of monumental proportions?

Sadly, for far too long, we've all been watching this bonfire of insanities stoked up by divisive, extremist politics of hate, Trumpism-Toryism nexus, if I may call it by that name. And now, what we are witnessing is just bedlam! The establishment should know better, when you sell your soul to the highest bidder, there's a debt to settle, and sadly, it's us, the populace, you and I Leti, we're among the mere mortals who suffer as we bear the brunt of broken politics and misgovernance. You should never have been kicked out of England. There is something called "due process," which should have been followed and exhausted first.

Hasn't our ignorance and fear of immigration got us into such a godawful mess? And what a shitshow of a government for exploiting that fear to shirk its own responsibilities. All ugly. All very ugly to repair now. And yet we have the nerve to call out other countries as banana republics! About time, we look in the mirror ourselves...

No one should be fooled by this anti-immigrant populism charade! Truth is, all UK is on the rocks as shortages bite and the eventual toll of Brexit is exacted. First, it was those long driver gridlock at Kent, the Christmas chaos of lorry drivers trapped in their vehicles as the rigours of the English weather set in. "It's not related to Brexit," we were told, by the psychophantic Brexshitmannia gutter press.

Ever since your departure Leti, now the nation must contend with recurrent high energy prices, and fuel shortages. The forecourts are empty as we speak. We have been sold out by a political racketeer. We need new leaders. Meanwhile the establishment's cronyism is on an all-time high, raging unabated as the Panama papers scandal and the recent Paradise papers attests to their well document sleaze and chicanery. Yes, this is beneath our dignity, but we must keep the larger imperative in mind, which is making more money till kingdom comes, chimes the psychophantic Tory Brexshit press in its usual propaganda tirades.

Keep on keeping on, my lovely. If anyone can win this fight and reinvent themselves regardless of geography, then there's only one *Letitia fucking John-son* who can do it and overcome adversity. You are the superwoman. You go girl! You know very well I admire your resilience, forthrightness, drive and unmitigated initiative. You can do this Leti! Continue pressing ahead!

All my love. Always,

Fari xx

Valediction Forbid Mourning

Fari My Love,

I cannot even know where to begin, my love. I gather your time was up. I received a heart-breaking phone call this morning from my Coventry sister of yesteryear, Emmy. I'm sure you remember Emmy, she used to visit us a lot, during our sojourn in Bicester. Good old Emmy saved the day, told me of your last breath last night. Call me insane. I'm totally out of it. I'm not sure why I'm even writing you an email, even though now I know you won't be able to get back to me. Maybe it's therapeutic to me, as I seek closure and a final valediction to you, my love. Equally, I am also sorry to learn of the tragic passing on of Maidei. May her soul find solace.

You taught me how to love again, Fari, without being judgemental of one's past misdeeds and transgressions; regardless of their sordid history, as was my case. "Personal baggage," you called it. How wonderful it was, we both fell in love that evening, when each poured their heart out to the other. That day lives forever seared in my memory and bosom, Fari, and will sure keep me going, when the chips are down as I miss you, going forward my love.

For this, I'm eternally grateful, Fari, and seek to eulogise and wish you well in the journey ahead, as you cross to the other side. Of all things Zimbabwean I treasure and hold dear, I'm glad you taught me about your cultural system of totems in relation to individual families. Thus today, deep down from the depths of Bangkok, Thailand, I pay homage to a great friend, lover and confidante invoking your very own *Gwai, Gumbi, Mukuruvambwa* totem.

Go well my lovely man, Fari. Loved beyond words, missed beyond measure, already!

Till we meet again. RIP Fari, my man.

Leti x

Acknowledgments

I wish to record a large debt of gratitude to an exceptional woman, of wit and great storytelling prowess, my mother Rudo Chatora, the greatest storyteller ever! In looking back, I realise you were the source of my early story arcs, not least your rich insights and profound knowledge of family history and oral tradition. You are a great inspiration. To my late father, John Chatora, how can I ever forget your inimitable library of books in our Dangamvura, Mutare home? Your penchant for books engendered an insatiable appetite for reading in me which continues to thrive to this day. Rest in peace, Pops.

I offer bottomless gratitude to my esteemed colleague, celebrated poet, editor, publicist, Tariro Ndoro for availing time to go through early drafts, making me to think much more expansively in terms of potential story arcs, and your on-point further readings pointers. Thank you for coming onboard and for your sublime work ethic which saw to it as you relentlessly trawled and checked my work with fine-tooth comb hawkish eyes. I can't thank you enough. I also wish to thank other colleagues: Memory Chirere, Stan Onai Mushava, Patrick Masiyakurima and Gift Mheta for equally giving critical input to early drafts of this work. Many thanks, folks. Much appreciated. My brother Arthur Chatora deserves equal credit for availing editorial input to the project. *PachiGumbi pedu, ngehwedu munin'ina*, as we always say. I love you kid brother, you're always there for me. I couldn't have asked for a loftier sibling!

In equal measure, I would also like to acknowledge my 2002 English Department Sakubva High colleagues in Mutare, Zimbabwe, particularly Wesley Mutowo *'Ngamura'* and Ray Damba *'Mabhachi'* among others for the friendship and camaraderie over the years, which engendered a passion and love for Literature as we bounced ideas off each other, teaching our sixth form classes at Sakubva High *Dangwe*. To my most senior brother, much venerated *big blaz* Fred Chatora, my uncle Sekuru Gracious Hwapunga, and longstanding friend and confidante, Agrippa 'Wasu' Nyamukondiwa, thank you for being my greatest cheerleaders. Your support keeps me going as I relentlessly

218

churn out those creative pieces. To Sekuru Evidence Mutumbu, thank you my brother, your cheerleading and constant support is nigh sublime and inspirational.

And finally, to Priveledge, for giving me a happiness I never knew existed. I love you with all my heart.

ABOUT
KHARIS PUBLISHING

KHARIS PUBLISHING is an independent, traditional publishing house with a core mission to publish impactful books, and channel proceeds into establishing mini-libraries or resource centers for orphanages in developing countries, so these kids will learn to read, dream, and grow. Every time you purchase a book from Kharis Publishing or partner as an author, you are helping give these kids an amazing opportunity to read, dream, and grow. Kharis Publishing is an imprint of Kharis Media LLC. Learn more at https://www.kharispublishing.com.

Author Profile

Andrew Chatora writes novels and short stories and hails from Zimbabwe. He received an MA in Media, Culture and Communication from UCL. His writing explores multifarious themes of belonging, identity politics, citizenship, and nationhood issues. *Where the Heart Is,* is his second novel following his highly successful debut novella: *Diaspora Dreams.* Andrew is principally interested in the global politics of inequality which he interrogates through his writing. When he is not writing, he is working on his PhD thesis on digital piracy, with Birmingham City University's School of Media and English.

New Book by Author Coming Soon...

Harare Voices and Beyond is the author's forthcoming book.

Read ahead the first chapter of the author's imminent book:

Harare Voices and Beyond

Synopsis

A drunken confession exposes a dark family secret. Rhys appears to have it all. A white Zimbabwean living in affluent Borrowdale Brooke area, he gets involved in a freak traffic accident, and therein unfolds a confession which unleashes a cathartic chain of events in the family's hitherto well-choreo-graphed life, and whose lived experience becomes microcosmic and an eye opener to Zimbabwe's seemingly closed, forgotten white minority commu-nity.

Through offering a rare insight into lives of the white community in post-independence Zimbabwe, *Harare Voices and Beyond* explores the dynamics of love, money, family feuds, identity politics, false philanthropy, and respecta-bility inter-alia. Two families' lives are inexorably linked in this fast-paced narrative which traverses multiple locations, pitting the seedy underbelly of Harare juxtaposed with the leafy northern suburbs and little-known Marina Thompson from UK Durham University all appears linked in a dramatic in-fused finale which leaves the reader numbed and shocked.

I

This is it for me and mother. It is most likely we are going to die. There's no other way the courts will let us off for the murder of my brother Julian. Mother's youngest son gone rogue. Whatever happens, Jonathan our defence lawyer has really done a brilliant job, eloquently pleading our case before High Court Judge, Justice Chatikobo.

"Your honour, this was an act of self-defence gone wrong on the part of my clients Doris and Rhys. Both plead culpable homicide in the face of extreme provocation. They have both exceedingly shown remorse for this mishap which will haunt and traumatise them for as long as they live.

"As we speak, my clients have been experiencing delirium and hallucinations, an upshot of this excruciating ordeal for them. Doris now has longstanding insomnia as her medical records submitted to court confirm and is now on chronic restorative medication. It is my submission to this court that it considers all the extenuating circumstances facing my clients and pardons them, for, they are not murderers but law-abiding citizens who got goaded into a tricky scenario, through no fault of their own.

"Prior to this, they do not have a criminal record, not two, not one, none at all on their record. Blameless stain! No blemish! So, they deserve a second chance; we all deserve a second chance in life."

Jonathan had persuasively argued and took a respectful bow as he resumed his seat in the packed courtroom. Both Mum and I gave him a thumbs up with our eyes.

"Excellent delivery Jonathan," I mumbled under my breath, as if fearing the judge would hear me.

"May the court rise as the judge leaves to prepare his determination," boomed the usher's sonorous voice; we all complied with his instruction.

That had been a few days ago, last Friday to be precise. I looked at Mother's haggard, emaciated, expressionless face and felt for her. Startlingly, she had gone downhill within the last eight months and had shrivelled into a wilted leaf, reduced to a pitiful shadow of her former self. A face etched with perpetual pain, a brow now creased with deep, furrowed lines of misery, worry and unhappiness. My mind flickered to the ebullient, effervescent Doris's persona of yesteryear whom I had been used to all these years. *Where had she gone, that vivacious, upbeat woman who had a ready smile for everyone, a big heart and larger than life personality?* I have the cheek to ask, as if I don't know the genesis of her ordeal. Blame it on Julian, but he is no longer here to state his case, is he? Perhaps I should give him the benefit of the doubt to state his side of the story, but just. Perhaps, that is for another day.

"Time to go back to court Rhys," the prison officer's gruff voice jolted me out of my reverie. I scrambled to get on my creased khaki prison garb, grabbed water from an old scrappy metal mug on my cell window and shuffled out as Warren, the prison officer, unlocked my clanging, metal cell doors and leg irons. The noise grated on me each time the heavy steel doors were opened. That hollow, annoying noise which went on and on, as if to remind me of my captivity status. I felt it; I was a caged animal and it hurt my self-esteem, yet this my newfound status.

"Your mother, Doris, is already in the prison van waiting for you. Better hurry up," remarked Warren. I shuffled awkwardly along the dreary, dingy, urine infested D section corridor of Chikurubi Maximum Prison, slowly navigating my way towards the exit under the hawkish eyes of the four other burly prison officers who had joined us and were escorting other prisoners to Harare Magistrates Court first. Then high-profile cases like mine and Mother's would be dealt with at the corner Samora Machel/Second Street ensconced, colonial looking high court building which, I must admit, still looked regal in the decrepit, disintegrating Harare infrastructure.

The Harare Jacaranda trees were a vivid show of purple adding on to the aesthetic ambience of the streets. Although decrepit Harare buildings made a mockery of its former epithet status: sunshine city, still, the blooming Jacarandas gave the city some much needed colour.

"Morning Doris," I exchanged greetings with Mother as I sat opposite her in the green prison van. She could only grunt and gave me a curt nod for an acknowledgment greeting. I wasn't surprised by this new change in Doris. Somehow, the past eight months' trial and incarceration, first at Harare Remand Prison, and later at Chikurubi, had sapped her energy. The once voluble woman cut a sorry representation of herself, for she had increasingly become morose, reticent and laconic.

"Cheer up, Mum, I know it's difficult, but whatever happens today, we get to secure some closure on this case which has dragged on for so long," I remarked as I flashed her a smile and tried to be upbeat, though inwardly my stomach was churning and constricting at the uncertainty of what lay ahead. Today was judgement day from Justice Chatikobo and it followed several gruelling weeks of intense sparring between our defence lawyers and the prosecution. The tetchy exchanges, which at times became ugly and heated, moreso our cross-examinations, had been brutal and adversarial, but we had emerged unscathed, at least those were Jonathan's reassuring words to us.

"Both you and Doris have done very well throughout court proceedings, believe me," Jonathan had consistently said, allaying our misgivings in his periodic debriefs to us.

That morning, as if to exacerbate our jarred nerves, the prison van took exceedingly long to navigate the traffic on the treacherous, pothole plagued roads of Harare. Because the van itself was like our jail, we could hardly see what happened outside; its windows were boarded up by tiny, barbed windows right at the top ends of the van. All we could feel as occupants was the constant discomfort and being jolted off our seats each time the vehicle hit a pothole or crater. And being handcuffed when this happened didn't make things any easier. I dare you, don't ever be in my position.

Once at the Harare high court, we had a brief moment to consult with Jonathan just before the expected 11:00 am verdict delivery time.

"Now, here are the likely scenarios which are bound to happen today," Jonathan said, speaking to us quietly in the private courtroom legal chambers where lawyers could confer with their clients.

"In the event of a guilty verdict, my learned colleagues and I will have recourse to studying the judgement so we can expeditiously lodge an appeal to the Supreme Court," Jonathan added.

"Should you both be acquitted, which I am hoping will be the case, then I will quickly proceed to Chikurubi to collect you both. Are we clear?" He spoke boring his eyes into both of us.

"Crystal clear, Jonathan," I replied. "And what does the time frame for an appeal look like, between a guilty verdict and you putting this in?" I asked. Perhaps the despondency in my voice was a tad too obvious, for it was a far cry from one who'd only been trying to be upbeat with Doris earlier on in the prison van.

"We should get our papers lodged and filed in within a two-week period at the latest, though I am still holding out hope for a propitious outcome," Jonathan replied.

"We do as well Jonathan, and in case things go the other way, please accept our utmost gratitude from the profoundest depths of our hearts, for what you've done for my son Rhys and me," Doris cut in. She appeared to have found her voice in the end, much to my surprise.

"No worries, Doris, you don't need to even say it," remarked Jonathan with a modest, peremptory wave of the hand. "Rhys and you have been through a lot these past eight months; you deserve a respite in the form of a favourable outcome. There's the court usher beckoning to us. It may well be the die is cast. Let me hear whether judgement delivery is ready."

"Judgement has been moved forward to 2:30pm this afternoon," remarked the court usher, peering at us over the horn-rimmed glasses he kept adjusting each time he spoke.

"How's that?" quipped Jonathan, clearly annoyed at this abrupt delay.

"No reasons have been offered, but this is Zimbabwe you know, where the wheels of justice turn excruciatingly slowly," he said in low tones with the last statement in a conspiratorial way to us, as if he was on our side and afraid to be overheard making those remarks.

"For crying out loud, my clients have suffered long enough for all these months to have their day of reckoning just pushed from pillar to post, just like that," remarked a visibly dejected and annoyed Jonathan.

"Well, we just have to wait, don't we?" Doris said. And so, we did wait, with bated breath, for our judgement hour, which was long drawn out. It was not until 3:45pm in the afternoon, a further delay of an hour and a quarter. Justice Chatikobo took his seat as we rose to our feet to acknowledge him, and then he commenced speaking, as the court room descended into ominous silence for a trial which had received national and global headlines. Some I can clearly recall, as they are permanently seared in my psyche: *"Murder most foul committed in posh Harare's Borrowdale Suburbs. A white Zimbabwean family, Rhys and his mother Doris, bludgeoned Julian Williams, Rhys's brother, after which they buried his body in their garden in a grisly murder which has shaken the opulent, leafy, affluent community..."*

jumped to my memory, snippets of some of these newspaper headlines furore surrounding our highly publicised trial in a country in which we, the white community, were a reclusive minority who tended to stay in the background in this southern African nation.

"And so, judgement will be reserved indefinitely, as I need more time to study the prosecution's and defence's closing arguments..." Justice Chatikobo's droning voice roused me from my late afternoon reverie.

Judgement reserved indefinitely? I was confused by these events unfolding before me. I glanced at Jonathan, who pretty much looked pissed off by the brief address from Justice Chatikobo who brusquely left the courtroom after his terse remarks.

That had been it, a dramatic end to a long, drawn-out day in which Doris and I had awakened looking forward to however difficult a day we hoped would give us the much-needed closure to a gruelling several months which had sapped us of our energies and resilience to live. But then, Justice Chatikobo had other ideas, the judgement reserved verdict. Even Jonathan, the best legal brains in Zimbabwe, had not seen this coming, as he commiserated with us thereafter. "Well, I am extremely annoyed at this whole judgement reserved thing, Rhys. I am absolutely fuming on your behalf, I am really sorry and feel for both of you," he said, trying to reassure us both.

"So, what does this mean to Doris and me? So many questions. Excuse me, Jonathan, but where do we go from here? How indefinite is a non-judgement?" I sarcastically quibbled, throwing the question back at Jonathan as if it had been his fault.

"Well, I wish I knew. I can only say, and here I hate to say it, but I can only repeat the usher's words, "This is Zimbabwe, where the rule of the jungle prevails, *donga watonga;* rule as you please, anarchy reigning supreme. Justice is for sale to the highest bidder. You know what, forgive my rambling. 'Reserved judgement' is bullshit stuff! We are at the mercy of this kakistocracy system now, and just have to wait until Chatikobo is ready with a judgement. Goodness knows whenever that will be."

"What about bail? Is there any chance all this circus can rumble on while we're out on bail?"

"Not a chance, I'm afraid, especially as it's a murder case. Besides, the high media interest in your case does you a disservice. So, as much as it pains me to utter these words, you are likely to stay in Chikurubi prison in limbo, without having a definitive end in sight. It could be weeks; it could be months we are talking of here, but hopefully not. Look, I'm fed up with all these antics. What this country needs is judicial grit, rigour and independence. Reserved judgements have become the recent "in thing," an abuse of power instrument at the disposal of this banana republic judiciary. I don't like them; no one likes them who's been at their receiving end. But that's the way it is, I'm afraid. I apologise to both of you once again. Will keep you in the loop on how things progress. This is Zimbabwe."

Jonathan was clearly deflated, and I felt for him as he left with a dejected air, his creased, scruffy, tweed suit underscoring a defeated man. Even his limp became more pronounced as he hobbled off, dragging one leg after the other. And even as we trudged out of the high court building and made that short walk back into the prison van belly, our leg irons clanging against the high court's pavement, I felt a dark, thick cloud of despondency descend on me, all this amid the harem of teeming journalists and clicks of their cameras taking shots of both Doris and me, swamped by a barrage of their ceaseless interview requests: "Mr. Williams, I'm from *the Zimbabwe Times*. Would you like to say a few words to this adjournment of your verdict today?"

"Do you think there is rule of law in Zimbabwe, given your nearly nine-month ordeal in Chikurubi prison, and now this?"

"Would you say you are being persecuted because you are white?" rang another question amongst a litany of ceaseless further questions thrown at us by these vultures.

"No comment," I quietly mumbled to them, my head lowered as I shuffled towards the prison van. *Golly, these fuckers, why can't they leave me alone?* I reflected as I negotiated the dodgy steps into the prison van, but I missed a step and was roughly propped up by the butt of an AK 47 and the rough, grimy hands of one of the prison warders.

***

CPSIA information can be obtained
at www.ICGtesting.com
Printed in the USA
LVHW010600301121
704726LV00010BA/728

9 781637 460849